Advance Prais
Mem(

"*Memortality* takes a concept we
worst nightmare. Innovative terro
—Bram Stoker Award-winner M
Mothman

"*Memortality* by Stephen Provost is a highly original, thrilling novel
unlike anything else out there. From the haunting prologue to the thrilling
conclusion, Provost has crafted an engaging, brilliant yarn that will keep
you glued to the page until the very end. Stephen is clearly an author at the
top of his game."
—**David McAfee**, bestselling author of *33 A.D.*, *61 A.D.*, and *79 A.D.*

"A rich and complex world, with an ever-twisting and an immensely
compelling story, *Memortality* is a terrific science fiction thriller that
imprints on your mind like an unforgettable snapshot."
—**John Palisano**, Bram Stoker Award-winning author of *Nerves* and *Ghost
Heart*

"Fans of *The Running Dream* will love Minerva, a feisty protagonist with
a special gift for helping the dead, who embarks on an action-packed
adventure as she attempts to save her loved ones."
—**Alexandria Constantiova Szeman**, author of *The Kommandant's
Mistress*

MEMORTALITY

Stephen H. Provost

Pace Press
Fresno, California

Published by Pace Press
An imprint of Linden Publishing
2006 South Mary Street, Fresno, California 93721
(559) 233-6633 / (800) 345-4447

Pace Press and Colophon are trademarks of
Linden Publishing, Inc.

ISBN 978-1-61035-289-5

135798642

Printed in the United States of America
on acid-free paper.

Library of Congress Cataloging-in-Publication Data on file.

In loving memory of Lorelei L. "Lollie" Provost, whose courage in overcoming the polio that left one side of her body paralyzed helped inspire the character of Minerva Rus. Mom, if I could, I'd bring you back in a heartbeat.

Contents

Preface

How many millions of people have lived, died and been left behind by history, their names and deeds whisked away to oblivion by the passing of time? The seventeenth-century blacksmith toiling in obscurity at his anvil. The medieval monk working silently away in an abbey. The triumphant war hero whose name—unlike those of Alexander and Bouidicca and Caesar—was never preserved in some ancient text. Or perhaps it *was* recorded . . . only to be lost when that text was destroyed by fanatics or burned with so many others in the fire at Alexandria's library.

Think of your own life. Perhaps you never knew one of your own grandparents, taken from this world before you even entered it. You will never know the sound of that person's voice, and you may know little about his or her life, other than what your parents passed along when they weren't too busy creating their own histories. Go back a generation further, or two, or three, and your ancestors are likely little more than names in the family Bible, if they're even that much to you.

No one can bring back the memories of those countless generations lost to history, but imagine for a just moment that you could preserve the memories of your own loved ones a little longer.

What if you could do more than that?

What if you could bring them back to life?

Motherhood
(1996)

The flowerpot sat on the windowsill in Mary Lou Corbet's apartment, its soil giving rise to green stems topped by golden blossoms, their petals spread in homage to the sun. Mary Lou's plump orange cat, Petrushka, curled his body around the flowerpot as he walked past, mewing, and nearly toppled it onto the desk where she sat, penning a letter to her only son.

She thought about Jimmy always, because she had to. Not just because she was his mother, but because his very life depended on it. Sometimes, a mother's love provides even more nourishment to an adult child than to a nursing infant.

Mary Lou waved the back of her hand at Petrushka, who jumped lightly down onto the desk, then into her lap, and began kneading her belly.

She giggled. You were never too old to giggle. Not even in the 76th year of a life that had seen so much sorrow.

"Silly boy," she chuckled, rubbing her knuckles gently near Petrushka's ear, then stretching both arms over him like an arching truss bridge and trying to settle her fingertips once again on her computer without disturbing him.

"My dearest son," the words on the screen began. "Know that you are in my heart and my thoughts always, as is your lovely bride."

Mary Lou still called Sharon her son's "bride," even though they'd been married for twenty whole years now. She always pictured her daughter-in-law the same way her son still thought of her: in the same white gown and radiant smile she'd worn on her wedding day. Mary Lou had known her long before that; Sharon had grown up right across the street, and there'd never been any doubt in Mary Lou's mind that, one day, this girl and her son would wind up spending the rest of their lives together.

Sharon wasn't just the perfect match for her boy, she was the perfect daughter-in-law, always offering to take her shopping or surprising her with a devil's food cake on her birthday. Some mothers insist no one's good enough for their little boy, but Mary Lou never thought that about Sharon. They were perfect for each other; for her, it was like getting two children for the trouble of one . . . not that Jimmy was any trouble, mind you.

Sharon was in her thoughts just as much as Jimmy was, but she knew she was getting older, and she wouldn't be around forever.

What would they do without her?

Like any mother, she worried, but she was convinced she had far more reason to worry than most.

A diesel truck rumbled by outside her window, exhaust trailing behind it. Mary Lou liked to sit at the window and watch the cars go by, but big trucks weren't supposed to be chugging along down residential streets. "Weight limit 6 tons," the sign at the end of the block read. She was about to shout something out the window when she remembered her task, remembered her son and his beautiful bride, remembered to focus on them and the email she was writing.

"My darlings: I woke up with a new ache in my shoulder last night. Nothing too bad, but please do hurry home. I miss you and I worry. You know I'm getting on in years, and I won't be here forever for you, so each day is precious to me. Please, you must hurry and find a special child of your own to be there for you after I am gone. You're trying, I know. That's why you're not here with me right now. You know these aren't just the words of some doting old woman who wants a grandchild in golden years. You have always given me more than enough love between the two of you. It's not for me, but for you—while you still have time and before I'm gone. Remember, I love you always. Mama."

Her finger hovered over the mouse for only a moment before she clicked it and the "send" button screen lit up on the screen. It was a new way of sending messages; she'd just discovered it in the last year or so, but she liked it.

The email was on its way.

Mary Lou Corbet stared at the photo of Jimmy and Sharon on their wedding day as she got up, while Petrushka jumped down from her lap in the same moment. Her eyes were getting heavy, and it was time for her nap. She needed one every day now, it seemed. Looking back, she couldn't imagine how she'd stayed up all night when Jimmy was fussing as a baby or, later, when she was working on some project for her business, Fireside

MEMORTALITY

Dressworks. Her dreams had been closer to nightmares back then, fueled by worries of losing her baby to some childhood illness or simply making ends meet to keep him fed and clothed.

Being a single mother had never been easy, and it was even harder back then, when whispers behind her back about "fornication" and "that bastard child" followed her down the street and into the grocery store, pharmacy, and post office.

Now, though, her dreams consoled her, because Jimmy and Sharon visited her in those dreams.

She picked up their photograph in its silver frame, turned, and carried it with her toward the bedroom, Petrushka tagging along, swatting at some gnat that whirred silently just beyond his reach. Mary Lou could have kept a second picture beside her bed, but then both photos might have become nothing more than "part of the scenery," fading into the background of her consciousness—something she could never allow to happen. She loved them that much, and she knew that, when she lay down on her perfectly contoured Reclin-o-pedic mattress, she would drift off to dream of them and, she hoped, their new child.

Every day, she checked her email for news of a new arrival, and every day, she was disappointed.

But then, one day, she found this:

"Great news, Mama! We've found a child—and he's perfect. Gifted. More gifted than any child we've seen, and you know how hard we've been looking all over the world. They've tested him, and his memory is perfect! He's three years old: the ideal age for us. We found him here in South Africa, and everything's private, so we'll have him today, maybe even by the time you open this email. It's been a long road, but we've done it, Mama. You can stop worrying now. We're coming home. Private plane. Private airfield. Everything's taken care of. Big hugs from me and Jimmy. —Sharon"

Mary Lou breathed a sigh of relief as Petrushka jumped silently up on the desk and onto the keyboard, dancing lightly on padded paws. Normally, she would have shooed the cat away, but today she didn't care. Everything was coming together so well, just as she had hoped when she'd given them part of their inheritance early to take this trip—to go on this quest. It had all been worth it for them to have a child of their own, something they couldn't do naturally. She didn't even look up when another diesel truck rumbled by outside and, right behind it, a late-model blue Ford Fiesta that, had she seen it, would not have been familiar to her. It wasn't from this neighborhood.

The car slowed as it came to Mary Lou's house.

The driver's side window rolled down.

The ever-curious Petrushka, perhaps sensing something, jumped off the keyboard and up onto the windowsill to look outside, then jumped away just as quickly, brushing the flowerpot as he did and sending it toppling to the floor.

The unfinished terracotta container shattered on the hardwood, but Mary Lou didn't hear it break.

Instead, another sound reached her ears.

Gunfire.

And, in the same instance she heard it, she felt it—slashing into her neck, her chest, the side of her face. Shock and searing pain hit her, both at once. Blood dripped from one open wound, fleeing from another. Two more rapid-fire shots missed, the bullets lodging in the plaster wall behind her, as Petrushka's legs whirred underneath him, sliding on the slick floor as he tore through the open door to the foyer, rounded the corner and vanished like a bolt down the hall.

The car sped up again and disappeared.

Mary Lou Corbet fixed her eyes on the picture of her newlywed son and daughter-in-law a couple of feet in front of her on the desk, willing herself to think about them and block out the pain. Her vision began to blur, but she hung on to the image, even when she was past the point of seeing and everything started to turn. She would hold them in her heart. In her mind. In her memory. Everything depended on it. She said a silent prayer that the child had been delivered to them in time. Only when she knew that could she let go. Only then could she be at peace.

She held on. Fiercely. Tenaciously. But the pain was too much and she drifted into a reverie, still holding tight to the image of Jimmy and Sharon. As she entered that brief way station of dreamtime between the living world and what comes after, they came to her: Sharon still looking as lovely as she had on her wedding day, Jimmy in slacks and a blue dress shirt holding a dark-haired three-year-old boy in his arms. The boy smiled and waved at her, and somehow, in this ethereal twilight dreamworld, she managed to smile back at him.

"Everything's all right, Mama," Jimmy said, trying to smile himself but his expression betrayed the grief he felt inside. "He's here with us. See?" He set the boy down and patted him on his back. "Say hello to your grandma."

The boy hesitated, then walked forward tentatively. He stopped just beyond her reach, and she extended her arms to embrace him, but though his legs weren't moving, he seemed to be retreating from her, getting smaller.

"I'll miss you so much, Mama," Jimmy said, his voice growing fainter now. "Thank you for always remembering us. We'll remember you forever. For all the good it will do. Dammit, Mama. If only we could show you how . . ." he burst into tears and couldn't say anymore.

Sharon put her arms around him, and he lowered his tear-covered face onto her shoulder.

"You can rest now, Mama," she said to Mary Lou. "We love you. Always."

Those were the last words Mary Lou Corbet heard in this lifetime.

Minerva
(2016)

"The accident is a lie."

"What do you mean? You keep saying that."

The face staring back at her was the same one she remembered from all those years ago. Kind, caring, patient. But older now. The playful smile the boy had once worn had vanished behind a mask she couldn't seem to penetrate now that he was a man. She hadn't seen him for years, but this was how she'd always imagined he'd look all grown up: the soft brown eyes, the pale complexion just brushed by a touch of sunshine, the auburn hair unkempt and uncut, cascading down across his left eye. She'd always stared at that; it distracted her. And he'd always noticed, brushing it back the moment she became aware of it.

His brow lowered slightly, as if to say, "You're staring." But he said nothing. Even the words he did speak seemed silent to her somehow, as if she were in a dream . . .

She moaned in her sleep and tried to turn her body, but the vice grip held her, the paralysis that had been with her since the accident.

In her dream, concern flitted across his face, apparent even in the dim glow of the candle that burned beside her bed. Its light had always comforted her, and at times, she'd stared into the flame as it flickered for moments on end, imagining she was a part of it. The thought of that soothed her, one of the few things in this world that did.

"Stay with me," he said, his tone resolute.

"I can't move," she protested.

"Yes, you can. All you have to do is remember how you felt before all this. Before the accident and the lies it's telling you."

"You're the liar," she whispered, and her voice whispered venom.

He looked hurt now, and pulled away from her, that resolve appearing to evaporate at the sound of her voice. In the same moment, he seemed farther away, the reflected candlelight that had danced in his eyes a few moments earlier now a fading glow that illumined little more than his forehead and the tip of his nose.

"I'm telling you the truth," he said, but she could barely hear him. A part of her wanted to believe what he was saying. Not a part—all of her. But in the instance that she acknowledged that desire, she was aware it could not be.

She tried to turn her body again.

Nothing.

Her jaw clenched tight, and she began to tremble with the effort.

"Not that way," he said.

"Then . . . *how*?!" Her voice was louder than she intended, and he pulled away further into the shadows.

"Wait," she said, softening her tone. "Don't go. You have to tell me . . . about the accident."

"It's not important now," he said, moving forward slightly again, into the candlelight.

"Not important? Then how do you explain this?" She nearly spat the words at him, and he averted his eyes.

"See?" she said. "You can't even bear to look at me. If the accident didn't happen, how did I get like *this*?"

He sat up straighter and held her gaze again, his eyes locking onto hers so that, this time, it was she who wished to glance away. But he held her there by force of will. "Min, you're beautiful."

No one ever called her that but him. Not her mother, not the social workers or counselors, not even Archer. She was always Minerva to them, or, in a condescending tone, Miss Rus. She usually liked it when he called her Min, but this time, it felt patronizing. Of course, any time he paid her a compliment, it felt patronizing.

"Now I *know* you're lying. I'm grotesque. And I can't move."

"Yes, you can." She wasn't even sure she heard him say it. The words were so soft they seemed but a silent wisp of unseen vapor escaping from between his lips. But she saw them move, and that was enough.

"How dare you!" she seethed, speaking the words softly, in measured tones as she fought to hold back tears. It wasn't a fight she was going to win . . .

Her eyes flew open. The candle by her bedside flickered as the overhead fan chain clinked like a metronome, the chain striking its light fixture dully like champagne glasses toasting her condition, her helplessness. Somehow, she'd managed to roll onto her belly, and now her sinewy arms thrust her torso upward and sideways, so she lay again on her back.

"Liar," she repeated softly to herself, blinking her eyes as she stared at the ceiling, the fan spinning hypnotically above her against the gray backdrop that told her daybreak was imminent. The dull, achy predawn light filtered in through blinds drawn tight against the sunlight. They always remained that way, midnight or noon. That way, no one could see in, and she didn't have to see what was out there, in the world beyond her own.

She stared down toward the foot of the bed and noticed that, somehow, her legs had become uncovered. The useless spindly appendages greeted her eyes and she winced, grabbing the sheet and pulling it over them so she wouldn't have to see. The sheet was wet, she noticed. The night hadn't been too warm, but somehow, she'd been perspiring.

A gentle knock came at the door.

"Minerva? Are you all right in there?"

It was Archer, thank heavens, not Jessica. For years now, she had refused to call her mother "Mom" or "Mother" or anything else that might seem even remotely endearing, because Jessica Meyer was anything but the endearing sort. Archer, on the other hand, was nearly always attentive and caring . . . except when he was caught up in one of those ridiculous video games of his. Then you'd sooner be able to lift Thor's hammer than pry him away from that screen and joystick. Or mouse. Or whatever it was they used these days. Minerva paid little attention to such things.

"I'm fine," she answered, her tone exasperated. She hadn't meant to say it like that, but most often, that was how she talked, whether the other person was friendly or not. Whoever it was, she just wanted to be left alone.

Archer came in anyway.

"I heard a noise," he said. "Like you were hurt."

"I'm fine," Minerva repeated, trying to sound as pleasant as possible.

The fan whirred methodically overhead.

"You don't look it," Archer said. "You're all pale and sweaty."

"In case you haven't noticed, I'm always pale. And I suppose if a girl can be ugly, she can sweat, too."

"Stop saying that. You're not ugly. I don't care what Mom says. You're okay."

"That's what *he* said, too," Minerva murmured, mostly to herself. "Well, actually, he said I was . . ."

"Who said what?"

She shook her head and glared at him. "No one. Nothing. And I don't give a . . ." She fired off an expletive, then stopped herself too late. "I don't care what Jessica says one way or the other."

"You shouldn't talk like that. If she hears you . . ."

"She talks like that herself all the time."

"That's what I mean. I don't want you to be like her."

"What's going on in there?" the voice rolled in at them from down the hall. "It's six o'clock in the freakin' morning!"

"Shi . . . eet," Archer said under his breath, and Minerva suppressed a smile at the irony of it.

"Nothing, Mom," he called back. "Just checking on Minerva."

"She can flippin' take care of herself! Do you know what happened to my goddamn cigarettes?"

"Is that all she can ever think about?" Minerva scoffed.

Archer shook his head and didn't answer.

"I'll find 'em for ya, Mom," he shouted back, then turning to Minerva, "Gotta go."

"It's not like I asked you to come in here in the first place."

He ignored her sarcasm. He had the patience of a saint, as Grandma used to say. The saying fit, even if Minerva didn't believe in saints or holy water or popes or sacraments. All a bunch of bull. But it occurred to her, as an afterthought, that she might need an exorcist right about now. These dreams she'd been having weren't exactly demonic, but they weren't exactly normal either, and she wasn't sure she wanted to keep having them.

She wasn't sure she wanted them to stop, though, either.

The fan whirred on. Clink. Clink. Clink . . .

9

Cigarettes
(2001)

Trees, telephone poles, and ranch-style tract homes whizzed by outside the window, a nondescript hodgepodge of suburbia. Minerva watched them. She was six years old, riding in the back seat of a gold-tan '94 Acura Legend, and she was thoroughly bored.

Smoke drifted back into her face from the driver's seat, and she tried to wave it away with her hand.

"I wish you wouldn't, Mom," she said to herself, but she knew she didn't dare say it aloud or she'd be smacked. It would be on the butt if they were at home, but if they were out, it would be a cuff across the face.

The boy next to her smiled, as if he were enjoying her discomfort. "She's just like a dragon with all that smoke, isn't she, Min?"

"Shhhhh! She'll hear you!"

Raven chuckled. She always wondered how he'd gotten that name. Wasn't it a girl's name? Maybe his parents had wanted a girl, or maybe they liked the bird.

"Do you like my name?" he asked.

That was weird. Had he been reading her mind?

"Ummmm. I guess so. Are you supposed to be a bird or something?"

"It's from something some Poe guy wrote. I guess it's really famous. My mom says she thinks I'll be famous, too."

"Like the kid on the cereal commercial?"

"I guess."

"You look better than him."

The car made a right turn. The tract homes gave way to a series of strip malls, muffler shops, and secondhand stores. No trees here, but the phone poles followed them.

"Where are we going?" Raven asked.

"Mom has to buy more cigarettes."

"Oh."

The brakes squealed as a stoplight changed at just the wrong time, and the Acura's front bumper wound up over the crosswalk line at an intersection. These cigarette runs could take forever. Jessica Meyer always insisted on paying the lowest price possible, but because the prices were always changing—usually going up—she had to drive all over town in order to find the best deal. In the meantime, she sometimes ran out of cigarettes, which was never good for anyone who happened to be in the car with her.

"Anytime now," she growled at the light, which nonetheless stayed red as cross traffic continued to whiz past in front of her, then finally stopped for turn-lane traffic, which also seemed to take forever.

"Want some gum?" Raven asked.

"Mom won't let me."

The light finally changed, and Jessica pressed hard on the accelerator, sending the car lurching, then flying into the intersection and beyond.

"Geez!" Raven exclaimed.

"Did I just hear you take the Lord's name in vain, young man?" Jessica snapped her head around, craning her neck as her dyed black hair flew across her forehead, but immediately seemed to snap back into place like a box-spring mattress.

"No, ma'am," said Raven.

"Mhmmm," she said, fixing him with a warning glare. "Well see that you don't, Mr. Smart Ass."

"Mom, the road."

The second the words were out of her moth, Minerva wished she could take them back.

"What did you say, you little . . .?" Jessica kept one hand on the steering wheel as she lashed out at her daughter with the other, latching on to her pant leg and tugging sharply at it. Minerva felt the seatbelt bite into her midsection then come loose. The mechanism been had damaged before they'd bought it (used), and she must not have secured it all the way.

"Mom!"

"Shut up!" The hand released her leg, shot up, and slapped her across the cheek.

"Mrs. Meyer!"

"Not you, too. I'm taking you home as soon as I get my ciga—"

Minerva saw it coming. So did Raven. You didn't need to be a grown-up to recognize something scary: another red light up ahead, looming over a raging river of traffic streaming down Huntington Boulevard.

Jessica spun around at the last minute, suddenly aware of what was happening. Pressing her back hard against the seat and her foot in the opposite direction against the brake pedal, she gripped the steering wheel tight and turned it slightly to the left, sending the Acura sideways, skidding into the intersection.

Minerva, free of her safety belt, ducked reflexively.

Raven, who'd never been wearing his in the first place, screamed.

The car's tires painted an arc the color of black chalk on the pavement, then the arc broke abruptly to the sound of metal crumpling, crashing, caving in on itself. The Acura rose up from the impact, its tires leaving the pavement altogether. Then the world went sideways and upside down. Minerva felt her head hit something and saw Raven flying toward the window, his body oddly contorted. Her mother, somehow still gripping the steering wheel, was embraced between her seat and the safety belt. Minerva closed her eyes and felt herself thrown against something hard, then a searing pain bit into her midsection, and spread down through both her legs.

The next thing she knew, the pain was gone—and so was everything else.

Paralysis

When Minerva's eyes came open, they were met with what seemed a near blinding white. Sterility. A man in a sickeningly teal-colored gown with a cloth cap of the same color bound tightly to his head.

"She's waking up." A seemingly disembodied woman's voice drifted to meet her ears from somewhere beyond her field of vision.

The man in teal looked up and walked slowly over to the bed, just as the woman's head—a moon-shaped face with a double chin—came into view on the opposite side.

At that moment, Minerva knew something was wrong. Not with them. With her. She couldn't move . . . couldn't even feel . . . her toes. Or her legs. Not anything from the waist down.

She struggled, or felt like she was struggling, to move them. Outwardly: nothing.

Panic flooded her mind.

"I can't move." She felt like she was screaming it, but her voice was hoarse and raspy, barely louder than normal.

"I can't *move*."

"It's okay," the woman said. "You're in the hospital, and . . ."

"Mom. Where's Mom?"

"She's down the hall, dear. She's going to be just fine."

"But I can't *move*."

"I know. Do you want . . .?"

"Where's Raven?"

The woman looked at the doctor, she but didn't say anything this time. The doctor, who hadn't said anything at all so far, didn't say anything now, either.

"My legs!" Minerva twisted her body to the right, trying to force her legs to move, but she couldn't even feel them to tell whether her body was working. She looked down at them: They'd moved only so far as her torso had pulled them.

"Mom!" she yelled.

"Shhhh, dear. She's resting now. You're here in the hospital."

"I don't care! I want . . ." she felt tears forming in her eyes.

This was all so wrong.

"Should we sedate her?"

The man shook his head. Did he ever say anything? She wondered again where Raven was. They'd been friends for as far back as she could remember, making mud castles together after it rained, playing Pin the Tail on the Donkey at birthday parties and exploring the contents of an old medical kit Raven said belonged to his grandfather. When she'd told her mother they were "playing doctor," her mother had yanked down her pants and swatted her hard across the back of the legs.

"You filthy child!" she'd yelled.

She'd tried to explain that they hadn't done anything wrong, that Raven's parents had said it was okay to play with the stethoscope and that little rubber hammer the doctor hit your knee with to make your leg pop up. Her mother wouldn't listen, though. She never listened. Sometimes, Minerva liked to pretend that Raven's parents were her mother and father. They were so much nicer. Then at least she'd *have* a father—and a real mother who loved her.

She squeezed her eyes tight shut against the tears. She didn't want to look at the nurse or the doctor anymore. They didn't care about her any more than her mother did. She hated them. She hated everything. Maybe if she could close her eyes tightly enough, where all she could see was the blackness, she could make her legs move and get up and walk out of here. Her arms shook violently, pounding the bed.

"Now, dear, please . . ."

She wished she could close her ears the way she could her eyes, to block that voice out.

"I think we *are* going to have to sedate her, Doctor."

From behind her closed eyes, Minerva felt the sensation of cold fluid entering her arm through the IV.

She wished Raven were here.

"I am."

The silent voice inside her own head that wasn't hers startled Minerva.

"Raven? Is that you?"

"Yeah. But I'm not supposed to be here. If the doctor finds out I'm here, he'll kick me out."

Startled, Minerva tried to open her eyes to see where he was in the room, but her eyelids were heavier now. She was getting used to the cold sensation entering her arm, so she didn't notice it as much. With effort, she forced her eyes open a crack. Everything was blurry now, but she thought she saw a figure standing near the doorway, dressed in dark clothes, about the size of an eight-year-old boy.

"Raven?" she whispered.

But the figure vanished. She wasn't sure whether it was because her eyes had fallen shut again or because he'd left the room.

Had he ever really been there at all?

School
(2002)

School was different now. Minerva had never been very tall, but rolling around in a chair all day long made it a whole lot worse. Other kids either ignored her, which was bad, stared at her, which was worse, or laughed and joked about her as if she weren't there—which she didn't want to be.

Even now, months after the accident, she'd sometimes believe she felt something in her legs. Without thinking, she'd push up on the armrests of her wheelchair and try to stand up, only to fall backward . . . and roll backward a few feet.

To make things worse, her mother seemed to want almost nothing to do with her. Not that she had ever been what anyone would call a loving mom, but now, it was almost as though her daughter didn't exist. When she did bother saying anything to Minerva, Jessica would turn her head away and start talking to the wall. It would have been funny if it weren't so insulting. This was her *mother*, after all.

"We're here," she announced, pulling the car to an abrupt stop in the school loading zone.

Minerva winced. Ever since the accident, even getting into the car with her mother was difficult. Whenever the car stopped abruptly, Minerva's stomach clenched and she felt like she might have to relive the horror of it all.

"Get out."

Minerva pushed open the door and waited for her mother to get the wheelchair out of the trunk. She always treated it like some terrible extra burden, lingering in the car for a few moments just so she could make Minerva wait for her. Why did she do that? Did it give her some sense of power? She wasn't the one who had been crippled by the accident. She could still walk. But that didn't stop her from acting like *she* had been the victim, like her life had been made so much worse by the fact that Minerva had dared to get hurt.

It wasn't like Minerva had wanted this. Had she been the one who ran that red light and wound up in wreck? If you asked her mother, she might as well have been.

"If only you had buckled your goddamn seatbelt," Jessica muttered. "How many times did I tell you to put it on? Did you listen? Do you *ever* listen to me?"

She wasn't talking to Minerva. She was talking away from her again.

She went around to the back of the car, opened the trunk, and hoisted the wheelchair out, dropping it like a heap of trash on the asphalt.

She swore—loud enough that a bunch of kids nearby turned to look at her. "See what you made me do to my shoulder?"

"Sorry," Minerva mumbled, staring down at the curb as she waited for her mother to bring the chair around.

"Here," she said, pushing the arms of the wheelchair apart and waiting.

"You have to put it closer, Mom."

Jessica swore again.

"Mom, please . . ."

"Fine!"

She pushed the chair a few feet more so it was just close enough, and Minerva thrust herself forward, catching the armrests. She let go of one and twisted her body sideways, trying to locate the seat beneath her paralyzed backside. Her chances of doing so were a flip of the coin. If her mother would only reach out a hand to steady her, it would be so much easier . . .

Her rear end hit the front lip of the vinyl seat and slid forward, sending her tumbling onto the sidewalk.

"Clumsy little . . ."

"Are you okay?" The voice, which came from off to one side, belonged to Mrs. Stebbins, Minerva's teacher.

Minerva nodded, but the tears in her eyes conveyed a different message. She couldn't feel her backside, but she knew it would be black and blue. It wasn't the first time this had happened.

Mrs. Stebbins reached down with both hands and lifted Minerva into the wheelchair.

"We'll take you to the nurse," she said.

Minerva's mother walked briskly around the car, stopping only long enough to slam the trunk shut before quickly opening the driver's side door and immediately thrusting the key into the ignition. A moment later, she gunned the engine, and the car squealed away from the curb.

"I'm sorry, Minerva," Mrs. Stebbins said.

Minerva didn't say anything. She was remembering a happier time, when Raven's parents used to drop her off at school. They'd done that most of the time, because even back then, Minerva's mother hadn't wanted to be bothered with the "chore," as she called it, of driving her to school. She lived several blocks from the nearest school bus route, and Raven's parents hadn't thought it was safe for a young girl to walk that far alone, so they volunteered to pick her up and drive her home each day.

She'd been jealous that Raven had two parents. Her own father had left when she was too young to remember; she didn't even know his name, because her mother only referred to him as "that person." (Archer would come along later, the product of an Internet flirtation that turned into a one-night stand with someone her mother called "that other person.")

Minerva's mother blamed her for her father's desertion, the way she blamed her for just about everything else, saying she had been a "burden" on him, but Minerva wondered if she hadn't treated him the same way she treated her. Raven's mom never treated his dad that way. She called him "my superhero," and he had a pet name for her, too, "Mrs. Sugarplum." They were always making jokes with each other that only they seemed to understand; or maybe they were the kind of jokes that only grown-ups understood, about the theater and politics and TV shows that came on past her bedtime.

Raven seemed to understand some of them, but whenever she asked him to explain, he promised he would someday . . . then never did.

Now she hadn't seen Raven or his parents since the accident—except for that one time in the hospital, when she was now sure she'd been dreaming.

For a long time, no one had even bothered to tell her Raven had been killed. It was like they were trying to spare her feelings because they knew she'd been so close to him . . . and because they thought a six-year-old was too young to figure it out. No one had even bothered to say, "He's gone to a better place," the way they had when her Uncle Tim had stopped coming to visit her mom every so often for beer and pizza nights. Her mother took her to visit his grave at St. Peter's Cemetery once. "This is what happens to people who drink too much beer," she told Minerva.

Never mind that she kept right on drinking Bud Light and Heineken herself after he was gone, not to mention boosting her cigarette intake to three packs a day.

She might have asked Raven's parents about him, but she never saw them, either. It was as though they'd vanished right along with him.

Minerva looked up as Mrs. Stebbins wheeled her past the Math Building and toward the main office. Out of the corner of her eye, she noticed a movement—a boy in a black T-shirt and jeans. She recognized him at once.

It was Raven. He wasn't dead, after all!

His eyes caught her gaze, and he lifted a hand to wave at her.

Then Mrs. Stebbins wheeled her around a corner, and he was gone.

Midnight
(2016)

Minerva had tried to find Raven again after that, and each time she did, she succeeded . . . after a fashion. She would catch a glimpse of him out of the corner of her eye, or in the midst of a crowd, but every time, something would happen and she'd lose sight of him. She was chasing a mirage over a flat, barren desert on a hot summer day—at least that's what it felt like. Being in a wheelchair didn't help matters; it wasn't as fast or maneuverable as a healthy pair of legs. She could remember playing hopscotch and climbing trees before the accident, and each time such memories visited her, she cringed. The accident had robbed her of so much: not only her legs, but her best friend, too. And now, without the use of those legs, she could never seem to catch up to him.

Once, when she was at home, she tried to call his house. As she was waiting for someone on the other end to pick up, she happened to glance out the window and saw him standing there, if only for a split second. He mouthed something that looked like, "Remember," then disappeared behind the rose bushes. At the same moment, there was a click at the other end of the line, as if someone had picked up. But the voice that followed was an automated recording: "The number you have reached is no longer in service. If you believe you have reached this recording in error, please check the number and try your call again."

She never did, not in the fifteen years that had passed since then.

After that, she thought of Raven less often, and his appearances became less frequent.

She'd stopped thinking about him at all when, one day, she saw him waiting in line at the school cafeteria behind Jenny Rudabaker, who was being her usual slow self in making up her mind between the chicken nuggets and the pizza bites. Minerva rolled up beside him and was about to say hello when she realized it wasn't Raven at all, just some other kid who looked like him from a distance.

After that, Minerva decided she must've been seeing this same kid the whole time.

"No, that wasn't me."

Minerva started at the sound of the voice as the candle flame flickered by her bedside. It was around midnight, and the room was pitch dark.

"Raven?"

"Now, *that's* me." The declaration was followed by a slight chuckle as a figure stepped into the dim light.

She shied away from him. He couldn't be here. It was impossible: She knew he was dead—that he'd been dead for fifteen years. Part of her felt afraid that he might be a ghost, and part of her felt afraid that—if he wasn't—here was a full-grown man standing in her bedroom in the middle of the night.

He was Raven, but he wasn't. His was the same boyish face she remembered, framed by the same, dark, wavy hair. The expression was that mischievous smile he'd worn years earlier, but she could see no sign of any hair on his chin—not even the kind that pokes its way out of a man's face after five o'clock (or, with some, after two in the afternoon). His body, however, had filled out: In that respect, he looked every bit of the 23-year-old man he was, even though he unaccountably wore the same "Legend of Zelda" T-shirt that had been his favorite back in third grade—just a few sizes larger.

"You still play that game?" Minerva asked, tentatively, trying to lighten the mood and avoid making him mad if he were some ghoul or zombie.

He shrugged. "Some things never change. Good games don't get old—even if good friends sometimes do."

Minerva looked down at her legs, her anger banishing her fear, then fixed him with a stare that could've melted the rust off a hundred-year-old pipe. "You think I look *old*?"

Raven's eyes widened. "That's not what I meant. I just meant it's been a long time since . . ."

"Don't patronize me," Minerva said. "What are you doing in my room anyway? I mean, we were friends a long time ago, but a guy coming into a girl's bedroom in the middle of the night? Hello."

21

Raven shook his head. "I'm sorry. I'm not here. Not exactly. Well, I am, but 'here' isn't really here."

"Look, I don't know who you think you are, but I haven't seen you in, what, sixteen years? And now you just show up in my room in the middle of the night like some psycho stalker? Or a ghost. Or . . . I don't know."

"We're not in your room. We are, but only . . . it's hard to explain."

"Fine. I don't care whether you're a stalker or a ghost or what you are. I don't care how you got here, just get the hell out."

"I can't."

"If you got in here, you can get out. I may not be able to run, but I've got one hell of a loud scream."

Raven raised his eyebrows. "I'm sure you do, but it won't make any difference."

"I'll give you to the count of three: One."

Raven was shaking his head, but he wasn't moving.

"Two."

"Let me finish that for you: Three. Do your worst."

Minerva let loose with a scream that should have accomplished the old cliché of waking the dead, or at the very least creating a small, localized tremor to make them toss and turn.

Raven stayed where he was, trying to suppress that mischievous grin of his. He was enjoying this.

Minerva kept up the scream for as long as she had enough breath to continue. But its echoes quickly faded into silence, and it was clear no one was running to her aid. She might have expected her mother to ignore her, but Archer was usually still up playing video games at this hour during summer vacation, and even if he'd turned in early, he would have heard her. Minerva could always count on him to check on her when she was upset. But there was no sign of him now.

"I hate to say I told you so . . ."

Minerva slapped her hand on the nightstand next to her, barely missing the candle, and began fumbling for her smartphone. The palm of her hand flopped around a few times on the wooden surface like a goldfish that had jumped out of its aquarium. Finally, it settled on the phone, which she snatched up, jabbing at the touchscreen with her finger as she kept a wary eye on Raven. He hadn't moved, which infuriated her because she wanted him gone, but also came as a relief because he wasn't coming toward her like some psycho with a knife.

The phone beeped, taking what seemed like forever to respond as she swiped the screen, then sent her eyes the following message. "Fooled you, didn't I? I'm all out of juice. Guess you're on your own, you pathetic cripple."

"What the hell did you do to my phone?"

Raven shrugged again. He was too good at that. "Nothing. I'm sure whatever you see there is your own doing, not mine."

His tone wasn't haughty or even satisfied, just matter-of-fact, as though he were stating the obvious.

"Very funny. I didn't program this piece of crap. Who do I look like? Steve Jobs?"

"When did you start talking like that? You sound like your mother. She always used to cuss like a sailor, too."

Minerva threw the phone at him, but it missed and shattered against the wall beside the door. Raven turned his back to her for a second, bent over and picked it up, then handed it back to her. The light from the touchscreen was still steady, and it appeared none the worse for wear.

"How . . .?"

"I guess you didn't really want to break it, did you?"

"Of course not, idiot. I was trying to hit *you* with it."

"It should be broken, though, and it isn't. Interesting how that works. You threw the thing hard enough to shatter it into a million pieces, but somehow it's undamaged. And it calls you a 'pathetic cripple,' which is pretty much how you see yourself. Be careful, Min. That's quite a gift you've got there. Everything's happening just the way you envision it."

He was smirking, as though he'd said something funny without bothering to let her in on the joke.

"By the way, that whole 'pathetic cripple' thing doesn't fly with me. That sounds like your mom, too: always playing the victim. Except she does it just to get attention. I'm afraid you really believe that about yourself."

Minerva looked for something else to throw at him. "Stop comparing me to my mother . . ." She had to nearly bite her tongue to avoid letting loose with another expletive. She wasn't about to prove him right. "If I could control everything that was happening to me, do you think I'd be paralyzed? Or do you think I'd have missed you when I threw that phone?"

"Of course. Because I ducked."

Minerva shook her head.

"Here's the deal, Min: You're dreaming. This is your dream, so things happen pretty much the way you want them to. That is, they happen the way you think they should . . . except when it comes to me, because I'm not a part of your dream—at least, not technically. I'm *in* your dream, but I'm still me. I can do whatever I want, within certain limits. For example, if I hadn't ducked, you would have hit your target with that phone of yours. And you wouldn't have been able to heal the bump on my head just by dreaming it away."

"You would have deserved it."

"Why? Because I wanted to visit an old friend?"

He pointed to a chair by the window. "May I?"

"I can't stop you. What do you think I'm going to do, jump up out of this bed and wrestle you to the ground?"

"Well, that might be fun," he grinned. "And you could, too. This is your dream, remember?"

"Ha ha. Very funny."

"No, I'm serious. Try it. Not the wrestling. I'll give you a raincheck on that. Just swing your legs over the side of the bed and stand up."

Minerva frowned, but she'd always been the curious type. It had gotten her into trouble opening an attachment from an email spammer promising free cosmetics if she'd "just click this"; as a result, her hard drive had been damaged beyond the point that any cosmetic fixes could cure. She'd learned her lesson . . . not. She was always up for a taste of newfangled exotic foods like chicken fried escargot and jalapeno margaritas. If some reviewer panned the latest TV show, she'd watch it just for kicks. And if some long-lost childhood friend who happened to show up in what might or might not be a dream happened to dare her paraplegic self to rise up and walk, she'd just have to give it a shot.

Pushing herself up with both arms, she focused her energy on the spot below her abdomen and sent those electrical charges from her brain down toward her legs that said, "Move!"

They did.

Before she knew it, she was sitting up on the side of the bed and, a moment later, standing in front of Raven.

"Nicely done!" he said, applauding softly.

Minerva stared down at her legs. Although she was clearly standing on them, they looked as spindly and pale as always, the muscles long since atrophied from years of disuse. A sudden panic flooded through her, and she felt the weight of her body collapsing downward on the frail appendages, her knees giving way like a sandcastle beset by a tidal wave of doubt. She barely managed to push herself back onto the bed an instant before she collapsed onto the floor, and a moment afterward, it dawned on her that she must have used those atrophied muscles in her legs to do so.

"That's a good start," Raven said. "Now try again."

"No way." Minerva glared at him but smiled despite herself. "Once is enough."

"For now."

Minerva said nothing for a moment, then replied, "Fair enough. I suppose if this is a dream—and I guess it's got to be a dream—it won't do any harm."

"Exactly."

Raven stood suddenly where he was and began striding quickly for the door. "I have to go for now," he said, glancing back over his shoulder, "but can we meet back here tomorrow night?"

"What is this? A date?"

He stopped momentarily. "Sure. If you want."

"I didn't say . . ."

But he was already gone. A date with her third-grade crush in her bedroom. Crush? Had he really been her crush? She guessed he had. She just hadn't admitted it to herself at the time. They'd been friends, sure, but she'd never thought about him being a crush. Maybe she was just projecting today's thoughts back onto her childhood. But that would mean. . . . She shook her head from side to side, her long, straight, black hair following her movements.

A voice interrupted her thoughts.

"Minerva? What did you do?"

She opened her eyes, suddenly awake.

Operative

Anthony Biltmore paced back and forth in his office, remembering. It wasn't the kind of office where you might expect to find a former CIA operative who'd made a killing on Wall Street by exploiting information he'd gained through a combination of espionage, bribery, and extortion. (Every bit of that was perfectly legal, at least according to the U.S. government, which paid him to do all of the above.) As far as the feds were concerned, he didn't exist. He was what they called a "ghost," which was why the even more covert agency that now employed him had stationed him way out in what they used to call the boondocks.

No address.

No public visibility.

Just an old, out-of-the-way motel that had been built in the late 1920s along an old, long-abandoned highway through an isolated ravine. They'd run it through this area because it was the path of least resistance, alongside the river that had carved out the canyon, only to discover that the river tended to flood during the rainy season, washing out the highway. More enlightened engineers had built a bypass some miles to the east, farther up another mountain in the range. When that happened, the motel suddenly found itself wanting for customers, and within a few months had shut its doors. The government had purchased the land and sealed it off with barbed wire and "no trespassing" signs.

Ignore the signs? Cut the wire? There were some trained Dobermans and Rottweilers waiting on the other side to deliver a not-so-friendly greeting. If you managed to get past them, there was another layer of barbed wire farther on and, past that, an abundance of poison oak, along with a well-hidden but extensive camera system that blanketed every square foot of the inner perimeter. Then, there was Anthony Biltmore, who, in addition to being an accomplished spy and con man, was lethal with his favorite weapon, the M39. On some assignments, he used a more compact firearm, but for protecting his territory, this was his only choice. He had invoked its firepower against a handful of intruders over the years, none of whom had survived.

If the authorities questioned him, he assumed the guise of a rancher and claimed the right of self-defense, and if it got beyond that, he appealed to a higher authority—one of his highly placed federal contacts, who could say the word and make the problem disappear. The cops stopped asking him questions and the dead men, as the saying goes, told no tales.

Apart from such rare unwanted guests, however, Biltmore (it wasn't his real name, merely an alias provided by his benefactors) was alone, and no one knew he was there. Even the feds seemed to forget he was there from time to time, although they had been kind enough to install a dedicated T3 line so he could keep tabs on the world at large. The world, however, couldn't keep tabs on him. Not only was Biltmore a spy and a marksman, he was an accomplished hacker, which enabled him to stay one step ahead of anyone who tried to infiltrate his fortress via the Web.

The agency had recruited Biltmore precisely for his multitude of talents, then had simply made him disappear.

He only stepped out of the shadows on those fleeting occasions when he was needed to do a job, and then only when the job couldn't be accomplished remotely. That had been the case with one of his earliest assignments: the termination of an elderly woman living on a fixed income in a small Santa Monica home. It was customary, when he was enlisted to do a job of this sort, that he ask no questions about the target's background or the reason for his involvement. Ignorance insulated him from the mess that often followed, and his employers were accomplished at covering their tracks—and his. Curiosity could be deadly.

In the case of the elderly woman, though, Biltmore had made an exception. He had hardened himself over the years, but not so much that the thought of shooting a 75-year-old woman in cold blood didn't create certain . . . reservations.

The assignment had arrived via secure electronic message, as all his assignments did, in this case from an individual known as TaniaX3iFy.

"New target acquired. Location: Santa Monica, California. Objective: Terminate. Your target is an elderly woman living on 21st Place," the message began, listing the specific address along with the longitude and latitude, so there could be no mistake. "She is the sole occupant of the home. Your assignment: terminating the target. Intelligence indicates she is likely to be in close proximity to the front window of the residence between 1300 and 1400 hours. Cover will be provided in the form of a non-fatal drive-by shooting in the area sixteen hours earlier. The vehicle you will use in the operation will match the description of the vehicle employed in that incident. The weapons will also match."

Biltmore hadn't been happy about that. He liked to choose his own weapons, but he understood the reasoning.

The message continued: "A member of the Guerrero Oculto street gang will be implicated in both shootings. The vehicle to be used in the operation will be delivered to you at 0800 hours on the morning of April 21, and the mission will commence and terminate the same day." April 21 was the next day. Biltmore studied the message for a moment, then typed the following reply to TaniaX3iFy.

"Query: Woman's name."

"Irrelevant."

"Query: Why is target being engaged."

"Classified."

"Query: Does she have any family?"

"No."

A straight answer. That was unusual. It might have meant TaniaX3iFy was being honest because she sensed it would ease his reluctance to take the assignment (not that it made any difference—he really had no choice in the matter, but TaniaX3iFy was certainly aware that a reluctant hit man was always less likely to succeed). On the other hand, it might have meant she was lying to him because she knew he'd hesitate at the wrong moment if he knew the truth.

No matter. He had the location, which was more than enough to investigate the matter himself.

"Understood and accepted," he typed, and the name TaniaX3iFY went gray, indicating the user was now offline.

Biltmore exed out of the message, called up a program he'd designed called Trenchcoat and typed in a code that brought up a prompt labeled "erase footprints." He typed a Y and hit "enter," then opened a secure-source browser and called up another program of his own design called Grail; in the search field, he typed the address he'd been given and hit "enter" again. Sometimes, a whole series of names would appear on the screen, belonging to each of a building's occupants dating back to the time of its construction. This time, there were just two. The first was the original owner, who'd been dead for forty years. The second was the woman he was looking for, including all the pertinent information: age (75), marital status (widowed, Elliot, deceased 1989), children (one son, James, deceased 1995), Social Security number, driver's license number and renewal date . . .

And, of course, the name.

He knew that name.

He'd stood up and started pacing then, just the way he was now. Then he sat down again, closed Grail, called up Trenchcoat and erased all record of what he'd just seen. On the screen, that is. His own memory was another story.

Regret

Biltmore had spent the past twenty years trying to forget what he'd seen on the screen that day, trying to forget that he'd gone through with the assignment despite what he'd found out. Of course, he hadn't really had a choice—at least that's what he kept telling himself. It was supposed to make him feel better about it, although it didn't seem to help much.

That had been a simple hit. Get in, get out, and move on to the next one. The fact that he hadn't been able to move on, not really, was what got to him. He'd immersed himself in more assignments ranging from corporate sabotage to cyberespionage against the Chinese, all the while trying to forget Mary Lou Corbet. Recently, though, that had gotten even more difficult. The assignments had begun to take on a narrower focus, and then there was the message from JulesB6s4R (he hadn't heard from TaniaX3iFY in several years) that "your assets are being dedicated to Operation Death Trap until further notice."

That had certainly caught his attention. Operation Death Trap had been the code name for his hit on Mary Lou Corbet. It was, as far as he'd known at the time, a one-off assignment. But if they'd resurrected that code name and had assigned him to the mission on a continuing basis, that could mean they were going to recruit him for more front-end work—what they called the messy business of eliminating "problem" individuals. It could also mean it had something to do with the Corbet woman.

Another electronic message had arrived this afternoon, and that's what had him pacing.

"New target acquired. Location: Calabasas, California. Objective: Infiltrate." More specific instructions followed concerning the target's identity and a more specific location, but there was nothing more on the objective beyond that single word. He was relieved that his superiors hadn't used the assignment classification "terminate," which was self-explanatory. There were others:

"Incriminate" (a euphemism for framing the target), "liberate" (extricate a less-proficient operative who'd gotten into a nasty mess), "confiscate" (steal something, either in the physical world or cyberspace; he was good at that), "invalidate" (discredit someone) and "disseminate," as in propaganda.

There were a few assignments he never received, because he either wasn't good at them or showed so little interest that his superiors got a clue and passed them on to someone with better social skills. Things like "facilitate" (working with another operative), "assimilate" (recruiting a new operative), and "mediate," a task his blunt manner made him a perfect candidate *not* to perform.

There was also "isolate," which his superiors had done to him. In fact, it was the way agency operatives generally did business: alone. Being antisocial by nature, he was fine with that. It was that same reclusive nature, however, that left him uneasy about his latest assignment. He'd never been assigned to an infiltration before, as it didn't exactly fall within his skill set. Schmoozing, rubbing elbows, and ingratiating himself to others—this was definitely not his forte. They'd never chosen him for such an assignment before, and he felt it odd that they should do so now . . . except for the title of the mission: Operation Death Trap. Only one explanation made sense: They'd selected him because he'd been a player in an earlier stage of the operation and they wanted to minimize their exposure by limiting the number of people involved. It was standard operating procedure, and it made sense—except for the fact that using an operative outside his area of expertise wasn't the best recipe for success.

He didn't like it, which was another reason he was pacing.

Under strict protocol, he wasn't supposed to contact his superiors other than electronically. The less contact he had with them, the less he could reveal if the mission was compromised. But protocol be damned. If he was going to do this job and do it right, he needed to ask some questions . . . and he needed to cover his ass.

He picked up his smartphone and dialed; someone picked up before the second ring.

"Baldwin's Curios, Books, and Collectibles. How may I help you?"

"I heard you have a signed first edition of *The Great Gatsby*. I'd like to purchase it."

There was a brief silence, then. "Password phrase confirmed. State identity."

"Triage3NxO1."

Another brief silence. "Identity recognized. Voiceprint match confirmed."

"Fine. Now let's cut the bull and . . ."

He stopped mid-sentence, interrupted by a beep and the sound of an old Phil Collins tune recycled as elevator music. A moment later, another voice came on the line.

"Hello?"

"Who am I talking to?"

"This is JulesB6s4R." It was a woman's voice. Somehow, Biltmore had always thought of Jules as a man, likely some British expatriate who wore a figurative stuffed shirt and had a last name like Verne.

"Okay, Jules. Do you want to tell my why the hell you assigned me to infiltrate some nobody in Calabasas? I've never been to Calabasas in my life, and I sure as hell have never been put on an infiltration. I think you've got the wrong guy here."

"You do realize this is a breach of protocol, Triage. This line isn't set up for frivolous inquiries. Ever hear of 911? That's what this line is, except secure, and only authorized personnel have access to it."

"Which means I really doubt I'm keeping anyone else from dialing in."

"Triage, there are more efficient uses of our time . . ."

"Indulge me."

Silence.

Biltmore forged ahead. "Are you going to answer my question?"

"Your personal background makes you ideal for this assignment, Triage. It outweighs any other considerations we may have about your conduct."

"Care to elaborate?"

What sounded like a sigh came through from the other end, and what came next confirmed his suspicions: This was all about Mary Lou Corbet, that seemingly innocent 75-year-old woman he'd shot to death two decades earlier. He had known before that in an entirely different context; he just hadn't put two and two together until the day he'd carried out the assignment. Now, there was another assignment, and everything he'd been struggling to push to the back of his memory these past twenty years was suddenly front and center again. This was, in fact, the very reason he'd been given this new assignment—which, as it turned out, was just a continuation of the old one.

"Welcome back to Operation Death Trap. Isn't this just my lucky day?" he snarled into the phone.

Then he hung up without waiting for an answer.

Come-On

Grocery shopping was one of those chores Jessica loathed. There was always too much to buy and too little cash in her bank account to make ends meet without resorting to the good ol' "R&R"—rice and ramen. Rice she could stomach. Ramen was another matter. She served most of that to Minerva (who hated it too) and Archer (who wolfed it down like he did everything else). The two of them were eating up all her money, and not a day went by that she didn't regret having them. Minerva especially. At least Archer helped out around the house and did as he was told. Minerva just lay there on her bed all day, reading or sleeping most of her useless existence away. It wasn't as though Jessica could have put her through college, and she couldn't kick her out. She was an invalid, after all. But at least she brought in a disability check. That was something anyway.

"Looking for something?"

Jessica realized she'd just been standing in front of the condensed milk for the past few moments, lost in her bitter reverie. She looked up, expecting to see a barely post-pubescent MarketMor employee in one of those tan smocks, only to be greeted instead by the sight of a man of medium height with dirty brown, slightly receding hair, dressed in a business suit.

She smiled slightly, despite her mood. "Butter," she said. "I don't think it's on this aisle, though."

The man nodded. "This way." He walked to the front of her cart, took hold of it and pulled it along; she had little choice but to follow him to the dairy section.

"Here we are," he said, smiling—though she saw it was an awkward smile, something he didn't seem entirely comfortable with.

"Thank you . . ."

"Carson. Bradley Carson."

"I know: 'But you can call me Brad.'"

"How did you know I was going to say that?"

"Look, Brad. I've been shopping here for five years, and not to brag or anything, but I've had my share of supermarket come-ons. Most of 'em start out with that lame old James Bond speech. Bond. James Bond. Why is it that every man over the age of 40 thinks he has to act like some kind of secret agent to get a woman's attention?"

"I don't know. I'm only 43, but I guess I qualify."

"Thirty-nine," she said, thinking that maybe if she told him her age, she could get him to leave her alone. Not that he was unattractive . . .

"Do I have it?"

The question caught her slightly off-guard. She was used to men flattering her by saying, "Well, you don't look it." His matter-of-fact air would have been off-putting if she hadn't found it so refreshing.

"What?"

"Your attention."

"I would say you do. But I'm supposed to be getting some butter."

Carson-Bradley Carson reached up onto the shelf in front of them and grabbed two medium-sized tubs of DairySmooth whipped butter and placed them in her cart.

"How did you know my brand?"

"Lucky guess. Well, good meeting you." He fixed her with a brief but intense gaze from deep-set hazel eyes.

"Yeah. You too. See you around."

He turned, and Jessica watched him walk away from her and disappear around the corner of the canned food aisle.

She purposely went in the other direction, her upper lip twitching slightly as it did when she was anxious. Reaching into her purse, she pulled out her grocery list and headed for the beer and wine section. A nice cold one was starting to sound pretty good, even if she could only afford the domestic piss water that tried to pass for beer. She grabbed one of those oversized "Magnum" cans and headed for the registers. Unfortunately, it was a Saturday, and the place was jam-packed.

She hadn't been in line for 30 seconds when someone came up behind her.

It was Carson.

Before she realized who it was, she had already looked at him. Part of her hoped he wouldn't notice her, but that part of her was trying hard to keep a lid on the other part of her.

"Hello again," he said.

"Hello."

"I didn't catch your name back there."

"It's Jessica, but you can call me Jess." She winced. That was as much of a cliché as the whole Bond-James Bond thing. If nothing else, they had clichés in common.

The line moved forward. Haltingly.

"Sorry. I'm not very good at conversation," he said, forcing that peculiar half-smile of his.

"Well, it's a market, not a business convention. You sure are dressed for one, though."

"Clothes make . . ."

". . . the man. That's a bunch of bullshit if ever I heard it." Did this guy talk in anything except clichés?

The woman in front of her, a gray-haired woman in a purple hat with a young, pudgy blond girl standing beside her, turned and shot her a glare. "Please. There are children present!"

"Well, lady," she shot back. "You'll be out of this line in five minutes and you'll never have to deal with my *bullshit* again."

The woman's eyes widened, and she turned back to face forward.

Jessica tossed her head slightly, as she did whenever she felt self-satisfied, her straight, black hair swishing like a waterfall.

"You're blunt," Carson said.

"And you're cute." Had she really said that? Geez. He was good looking and all, but was she really that desperate? Still, a man wearing a suit that nice—good god, was it an Armani?—had to be worth something, and even if he turned out to be lousy in bed, she could put up with it if he turned out to be a reliable sugar daddy. And if he turned out to be good in bed . . . Her mind had begun to swim with possibilities.

"Did you find everything okay?"

She looked up at the checker, a middle-aged woman with a tattoo across her arm that read "Loverly" and who thought she could look hip by dyeing her hair green.

"Oh. Sure. Yeah, that's it," Jessica said.

"Just run hers and mine through together."

She looked back at Carson, startled, but just said, "Thanks." She had never been one to object if someone else wanted to pay for her.

Not only did the checker ring them up together, she also put their bags in the same cart, so she had little choice but to walk out with him. Not that she was complaining at this point.

"My car's right over here," she said.

She clicked the electronic device on her keychain twice, the trunk popped open, and she watched as Carson loaded the bags into the storage area. She winced slightly as she realized how messy it was: an old grape slushy cup, a half-read romance novel, a box of tampons that she kept in the car for emergencies and a flashlight with a broken-out bottom that had left a couple of batteries to roll around annoyingly.

Carson didn't flinch at any of it. He didn't seem to notice or, if he did, he was gentleman enough not to react. Jessica wasn't used to dealing with gentlemen. It was a nice change of pace.

"All in," he said, reaching up and slamming the trunk.

He reached out, as if to shake her hand, but took her left hand instead.

"No ring," he remarked, fixing her with that intense gaze once again.

Her own eyes met his and didn't waver. "Would it matter if there was?"

He waited a moment before answering, then said, honestly, "No."

"How about we go somewhere," he said. "I know a good Italian place, Agostino's . . ."

She smiled and put a finger to his lips, feeling his breath brush gently across its tip. "I've got a better idea. Why don't we go to my place ... and get to know each other better."

Progress

Minerva set her book on the nightstand earlier than usual and closed her eyes. She didn't want to admit to herself that she was excited at the prospect of seeing Raven again, because everything sensible inside her was telling her not to expect anything. Of course, she told herself, last night had only been a dream, and if he happened to appear again tonight, it would only be because she was thinking about him as she dozed off.

Still . . .

She closed her eyes, trying to let herself drift off, then suddenly opened them again, as she felt a tingling in her legs.

This was impossible. She hadn't felt anything there since the accident.

"The accident is a lie."

She looked around frantically, and there he was, sitting in the same chair by the window that he'd occupied the previous night, staring at her, hands clasped in his lap and chin slightly bent forward.

"Comfy," he said, lifting his head and smiling.

"You're here."

"I'm not in the habit of breaking dates, especially with beautiful women who've just come back into my life, such as it is, after far too many years."

She scowled. "This isn't really a date, Raven. You're just a dream, after all."

"Correction. This is a dream. I'm in it, but I'm not part of it. I could walk out that door in the next moment and you'd go right on dreaming."

"Maybe, but your leaving would just be part of the dream, just something in my head."

"If that's true, you can make me vanish just by wishing it. Go ahead."

She said nothing, and he didn't move.

"See?"

"Maybe I don't want you to leave." She scowled again. She hadn't really wanted him to know that. He'd tricked her into saying it.

"That's progress," he quipped. "Last night, you threw a cellphone at me. Now, sit up on the bed again, like you did last night."

This time, Minerva didn't hesitate. She swung her legs out over the side of the bed and sat up, facing him, just a couple of feet away. She still felt the tingling in her legs, but she was more aware of Raven. His eyes were studying her intently, as if searching for something. Then, a moment later, he nodded slightly in apparent confirmation that he'd found it. He unclasped his hands and leaned forward.

"Give me your hand."

She did, and he smiled, holding it in both of his. His skin was softer than anything else she could remember touching, even more so than the velvet cloak hanging in her mother's closet or the silken fur of her old calico cat, Samantha. They were lighter, too, as though his hands were being suspended from some invisible marionette string that hung there as she held them. His smile was both joyous and melancholy at once, while his eyes, nearly half-closed, seemed moister than they had been.

"What is it?"

"It's just been . . . so long . . . since I touched someone. Anyone. And I'm so glad it could be you."

She felt in her own hands, as they rested in his, the same tingling feeling she felt in her long-dead legs.

Suddenly, she flinched and withdrew them.

"What's happening here?"

He shook his head quickly from side to side, as if shaking off a chill. "I'm sorry. Please, Min, don't be afraid. It's only me."

She stared at him warily, his features shadowy in the flickering light of her candle. Her tone, when she spoke, was flat. "Is it? Really? What are you doing here, Raven, or whoever you are. And what do you want from me?"

"Just that you never forget about me."

It seemed an odd request. "Well, I don't think there's any danger of that," she quipped. "You're making a lasting impression here, that's for sure."

"Promise. It's the only way I can help you."

"Help me? How?"

"Help you get past the lie of the accident."

She sat up bolt straight and stared straight at him. "That accident left me crippled, you jerk. It's one hell of a lot more real than this messed-up dream."

Raven shook his head decisively. "No. It's not. That's where you're wrong. But you have to remember, or I can never help you."

"Remember what?"

"Me."

"You're right here in front of me. Duh."

"I mean, after I leave tonight. After you wake up. Please say you'll let me come to you again. And promise me you'll never forget me."

"I can't, even if I wanted to. You're making sure of that."

"So promise me." His eyes grew softer, and his head tilted slightly to one side. "Give me your hand again."

Against her better judgement, she did, and she felt the soft lightness of him again, the tingling in his hands that ran across her palms and up into her arms, coursing down through her body to meet the tingling in her legs. It felt exhilarating, almost like life itself, but with something missing. She couldn't put her finger on what it was. She felt her shoulders relax as he took her other hand in his.

"Now," he said, "remember what it was like to walk. To have the use of your legs. Focus on what it felt like."

He stood to his feet, and she felt him gently tugging on her arms, drawing her up to meet him. She didn't resist, and her legs, as if magically, complied.

"How is this possible?" she breathed.

"It just is. You'll understand soon, Min. Just give it time. And promise me you won't forget."

She felt his chin resting on her shoulder as she allowed him to pull her close in an embrace that seemed ethereal, like something from a dream.

But then, this was a dream.

"I promise," she whispered.

And she felt a drop of moisture on her shoulder.

"Thank you."

Breakfast

Minerva was jarred awake by a loud noise invading her dream. At first, she couldn't tell what it was; muffled voices seeping through the wall and into her semi-consciousness. They weren't words, really—more like grunts and moans, and then something louder, more insistent.

Her mother was having sex.

"Great," she said under her breath. "Jessica's found someone else to bed. Or con." She chuckled to herself. No skin off her nose. If anything, whoever was in there with her would keep her mother distracted. It had been bad enough when the woman had ignored her as a child, but these days she'd traded neglect for a steady stream of verbal abuse.

"You useless little bitch. I can't believe you came out me. I'd just as soon stick you back up inside me so I wouldn't have to deal with you, but I'd probably catch something, you worthless . . ."

That was just one example.

Maybe 'getting some' would improve her attitude—even if it was only temporary, until Mr. Wonderful realized all he really was to her was a dick attached to a wallet attached to a bank account. That bank account would be drained before long, if she knew her mother, who might not have invented the term golddigger but had probably applied to have it trademarked.

She rolled over and went back to sleep, expecting to find Raven waiting for her again in her in the depths of her slumber. The next thing she was aware of, though, was a beam of sunlight knifing its way into her room past a frayed edge of curtain.

"Breakfast."

The voice on the other side of the door belonged to Archer. He knew better than to come into her room unannounced. The time he'd come in while she was sleeping and squeezed a wet washcloth over her forehead, announcing "Chinese water torture" had been the last time he'd tried anything like that. No, she hadn't thrown a cellphone at him, but the scream she'd let out as she sat bolt upright in bed not a foot away from his grinning face had convinced him: Startling his big sister wasn't the safest course of action.

"Come on in and help me then," she said.

The door opened and Archer danced in, a ball of too much energy for however early it was. She looked at the clock: 9:45. How did it get that late?

Archer went to the closet and grabbed a muted rose-colored top to go with a pair of loose-fitting pants, while Minerva rolled over and pulled a pair of panties from the drawer in her nightstand. She didn't mind having her little brother help her change; she could do it herself—and usually did— but it was a lot easier when you didn't have to yank your lifeless legs around and contort yourself into enough positions to impress a yoga master.

She handed Archer the panties, and he went to the foot of the bed, drawing aside the covers and putting her feet through the holes one at a time. Then he guided them up under the sheet to just above her knees, where she grabbed them and took them the rest of the way.

"Thanks, Arch," she said.

"Mom's making sausages and biscuits and gravy," he announced, repeating the drill with her pants and handing her the shirt. He turned away as she pulled a sports bra out of the drawer, used her muscled arms to push herself into a sitting position and slipped it on over her head.

"That's a switch. When was the last time she made breakfast?"

"Can't remember. But there's some guy here. I think she's trying to impress him."

"With her cooking?"

"It's better than cereal."

"We'll see."

He laughed as he went over to the window and drew back the curtains. "I know you don't like too much light in here, but it's like a mausoleum."

"Where did you learn that word?"

"School. It was one if my spelling words last year. I got it right, too."

Minerva smiled. "Good for you."

She positioned herself on the bed, then transferred herself into the wheelchair that sat beside it. Archer ran around the back and took the handles, opening the door and wheeling her out of the room and down the hall. Like getting dressed, propelling herself from place to place was well within her ability—part of the reason she'd developed those muscles in her arms—but Archer seemed to enjoy helping her, and she liked being treated to a free ride. It wasn't as though anyone else was going to give her one.

"There you two are," Jessica smiled. Yup, she was trying to impress this guy, all right. Her disposition was usually about as sunny as a total eclipse. "Have a seat: Breakfast is coming right up. I'd like you to meet Bradley. I have a feeling you'll be seeing him around quite a lot here from now on."

She was really turning it on: charm plus expectations could be a potent combo. She must really have her sights set on this guy.

"Brad, these are my children, Archer and Minerva." Whenever she introduced them to anyone, which was hardly ever, she always mentioned Archer first, even though she was the oldest. It was a subtle dig, but it was better than "this is my pathetic, worthless daughter."

"Hi," she said, forcing a half-smile. It couldn't hurt to make nice if he was inducing this level of phony politeness from Jessica.

The man smiled. "Hello, Minerva," he said, and left it at that.

Man of few words. Interesting. He didn't seem too enthusiastic about being here. Minerva had heard plenty of enthusiasm through her bedroom wall the night before, but then again, some guys would hop in the sack with anything if they were hard up. Maybe this guy was one of them, although he seemed a bit more put together than the guys her mother usually brought home from the bar. His dress shirt had a few wrinkles, probably from being tossed in the corner while he and Jessica did the nasty, but it was a dress shirt, not a leather jacket or a Slayer T-shirt, and that alone was quite a contrast.

"So, what do you do, Bradley?" she asked.

"Minerva, it's not polite . . ." Jessica began.

"C'mon mother, I'm showing an interest. It's more than you do whenever I introduce you to one of my friends."

Oops. So much for being nice.

"Uh-oh," she heard Archer whisper.

"Friends?" Jessica said sarcastically, all the previous sweetness draining from her voice. "What friends?"

Minerva gritted her teeth. The brief struggle to play nice had just flown out the window. "Yes, Jessica, I do have them. And they're not just friends with benefits like Bradley here." Then, turning to him, she added hastily and with sincere regret, "Sorry, no offense. It's a mother-daughter thing."

Bradley said nothing, but the expression on his face looked more awkward than offended.

Her mother all but sprinted around the kitchen table to Minerva and grabbed the handles of her wheelchair, yanking backward, then thrusting her forward, out of the kitchen.

"Excuse us," she said curtly over her shoulder.

She whisked Minerva through the door to her room and all but slammed it behind them, then pivoted around and bent over, so the heat of her breath was in her daughter's face.

"How dare you?" she seethed. "That man out there is actually a decent human being—unlike some lazy little nobodies I know. Bradley could be our ticket out of this hellhole, but what do you care? You'd just as soon sit here in this room and rot the rest of your life away like a corpse. Well, just keep it up and you'll be one soon enough."

"Sorry," Minerva said, averting her eyes, and she actually meant it—not because she gave a damn about her mother's ambitions, but because of something Raven had said about her behaving like Jessica. She didn't want to turn into some clone of her mother.

"I'm afraid 'sorry' won't cut it this time," she spat, rearing back with her right hand and letting fly a hard slap across Minerva's face.

Minerva fought back the water behind her eyes, curled her lip briefly, then forced herself to relax. This would not end well if it kept going this way.

Jessica bent forward again and whispered in her ear. "You don't even know what it's like to have a man inside you, to wrap yourself around his flesh and make it part of your own. You don't know what it's like to absorb him so he loses himself in you and you can do anything you want with him. Why? Because you can't *feel* anything down there, can you, Minerva? If you were a woman, you would understand what I'm trying to do here. But you're not a woman at all. You're an 'it.' You'll never know what it's like to take a man, because no man will ever want you."

She stood up straight and stared down at Minerva.

Minerva met her gaze, holding it steady but keeping her expression an emotionless mask.

There was a soft knock on the door.

"Yes?"

Bradley Carson opened it. The expression on his face still appeared awkward, but Minerva was starting to think that was his standard look. "Sorry to interrupt," he said flatly. "But I'm afraid I have to be heading out."

"Damn," Jessica said, before she realized she had said it aloud. Then the saccharine sweet smile returned to her face. "I'm sorry Minerva made a scene, Brad. Really, I am. I'm sure she really likes you."

I don't know whether to like him or not, Minerva thought. *Unlike some people, I don't sleep with someone before I actually get to know him.*

"No worries," Carson replied with a half-smile.

"I just wish I didn't have to spend the day with her when she's like this," Jessica complained. "She's impossible to . . ."

"Well, then, why don't I take her off your hands for the day."

Minerva sat up straight and stared at him. "Ummm . . ."

Jessica's face brightened, and this time Minerva could tell the smile wasn't forced. She'd take any opportunity to be rid of her paraplegic burden for a day.

"Don't you have to work?" Minerva asked. She didn't know this guy from Adam, she didn't enjoy going out, and she had no idea what to expect from him. Sure, he wore a dress shirt and slacks, but that didn't mean he wasn't some kind of psychopath. Hell, at best he was an idiot. Anyone who slept with Jessica would have to be.

"It's no trouble," Carson said. "I'm a stockbroker. Online trading. I do most of my work from home."

Oh, brilliant. This guy's going to take me to his house? What kind of mother lets her boy toy take her daughter to his house after a one-night stand? But then, she'd forgotten: Jessica wasn't a mother but a parasitic sociopath.

"Look, I'm not really sure . . ."

Jessica interrupted her. "That would be wonderful, Brad. You're an angel."

"But . . ."

"Don't worry, I'll take good care of her. Keep her occupied. Maybe take her to the pier and work on my laptop from there."

They were talking about her as if she wasn't even there. Wonderful. At least he was talking about taking her someplace public, which meant he wasn't going to abduct her and throw her into his basement or something—if he wasn't just saying that for her mother's benefit. The irony was, Jessica would probably applaud him if he made her disappear for good.

"It's settled then," Jessica said. The accompanying smile was, again, sincere. "Get your purse, Minerva, and wipe that frown off your face. You're a pretty girl when you smile, dear."

"Yes, she is," Carson said. "The image of her mother."

Minerva couldn't help wincing as Raven's words about her behaving like her mother came back into her head. *Just great. I can't escape this woman except with the help of some strange guy who's just spent the night with her.*

She remembered Raven again, and the thought of him calmed her. She glanced over at the window as Carson wheeled her out of the room, and for a split second, she would have sworn she saw her childhood friend there, all grown-up now, his face clouded with a nearly panicked look of concern.

Then he was gone . . . if he'd ever been there in the first place.

Taffy

The marine layer defied the sun, its presence putting a damper on a visit to the pier for those who had ventured out. It was nearly noon by the time they got there, but it was becoming clear that—even though it was Thursday—the sun was intent on taking a holiday. That was fine with Minerva. She'd always liked cool, damp days; they made her feel at home—or how she wished home would be, if she'd had a choice in the matter.

Seeing the pier was a relief; at least this Bradley hadn't been B.S.'ing her about where they were going.

"You haven't said much," she said as they pulled into a parking space underneath a palm tree in the lot just north of the pier. On a warm summer day, there wouldn't be a spot to be had here, but today, the lot was barely half full.

"You haven't exactly been wordy yourself." Carson got out of the car, retrieved her wheelchair from the trunk and brought it around to the passenger's side, opening the door for her.

"Hello? I'm in a car with some strange guy who just boinked Jessica—who, in case you haven't noticed, doesn't exactly inspire much respect from yours truly."

A seagull flew overhead, giving a loud cry before banking sharply and heading out over the ocean.

"I noticed," he said, and left it at that. She'd expected him to defend Jessica.

They headed toward the pier, whose attractions included an aquarium, vintage carousel, and solar-powered Ferris wheel.

"What do you do?" he asked.

"Not much. Just sit around mostly and read a lot. I'd like to be an writer at some point, but I've only written a few poems and one book, which is garbage." She wasn't quite sure why she was opening up to this guy, except that he seemed a little like her. Quiet. But not in a creepy way; it was more like he just didn't want to litter a conversation with too much nonsense.

"Impressive. A lot of people never finish reading a book, let alone writing one. And you're how old?."

"Twenty-one. Old enough to drink, and old enough to write a book, even if it's a lousy one."

"Maybe it's not so bad. I wouldn't mind reading it sometime."

Carson gestured to a saltwater taffy shop, and they stepped inside. Minerva noticed that some of the paint had chipped on the walls, which were decorated with colorful cartoon animals: a purple elephant blowing bubbles from its nose, a pink kangaroo wearing boxing gloves and smiling incongruously at a turquoise bear in a police uniform.

"I remember these," Minerva said, more to herself than to Carson. "From when I came here as a kid. There used to be a green frog wearing a crown over there." She pointed to a display stand loaded with touristy knickknacks that obscured a portion of the wall to the right of the counter. "And I remember they used to have a stork with a mailman's cap carrying a baby; it was painted on the ceiling, but they must have painted over it because it's not there anymore."

Carson looked at her blankly. "Those paintings you're talking about haven't been there for as long as I can remember, and I've been coming here since kindergarten."

Minerva looked at him. "Sorry, but you're wrong. I was here, and I saw them. I don't just make things up like that."

"I didn't say . . ."

"Look, you don't know me real well, but I'll let you in on a secret: I've got what people call a photographic memory. I don't forget things. Anything."

"Eidetic."

"Yeah, so I remember this like it was yesterday. I could tell you who was behind the counter the last time I was here: a guy named Waldo in his mid-40s who looked a little like a walrus with a bald head and a thick mustache. He was wearing blue overalls that didn't fit him very well, and he had a cold or something, because he kept sneezing. Jessica wouldn't buy me any taffy because she said she was afraid I'd catch something, but I'm sure she was really just being cheap."

"I'm sure you're mistaken, Min. I've got a pretty good memory too, and . . ."

"Minerva. It's Minerva. Only one person gets to call me Min, and you're not him. I really don't care if you believe me or not about this place. I know what I saw, and I'm not going to sit here and argue about it with Jessica's boy toy."

She turned away from him, toward the counter and a long row of plastic containers holding various flavors of saltwater taffy. She knew right where the one she wanted would be; they hadn't changed it in fifteen years. Caramel Swirl, her favorite, was at the end of the row on her right. She wheeled herself a few feet until she was in front of it, then grabbed a small white wax-paper bag in one hand and the plastic scoop in the other, plunging it into the container.

The smell of the shop, its sugary sweetness mingling with the sea air that drifted through the front door, brought back even more memories. She'd come here with Raven and his parents the weekend before the accident. Unlike Jessica, they didn't begrudge her a handful of Caramel Swirls—a few handfuls, actually. "A treat for a little girl who deserves it more than any other little girl in California," Raven's father had said in exactly those words.

Raven had been partial to the Black Licorice at the other end of the counter, and she remembered seeing him there, dumping one scoopful after another into his bag until it was all but overflowing. She could picture him intently balancing the bag against his chest with one arm as he tried to coax just one more piece of taffy into the opening.

In that instant, he saw her looking up at her, holding a finger to his lips, and she noticed that the bag was gone. Raven, meanwhile, wasn't an 8-year-old boy anymore, but a 23-year-old version of his former self.

She blinked, expecting him to disappear as he had each time she had glimpsed him in the past, but when she looked again, he was still standing there. This time, she wasn't going to let him slip away. Turning her wheelchair, she pushed down and forward on the wheels, not taking her eye off the figure of her childhood friend. For an instant, it occurred to her that this entire episode might be a dream . . . but that idea flew out the window when she felt a hand come out of nowhere and clamp down on her arm.

It was Carson.

Knocked off balance, her chair tilted slightly and she nearly fell sideways.

"Hey! What the . . ."

"Sorry," Carson said, looking down at her. "I didn't mean to startle you."

"What the hell do you think you're doing!" His hand was still on her arm, and she shook it loose.

"Your mother asked me to look after you, and I didn't want to let you get too far away. This is a big place, and it would be easy to lose track of you."

Minerva shot him a withering glare. "In case you hadn't noticed, I'm not a child. And you're sure as hell not my father. And no one—I mean *no one*—puts his hands on me without my permission, got it?"

"Sorry," he said again. "Where were you going?"

He'd let go of her hand, but he was standing in front of her now. Through it all, she hadn't taken her eyes off Raven. Why hadn't he come over to intervene? What was he waiting for? She was hoping he'd have a car and could get her out of here.

"Didn't you hear me?" she said to Carson. "Do I look like a two-year-old to you? This isn't twenty questions, and I'm not playing games. Now get the hell out of my way."

"I think I should just take you home."

"I'm not going anywhere with you. I'm staying here with Raven."

"Who?"

"I told you, this is *not* twenty questions. *Move!*"

He didn't.

So she did. Faster than he could react, she put both hands on the wheels, shoved off and catapulted herself toward him, in the next moment freeing her hands and letting fly with a right cross into his gut as she hit him. What she lacked in leverage she made up for in the velocity of the wheelchair and her own strength, which was considerable. The muscles in her immobile legs might have atrophied, but she'd built up the ones in her arms to compensate. The force of her blow didn't hurt Carson, but it sent him back on his heels and off balance, staggering into a display of jellybeans that proceeded to scatter across the tile floor.

Minerva didn't stop to survey her handiwork, although the clerk and a young couple in the store had their eyes fixed on the scene. Instead, she maneuvered around Carson and continued forward, to where Raven was still standing, then raced by him, calling, "What are you waiting for?"

He followed.

She glanced behind her to see the store clerk standing in front of Carson, barring his path as he tried to follow her. Hopefully, he would hold him there long enough for them to put some distance between themselves and him.

"Where the hell have you been?" she said, as he dashed ahead of her and opened a side door to the shop. "And why didn't you help me out back there?" She was out of breath, in part from exertion and in part from the panicked certainty that Carson was right behind them.

"It's complicated."

"Isn't everything." It was sarcasm, not a question. "Where's your car. Let's get out of here."

"I'm afraid I don't have a car."

"What?! You're 23 years old and you don't have a car? Do your parents still drive you around or something?"

"My parents are dead."

She stopped suddenly, forgetting Carson for a moment. They'd turned a corner, and she wheeled herself into a narrow alley between a couple of buildings. She looked up at him and saw a vacant sorrow in his eyes. "Hey, I'm sorry. I didn't mean . . ."

"It's okay. You didn't know. There's a lot you don't know. But I want to thank you for meeting me here. Your bedroom was a little . . . awkward."

"How do you . . .? That was a dream."

"I told you: It was your dream, but I was real. I was there, just as much as I'm here with you right now."

Minerva glanced furtively around the corner and caught a glimpse of Carson, but he hadn't seen them coming this way and had turned in the other direction. He'd be back, though.

"Whatever," she said. "But I didn't get any message asking to meet you here. Not that I'm sorry you showed up . . ."

"That's good to know," he smirked.

"Listen, we've got to get out of here before he comes back. Do you have any cash? Could we get a cab or something?"

Raven shook his head and pulled his pockets inside out as illustration.

"No car? No money? Not even a cellphone? So how did you get here."

"You brought me here. I wish I could help you the way you're helping me, but I can't. Not yet anyway. I think you're better off going back with him."

"Him? You've got to be kidding! I just punched him in the gut and ran over him. What do you think he'll do to me?"

"Nothing."

She stared at him, waiting for him to elaborate. His habit of being mysterious about everything was getting old.

"I was watching him back there. He wasn't acting like someone who wanted to hurt you. I'm not saying he has your best interests at heart or that you should make a habit of hanging out with him, but from the way he reacted, he *is* trying to protect you. At least for now. My guess is he's using you for something, probably to impress your mom. So play nice and apologize for losing your cool. If he's using you, use him—as your ride home."

"If you're stranding me here, I'm not going to forget this." For the first time she could remember, she was angry with him.

His reaction startled her. "Good," he said. "I don't want you to." Then he startled her again and bent down to her, taking both her shoulders gently in his hands. His touch tingled—it was the same sensation she'd felt in her legs during that dream. She opened her mouth to speak, but before she could say anything, his lips were pressed softly against hers, one hand reaching around the back of her head and stroking her long, dark hair. She didn't resist. The taste of him was sweet; she'd never tasted anything like it before.

After a moment, he pulled back and gazed at her. His eyes were lighter than she remembered from their childhood; they were almost translucent.

"I wanted to do that when we were kids," he said, looking away from her. Was he blushing? "My parents were so happy together, and I imagined that one day you and I would be the same way."

Minerva didn't know what to say. The anger had drained out of her, but it had left her even more confused than before. "Please, don't leave me here," she said.

"If there's one thing I know about you, it's that you can handle yourself," he said. "If I could help you, I would. There's nothing I want to do more. But I can't. Not now." He glanced around the corner and saw Carson's shape down the alleyway, coming back in their direction. "He's coming back. I have to go. But I'll see you tonight—in your dreams—and I promise I'll explain everything. Just don't forget me. The more you think about me, the more I'll be able to help you."

She shook her head. What was he, some sort of narcissist? He didn't act like it. He seemed like the Raven she remembered, except . . . he had turned out to be one hell of a kisser.

As if reading her mind, he bent down again and kissed her lightly, fleetingly on the lips. "See you soon."

Then he turned away, pivoted around the corner and was gone.

Fair Trade

Minerva didn't say anything on the way home. She didn't apologize the way Raven had wanted her to. She wouldn't do that. But, though she hated the fact that Raven had been right, she was relieved to find that Carson didn't seem angry at her for hitting him or interested in getting back at her for it. When he found her in the alley, he was acting the same way he had before she'd gone off on him: cool, unaffected and not very talkative. That suited her just fine. She had no desire to hear anything he had to say, and the few times when he tried to start a conversation, she wouldn't respond. Not a word. Not a glance. Not a movement . . . though she gave him an earful inside her head.

"Who was it you were trying to get to back there?"

None of your business, Mr. Nosy Ass.

"I'm sorry the day didn't turn out the way I'd hoped."

And just how was that? Were you going to kidnap me? Rape me? Over my dead body.

"Next time, things will go better, Minerva."

Next time? What have you been smoking?

When she wasn't mentally cussing him out—and even when she was—she was thinking of Raven. In some moments, she was remembering the kiss they'd shared (yes, she had reciprocated, even though it had taken her by surprise); in other moments, she was wondering what was wrong with him—why he hadn't defended her; why he had left her there; what he seemed to be hiding. He said Carson was using her for something, and she suspected he was right, but Raven seemed to be using her, too. Except he was nicer about it. And he was Raven. That counted for a lot.

Carson pulled the car in, and she had the door open before he could shut off the engine.

"Back so soon?" Her mother had opened the front door when she'd seen them drive up. She didn't work. Instead, she lived off alimony, government payments she received as a caregiver and a side part-time accounting business she operated out of her home. If someone like Carson came along and decided to spend money on her, so much the better. It was more than worth the trade-off to have sex with these transient "sugar daddies," even if the sex was bad. It wasn't like prostitution—not really. At least that's what she told herself in order to justify it. She deserved a steak dinner, a glass of wine, and a few trinkets of jewelry every now and then.

"Sorry, Jess," Carson said, as he wheeled Minerva in through the door. "The pier was mobbed, so I thought it would be better to just come back here. Do you mind if I hang out here for the day?"

Jessica smiled. "It'll cost you," she teased.

"Name your price," he said, playing along.

"Dinner and another late night with yours truly. If you're a good boy, I might even let you stay over."

Minerva thought she might vomit listening to the two of them. She didn't know who was worse: Jessica for her blatant manipulations and innuendo or Carson for falling for it . . . if he was falling for it. He seemed smarter than that.

Carson nodded. "A more than fair trade."

"I'm going to my room," Minerva announced, not really caring if either of them heard her.

Neither one responded.

Closing the bedroom door behind her, she rolled up beside the bed, transferred herself in and lay there, staring at the ceiling. A few moments later, she heard another door close and, shortly after that, the sound of groans and bedsprings squeaking in rhythm. She pulled a pillow up over her head, but she could still hear them. Couldn't they at least keep it down a little? At that volume, the neighbors would hear. She threw the pillow off and, glancing at the open window, realized the noises weren't coming through the door but from the *outside* and around the corner—Jessica's window was obviously open, too. The neighbors would *really* be able to hear *that*.

The noises lasted far too long before they finally stopped, replaced a short time later by the sound of voices in conversation. They clearly didn't realize their window was open, because they were making no effort to lower their voices, speaking in conversational tones. She could hear them as clearly as if they were standing just across the room.

"I'm worried about your daughter, Jessica."

"Why? You barely know her. I'm her mother, and I don't even worry about her anymore. She's a lost cause. Worry about me."

"Jess, I'm afraid she's got emotional problems."

"Like you're telling me something I don't know? That little nutcase has been trouble ever since the accident. From before that, really. She's got attitude, but you'll get used to it if you stick around."

Carson ignored the invitation to declare that he did, in fact, intend to stick around. "There's more to it than that," he said. "I think she's hallucinating. She's remembering things from childhood that weren't there, and said she saw somebody named Raven in the taffy shop. Ran me over with her wheelchair to get to him."

Minerva heard her laugh then. "Then she *is* hallucinating. Raven's been dead for fifteen years. He was with her in the car when it happened—the accident." Even though she knew, by this time, to expect nothing more, Minerva was still hurt that there wasn't even a hint of guilt in Jessica's voice. *She* was the one who had emotional problems. The woman was a sociopath.

"I have a friend who's in practice—a psychiatrist—who I think might help her," Carson said.

"Oh, I've taken her to shrinks. They never help. Besides, I don't have money for that crap."

"He's a friend. I think if I ask him, he'll see her as a favor. Besides, what can it hurt to try? This guy is good."

"Well, if it won't put me out any . . ." Yep, that was Jessica, all right. As long as it didn't cost her, she was willing to try anything. "It would get her out of the house." *And out of my hair*, Minerva was sure she was thinking.

"Then it's settled. I'll call him in a few minutes and see if he can squeeze her in tomorrow."

"If you want, go ahead. I still don't get why you're concerned about her though."

"She's your daughter."

Jessica didn't say anything for a moment, and Minerva suspected she was taken aback. A man talking about investing that much in a "relationship" that still was barely more than a one-night stand? She wasn't used to that.

"Suit yourself," she said finally. "It won't do any good, but if you want to try, I won't stop you."

Great. There her mother was making decisions for her again, without so much as asking her opinion about it. Didn't she have any say in the matter? Did her disability somehow render her incapable of making her own choices? To Jessica's way of thinking, it sure seemed to. On the rare occasion when she took an interest in Minerva, it was either to control her or to dismiss her for her own convenience—usually both. This time was no exception, but if Jessica was being Jessica, that didn't excuse Carson for sticking his nose in her business. Who the hell did he think he was? Jessica was throwing herself at him anyway. It wasn't as though taking the cripple off her hands for a day at the shrink's office was going to win him any brownie points he hadn't already earned.

It was just afternoon, but Minerva was tired already. A nap was just what she needed to escape.

She fell into a fitful sleep and, when she woke again, it was dark outside. It was only then that she realized Raven hadn't visited her in her dreams.

Therapy

Dr. Fitzgerald was a middle-aged man with close-cropped, graying hair that clung to the sides of his head like bristles. He wore glasses, which he habitually took off every few moments and gnawed on with his teeth. He had a musky odor of aftershave. And he talked too much.

Minerva didn't want to talk at all.

"Tell me about your friend."

"There's nothing to tell."

"His name is Raven?"

"Yes." Carson must have told him the name.

"He was with you in the car at the time of the accident."

"Yes." Jessica had obviously been talking to this quack too . . . or had said something to Carson, who had passed it along.

"Minerva, Raven has been dead for fifteen years. He died in the accident. You know that, don't you?"

Minerva stared at him. "I never heard of a funeral, never saw a death notice. But I did see Raven at the pier. I talked to him." *He kissed me.* She wasn't going to go as far as to tell him that. She was telling him too much already, but she felt like she needed to defend Raven and, more than that, defend herself from this shrink who seemed to be building a case right before her eyes to label her as crazy.

"Have you seen him, other than that one time on the pier?"

"Only in . . ." She stopped herself; she was going to say "my dreams."

"Yes?"

"Never mind."

"This is important, Minerva."

She wanted to tell him to F-off, but then pictured Raven saying she was behaving like her mother. Instead, she said, "Look, Doctor Fitzgerald, I'm sure you're very good at what you do, but really, I don't need your help. I don't need you asking me about Raven and then telling me he doesn't exist. I don't need to defend myself to you or anyone else."

"No, you don't. You're right about that."

"Then why are we here?"

"I've been told you have an eidetic memory. That's not often found in people of your age, but it means you should be able to remember everything accurately. If you don't remember Raven's death, that could be because you've blocked it out . . . or because false memories have been introduced in its place. I will be candid with you: Bradley told me you had memories from the pier that weren't how he remembered them. You were with Raven when you were at the pier before, in your childhood, weren't you?"

Carson *couldn't* have told him that. Maybe this Fitzgerald had just figured it out himself, in which case he was sharper than he looked. Or maybe he was just grasping at straws and made a lucky guess.

She nodded slightly, before she could stop herself, then shook her head vigorously from side to side. "Look, I'm the one with the photographic memory. Shouldn't that count for something? Have you ever thought that your friend Bradley is mistaken? Or does he have an perfect memory, too?"

"We're talking about you, here, not Bradley."

"You're twisting it."

"You were close to Raven, weren't you?"

"He was my best friend."

"So naturally, you want him to be alive. Do you have a boyfriend, or a girlfriend perhaps? Anyone with whom you share a romantic attachment?"

"No."

"Friends?"

"Just online. I stay in my room mostly. No one wants to hang out with a cripple. It's too much trouble."

Fitzgerald nodded as if he had just cracked the combination on the safe at Fort Knox. "Then the memory of Raven must be comforting to you. It makes sense that you've brought him back into your life now, as an adult, as a source of consolation and support."

Minerva rolled her eyes.

"I'm trying to help you, Minerva. But you need to accept your reality before you can begin to heal. Raven is dead. We'll work through this, you and I, I promise you."

Go to hell.

"In the meantime, I want you to do something for me: If you find yourself thinking about Raven, push him from your mind. Think about something else. Is there something you enjoy doing that you could use to focus your mind?"

"I write sometimes, when I feel like it. But don't ask me to stop thinking about Raven. You don't just forget a friend—especially if you're like me and you don't have many of them."

Fitzgerald ignored that and focused instead on the first part of what she'd said. "Then write. Make up stories. Be creative."

"I'll do that," she said. "But I won't forget about Raven."

"In time. All in time," Fitzgerald answered. God, he was haughty. "I want to see you back here Thursday, and then three times a week for the foreseeable future. Bradley's already agreed to bring you to your appointments.

Minerva wondered what would happen when Jessica's appetite for money, jewelry, and fancy dinners wore out its welcome with Carson. The appointments would stop, because Jessica sure as hell wouldn't pay for them. Minerva gave it a week—two at most. She could play along until then. But she wouldn't forget about Raven. Fitzgerald could analyze her, hypnotize her, or lobotomize, but whatever he did, she would never forget Raven.

Visitor

Biltmore heard a knock at the door. What the hell? How could someone have gotten onto the property without him knowing it? Someone must have disabled or bypassed the security system—no mean feat unless . . .

He glanced again at the closed-circuit monitors. There had been nothing unusual a moment ago, but now the front-door camera showed the figure of a woman standing outside. She was alone.

"Who's there?" Biltmore shouted.

The woman's voice answered: "I heard you have a signed first edition of *The Great Gatsby*. I'd like to purchase it."

. . . Unless the person involved were a fellow operative.

When Biltmore opened the door, a lithe woman in a pantsuit who looked to be in her mid-thirties was standing on his doorstep. Her dark crimson hair had been straightened so it fell like sheets of rain on both sides of her pale face, down beyond her shoulders, and her tight lips forced a thin smile as she greeted Biltmore.

"Jules," she said, extending a hand. "Your contact."

"I know. Pleased to meet you."

"May I sit?"

"Of course." He brought her into the living area—what used to be the motel's office—and gestured toward a brown, overstuffed loveseat off to one side. He slept in one of the old rooms but did his work from here.

"I can see from your face that you're surprised to see me," Jules said, brushing her bangs away from her eyes. "You're asking yourself, 'What is *she* doing here?'"

"The question *had* occurred to me. You weren't exactly thrilled when I called you about this assignment in the first place . . ."

"And you weren't expecting to see me show up on your doorstep."

"No. It isn't, as the top dogs like to say, protocol. In all the time I've done business from here, no one's ever come out to check on you."

"Well, as they say, protocols are made to be broken. And I'm not here to check on you, I'm here to brief you. This is a complex assignment—so complex that the decision was made to loop you in on the particulars. This is a big one, Triage. There's no margin for error, if you know what I mean."

"I'm not allowed to muck it up."

"Correct."

"Have I before?" He walked over to a refrigerator, reached in and pulled out a ginger ale. "Want one?"

"I'm fine. And no, you haven't—mucked anything up, that is—but there's a first time for everything, and this can't be it."

"Fine, fine. Some big dog's got his panties in a wad because his tail is on the line if this doesn't work. I get that. Just get on with the briefing. You want to talk all grim and serious? Tell it to your pooch after he shits on your rug. Don't waste it on me. I've got better things to do with my time."

She laughed. "Very well. Maybe you'd better give me one those beers after all."

"It's a ginger ale. I don't drink on the job."

"Never mind then. I do, but we'll keep that between us, okay?" She opened her briefcase, pulled out a laptop and flipped it open. "It's all in here. I couldn't risk transmitting it to you, even over a secure line, so we decided to deliver it in person."

Biltmore sat down beside her as the program loaded. "I'll walk you through it verbally and then I'll leave it with you. I trust you won't 'muck it up' by losing track of it."

He glared at her.

"Then here's some background. When we enlisted you for Operation Death Trap, you probably thought it was a one-off hit. We did, too, actually. We didn't realize the extent of the situation until much later."

"Situation?"

"Yes. I'm sure you wondered why we asked you to kill some 75-year-old woman in Santa Monica who had no criminal record and no ties to anyone of any importance."

"I do my job, but . . ."

"But you did wonder. If you didn't, I'd wonder about your value to us as an operative. The woman, Mary Lou Corbet, had a son named James and a daughter-in-law named Sharon. They were killed when their plane went down in 1988 over the Pacific Ocean on their way home from a two-week vacation on Maui. Their bodies were never recovered."

That was odd, Biltmore thought. He'd known Mary Lou Corbet casually before any of this had taken place: She'd worked as a babysitter for him and his older sister when he was in kindergarten. Once or twice she'd brought her son along with her. He was much younger then, but he could still tell it was the same person he'd run into many years later with his wife and mother—Biltmore's old babysitter—on a grocery run. He didn't know the exact date, but he did know one thing: It was years after 1988, when James and Sharon Corbet had supposedly been killed.

"But I saw James Corbet after that, sometime after 1990. And yes, I'm sure it was him. I know he didn't have a twin brother running around loose somewhere—I checked."

"Of course you did." Jules's tone was a little too patronizing for his taste. "And no, he didn't have a brother. That was him . . . sort of. The reason we ordered the termination of Mary Lou Corbet was on a need-to-know basis then. We didn't think you'd ever need to know, but now you do. And it's simple: She had used an illegal technique to resuscitate James and Sharon Corbet and was continuing to use it to maintain their existence."

Biltmore looked at her askance. "Resuscitate them? Are you talking about some bizarre Nazi-style experiment to bring back the dead? Wait, you said their bodies were never found."

"They weren't. The James Corbet you saw was the product of the technique Mary Lou Corbet used. It was still him, but not in the body that went down with the plane."

Biltmore shot her a look that clearly said he thought she'd lost her marbles. "So you're telling me there's a law against bringing someone back from the dead? I guess someone better arrest the dude upstairs for that trick he supposedly performed with Jesus." He was, understandably, less skeptical about the legality of what had taken place than about the fact that it had (supposedly) occurred.

"Oh, there's no law against it. Illegal isn't precisely the term. It's about agency policy. Not widely known, but I can show you chapter and verse if you'd like, Triage."

Biltmore winced. He hated that code name; it always reminded him of one of those casualty scenes he'd seen on reruns of *M*A*S*H*. It was bad enough that Anthony Biltmore wasn't his real name, any more than Bradley Carson was. Security precaution or not, it had gotten to the point where you couldn't tell his aliases without a scorecard.

"But to the question you so conveniently forgot to ask, the technique Corbet used is not only effective, it's been used by certain 'gifted' individuals for millennia. Have you ever heard of necromancy?"

Biltmore was taking a drink of his ginger ale when she said it. He laughed impulsively, and some of the liquid went down the wrong way, causing him to cough and sputter.

"See what you get for laughing, Triage," she joked. "People have been burned at the stake for being necromancers, and it wasn't just an accusation. They really were able to bring the dead back to life. It doesn't have anything to do with witchcraft or the devil or some magical blend of herbs. These 'gifted' people discovered that simply by focusing their minds intently for an extended period, they could bring back loved ones who were dead and buried.

"But they could only keep them here for a short time, no matter how hard they tried. Only in our own lifetimes did someone discover how to . . . enhance the ability. Most people don't have the discipline to maintain that focus, or, just as important, the ability to visualize the person in their mind's eye and create the necessary projection. People with eidetic memories do."

"Then it's all just a projection? A *Star Trek* hologram created by a few deluded mind freaks?"

"That's what a lot of people thought at first, but it's not. The people that get brought back are the actual 'ghosts' of the ones who died, with all their thoughts, memories, and character traits. And they're corporeal. You can shake their hand, photograph them, even feed them a seven-course meal. The only catch is they can't stick around after the gifted individual stops thinking about them intently. They'll linger for a short time, but once the link is severed, they'll eventually fade away. In a way, the gifted person is like a history book: When the library in Alexandria burned down, all those works were lost forever."

"And once the gifted person is eliminated, the undead person goes back to being dead. Let me guess: Mary Lou Corbet was one of these 'gifted' sorts who was grieving over the death of her son and his wife . . ."

"Yes. And the grief was so pronounced, it activated her gift. As with most people in mourning, she was fixated on the thought of her lost loved ones. That fixation is what brought them back to her, and when she realized what she had done, she continued to focus on them, keeping them 'alive,' so to speak."

Biltmore shook his head. It wasn't like the government to funnel resources into this sort of hokum—the twenty-year remote viewing experiment notwithstanding. That had been deemed a failure, but now the agency was apparently keen enough on this idea of 'gifted' people with eidetic memories to go around killing people over it.

"Christ! How many reanimated corpses do we have walking around here?"

The question was meant to be rhetorical, but Jules answered it anyway. "Our best guess is a few dozen, but no one's really sure. Most of the time, the 'gifted' don't even realize they can do this—we do our best to keep a lid on that, which is why you weren't told about any of this twenty years ago. They usually figure it out by accident, the way Mary Lou Corbet did, and most of those don't realize they have the power to keep their loved ones with them through the force of will. When the departed return, they pass them off ghosts and hallucinations. They report these to their friends, who then, through the power of suggestion, start 'seeing' similar phenomena at supposedly haunted houses and the like."

Biltmore shifted in his seat. "And when one of these 'gifted' people figures out how to harness this power . . ."

"We eliminate them. Hence your assignment to terminate Corbet."

"For God's sake, she was just an old lady!"

"And a huge security risk. Think about it. What if one of these 'gifted' individuals was a radical Jihadist who'd known Osama bin Laden. What if this person decided to focus his energies on bringing bin Laden back from the dead. You can imagine the repercussions. It's even possible one of them could immerse himself in historical data to such an extent as to bring back Hitler or Stalin or Mao Zedong. Maybe even Attila the Hun. No one's done any of that yet, but we're not about to test the limits of this thing. It's too risky."

"So you just kill off little old ladies from Pasadena or Santa Monica. Brilliant."

A tight-lipped smile crossed Jules's lips. "You're the one who killed her, no questions asked. A little late to start questioning now."

"People get smarter as they get older. If they're lucky."

"Then you're smart enough to know that you're in this now—you have been for twenty years—and there's no getting out."

Biltmore's expression was grim, but he said nothing. "I take it 'this' wasn't finished when I put a bullet in the poor widow Corbet's skull."

"I wasn't with the agency then, but from what I can gather, they thought it was. As it turned out, though, the woman had been in failing health before that little accident you arranged, and she had set up a contingency plan to keep James and Sharon alive in the event of her passing. She'd urged them to adopt a child abroad, using phony passports, and bring that child back to the States with them."

"What would that accomplish?"

"If the child were gifted, he could preserve James and Sharon after Mary Corbet had died. A very young child thinks of little else but his parents, so he wouldn't even have to be trained. He'd naturally keep his adopted 'ghost family' alive."

Biltmore drained the last of the ginger ale, crushed the can in his right fist and threw it across the room at a recycling container. Bull's-eye. "Now you want me to kill this kid—well, he'd be grown up by now—is that it?"

"Not exactly."

"Then what am I doing, exactly? I suppose this is why you needed to brief me."

Jules nodded and put her hand on Biltmore's knee, which wasn't an entirely unpleasant experience. She looked him in the eye, then gestured toward the laptop screen on the coffee table. "This is the individual you will need to focus on." He recognized the picture on the screen immediately.

It belonged to Minerva Rus.

Assignment

"First you ask me to kill a sick old lady, now you want me to off a cripple?" Biltmore was incredulous.

Jules shook her head. "Not necessarily. We don't think she realizes she's gifted—yet. But that could change quickly. That's why you were instructed to take her to Fitzgerald. He may be able to keep her from resuscitating the Corbets' adopted son."

Biltmore did a double-take. "So he's dead, too?"

A lucky accident. He was killed in a car crash when a certain single parent failed to stop for a red light, and her car wound up upside down in the intersection."

"Jessica."

"Yes. The boy, Raven Corbet, was killed instantly. We thought that was the end of it until we uncovered information that Minerva had shown signs of being gifted. Don't worry: We won't order her terminated unless we have to. If Fitzgerald can persuade her not to fixate on Raven, we might be able to stop this before it gets started, and no one will have to get hurt."

Biltmore bit his tongue. He wasn't about to let on that Minerva had already seen Raven at the pier. For one thing, he liked her, and for another, he still wasn't sure that this whole thing was anything other than a case of agency paranoia run amok. "No one will have to get hurt," he echoed, but his was a determined statement, not mere repetition.

"Good. We're telling you this so you can make sure that doesn't happen, but if things get out of hand, we'll need you there to execute the terminate order. Do you understand?"

Biltmore nodded and repeated to himself: *No one will get hurt.* In his mind, this was a chance to redeem himself for the hit on Mary Lou Corbet twenty years earlier by making sure nothing happened to Minerva Rus.

He stood up, walked to the refrigerator, and grabbed another can of ginger ale. "Sure you don't want one?"

"Maybe this time," Jules said.

Biltmore grabbed a second can and handed it to her. "Good to know your stomach gets a little queasy about this kind of thing. I'm not allowed that luxury," he lied.

"And you think I am?" she laughed. "Besides, this is your second can."

"I like the taste."

"If you say so." She flipped open the pop-top. "Anyway, detailed instructions are all on the laptop—encoded, of course. Return it when you're done or destroy it if you're compromised."

"How long do you think this will take?"

"What's wrong? Getting tired of Jessica Meyer already? The boys who brought us intelligence on her said she's a real wildcat in bed."

"I hear the same thing about you," he quipped sarcastically.

"I don't know how you would. You're the only one on the inside who's ever even seen me. You should feel privileged." She smiled wickedly. "But to answer your question: as long as it takes. We'll need you under cover until we're sure the Rus girl has no intention of bringing Raven back from the dead. When we're satisfied, we'll pull you for a lower-level observer who won't need to spend as much time on the case."

"Thanks," he said, half-grateful and half-sarcastic.

"One other thing: Don't come back here again until you're done. I want you in that house 24-7. I don't care how much you have to sweet-talk Madame Jessica, get yourself in and stay in."

Great. If this dragged on too long, he might have to do something like propose to her. That whole thing about being a wildcat in bed was a bunch of bull, and even if she had been, her caustic personality would have spoiled any potential fringe benefit.

"Shall I see you to the door?"

"Don't bother. I can see it from here."

"It was just a courtesy."

"You're an agent, not a doorman, Triage."

Biltmore crushed the now-empty second can of ginger ale and flung it in the direction of the recycling container.

This time, it missed.

Tingling

When the doctor told Minerva not to think about Raven, it had the opposite effect. That was usually what happened when people told her to do something: She found a way to do the exact opposite. Yes, Raven had told her to remember him, but that was different. She *wanted* to remember him herself, regardless of what he said . . . and not just the way he had been when they were children, but the way he was now, grown up and coming to her in her room every night. Yes, it was only in her dreams, but she'd seen him in the waking world, too, there on the pier. Dreams were dreams, but whatever the doctor might say, she hadn't been imagining *that*.

To hell with him, she said to herself, and thrust the image of Fitzgerald from her mind, replacing it with Raven's likeness.

Night had fallen, and the candle flickered on her bedstand, its comforting presence quieting her like a sliver of sunlight that had come down from the heavens to dance beside her bed. The house was still; Jessica and Carson had gone out to dinner at McKay's, that swanky place downtown, and Archer was down the hall, occupying himself with the latest online game. The window was still open, and moonbeams crept in on a gentle breeze that wafted the drapes aside, then cradled them back again and repeated the process. The air blew cool but not cold, neither the frigid burst of winter nor the stale listlessness of most summer nights.

Minerva could hear the sound of a branch from the tree outside being blown against the window. Its light cadence was rhythmic and insistent . . . a tapping that continued even as the breeze subsided for a moment. Perhaps she had been mistaken. Maybe it was a woodpecker. . . . But then, a moment later, she heard a half-whispered voice.

"Hey. Do I have to keep tapping on this stupid window all night, or are you going to let me in?"

It was Raven.

"The window's open," she answered.

"Well, I didn't want to come in uninvited," he said, climbing through. He was dressed differently tonight, in a dark-blue buttoned shirt, dark jeans, and a leather jacket. She had to admit she liked the look on him.

"That didn't stop you before."

"Well, that was different. That was a dream. You were dreaming of me, so I appeared. But I was really there—more than just part of the dream."

"Just like now."

He chuckled softly and shook his head. "No, Min. You're not dreaming now. I really am here."

Minerva stared at him. She had assumed she'd nodded off, but he was right: This didn't feel the same as before. *He* seemed the same—even in the dreams, he had seemed somehow sharp and in focus, while everything around had felt more ethereal, less concrete. She had assumed it was because she had been focused on him, but now the sense of Raven being set against some dreamscape had vanished. Everything else seemed just as real as he did.

He took maybe a step inside the window and stopped. She wasn't sure why. "You don't have to stay over there, Raven. Come here and sit on the bed. I won't take it the wrong way."

"What way is the wrong way?"

"Like you're coming on to me."

"I'm sorry you think that's the wrong way, because I wouldn't mind doing that, but I'll stay right here where I am, thank you."

She furrowed her brow and pursed her lips together, curling them up to one side in something between a smile and a scowl. "I don't get you, Raven. If you're trying to be a tease, you can cut it out, because I'm not *that* interested and you're not very good at it."

Raven smiled back at her, without the scowl component. "I want you to come over here."

Minerva was silent for a moment, then reached for the silver bar that had been installed beside her bed to pull herself up. She started to pull herself toward the wheelchair.

"Not that way."

"I'm not going to get there any other way."

"Sure you are. Remember in your dream, when you stood up? You can do that here, too. All you have to do is focus and remember what it was like to walk. Just keep your eyes on me and feel the tingling in your legs. It was there before, in your dream, wasn't it?"

She nodded slightly. "How did you know?"

"Because at first I felt that tingling too. But I can explain that later. For now, I want you to focus on my eyes and, with your mind, make that tingling spread down both your legs until it's more like an ache, then a piercing pain. The pain is good. It means you're feeling. Don't shrink from it, or you'll lose focus. Embrace it like a long-lost friend."

Despite her misgivings, Minerva did as he asked. She was afraid of wanting too much to trust him, but then, she *did* trust him. She always had, even when they were kids and he was playing hide-and-seek with her in that old abandoned house on Marberry Drive. Besides, she was feeling that tingling in her legs again, and the more she stared at him, the more she thought about it, the stronger it got. It grew into an ache, as if she had just run a marathon, even though she knew her muscles had atrophied long ago. How was this possible? Was she just imagining it?

The ache was throbbing now, as if the blood in her veins were welling up and pulsating feverishly in both legs, willing them to reawaken. Just as Raven had said, the ache was becoming a pain. It felt almost as if her legs were going to explode, while at the same time, sharp daggers were piercing her calves, her thighs, her feet, and even her toes. Her first instinct was to recoil, and she winced, balling up her fists against what was becoming nothing less than agony. She wanted to close her eyes against the pain, but she willed them to stay open, to stay in contact with Raven—not just because he had asked her to, but because she feared that, if she looked away, he would vanish.

Amid the pain, she felt a twinge—an involuntary spasm in a muscle she'd forgotten was even there. Then, almost immediately, another. It felt like muscles shriveled and wasted from disuse were somehow rebuilding themselves, sinew upon sinew, fiber upon fiber. It was impossible, and for a moment, Minerva felt sure she had been mistaken and that she was, indeed, in a dream once again.

In that moment, her purpose wavered and the pain subsided . . . but so did all the other sensations.

Quickly, she refocused, and they returned. Dream or not, she would not let this chance pass her by.

Raven's lips were moving, saying something, but her mind blocked it out. No distractions.

Only his eyes. Her body. Awakening anew.

He was nodding his head slowly, and she felt the pain begin to subside, slightly. Gradually. She willed her hips to move sideways, barely noticeably—a few inches at most . . . then a few inches more. She felt strength returning to her, in a trickle at first, then a steady flow, her heart beating stronger, sending blood to nourish her hips, thighs, calves, ankles, feet. She felt it all now and, in a sudden rush, urged herself to swing her legs over the side of the bed and sit up, facing Raven.

Her toes touched the carpet, and she felt it for the first time in fifteen years.

"Now relax," she heard Raven say. "You've done it."

"How?"

"You always could have. You just didn't know. Min, you are one of the Gifted. Now stand up and walk to me."

Still in disbelief, Minerva pressed her feet against the floor, put her hands on the bed, and tentatively pushed up, an effort made in concert with newborn leg muscles that tensed now and constricted, then lengthened . . .

She stood. Unsteady and angular at first, like a fawn just now emerged from its mother's womb.

One step and, still upright, she took a second, and a third, until she reached the place where Raven stood.

He took both her hands, his gaze never having shifted from her eyes, and smiled. "There. That wasn't too hard at all now, was it?"

He let go of her hands and drew her to him in a soft embrace. It felt comforting. Safe. She drew in close and laid her head on his shoulder; her legs, unused to holding her weight, relaxed as she allowed her body to rest against his. The tingling in her legs had stopped, but she felt the same sensation as she came in contact with him—in the palms of his hands, his soft breath cascading down across the side of her face . . . . She let her arms move up underneath his jacket, running them up his back, and feeling it there, too. It was as if life was somehow escaping him at every moment, but being replenished from somewhere. But where? Of course, this was crazy; she was merely imagining this.

She looked up at him, into his eyes, and saw him already staring back at her. It was a look that blended understanding with questioning, as though he knew part of what she was feeling in greater detail that she would have thought possible; yet in another sense, he seemed still unsure, probing her eyes for a sign of . . . something.

Minerva tilted her head back and pressed against the floor with her toes. What a sensation it was! Then there was the sensation that followed—the feeling of her lips on his. The tingling she'd felt before spread across the surface of her skin and burrowed its way inside her, warming her entire face. Instinctively, she opened her mouth to take in more of it, to draw his sweet breath into her own mouth, to feel the warmth of his soft, moist tongue on hers.

She felt her arms draw him closer in, assuredly; his question had been answered. Her own arms tugged at his shirt, pulling it up and untucking it, allowing her hands to find their way up the naked flesh of his back.

The tingling was a crackling now, spreading through her and igniting a shiver that traveled the full length of her body.

She had imagined her first kiss—and yes, this was her first. No one had wanted her before, when she was crippled. Would even Raven have wanted her like that? He had kissed her on the pier, but she had chalked that up as much to give sympathy and comfort as anything else. She pulled back slightly, but not completely, drawing her lips away from his but allowing herself to remain there in his embrace. Despite her questioning, she still felt safe there.

Then, as if in answer to her still unspoken question, he said to her, "I've been wanting to kiss you like that for longer than you know."

Yeah, right. That would have been her normal response, but this time, she didn't voice it. In case she was wrong. She had an inkling that she was, and a near-desperate desire to be. Still, she'd become so accustomed to shielding herself with sarcasm, it had become almost an instinctive response. "Well, you're not very original," she said, chuckling softly. "That line's right up there with, 'I've been waiting for you all my life.'"

Raven smiled, the candlelight dancing across his eyes, and chuckled himself. "Actually, I have been," he said. "Just waiting for you to remember me."

He leaned over and kissed her again, his lips soft and, if possible, even warmer now. The tingling was insistent. She'd heard people talk about a magical kiss, but somehow she'd never imagined it might cause such a tangible physical sensation. She reached up and touched his dark hair, flowing willowy down to near his shoulders. It was nearly as dark as hers— hence the name his adopted parents had chosen for him. She remembered noticing the similarity as a child, just as she remembered discovering the closeness of their names: Every letter of his was contained in hers, with only the "M" and the "I" being absent. She'd teased him about it, saying, "I M Raven, not you!" and "You are Mi Raven." They'd joked about being twins separated at birth and, back then, had been closer than most siblings. She was glad they weren't siblings now.

"You are Mi Raven," she said aloud, before she even realized she had voiced it. She looked away, embarrassed, but felt his fingers softly on her chin, turning her head back toward him.

"Yes, I am," he said simply. "And I always will be."

The tingling grew into a crackling again, this time coming from his finger-tips as they rested against her face, cupping her chin first, then brushing her cheek; it was as if gentle sparks were cascading from a the hand of a wizard at rest, a powerful mage releasing energy without even knowing it.

She brought her lips up to meet his again, more confident this time, more insistent. She opened her mouth to drink in the sensations he offered, but more than the sensations: the feelings behind them. When she felt them, she surrendered to her own feelings, pulling him even tighter against her body, as though closer could never be close enough. She pulled away just long enough to bring her hands up to his shoulders and slide his jacket off, sending it falling to the floor as he released her from his grip for the same brief moment.

Before he could pull her close again, she was unbuttoning his shirt, slowly, first the top button, then the next, and then more hurriedly, feeling anxious to press up against him again. When she did, the coarse chest hair tickled her but—was it possible?—tingled and sparked with the same life energy that seemed to race through his entire being.

She kissed his neck, squeezing his flesh softly between her lips, then biting playfully with her teeth.

She felt his hands make their way underneath her pajamas and in that instant realized she was wearing the same blue Smurf pajamas she'd had since she was a high school sophomore. *I must look ridiculous*, she thought, but that thought fled from her consciousness as she felt his hands exploring her shoulders, running down her arms, caressing the small of her back.

Minerva closed her eyes, abandoning vision and yielding to the sensation of touch, tumbling backward with him in a spinning whirlpool of countless caresses. Tangled together, pressed against each other. Moving. Embracing. Tasting. The tingling, the crackling sparked electrically between them, tossing them about like leaves on rolling tide, raising them up to a crest, then crashing down over them and submerging them in the depths of which they were barely conscious. Then, at the last possible instant, they rose, gasping for precious air, only to willingly dive back to the depths and remain there and open themselves to one another, where no one could sense them except their own joined awareness.

They emerged finally, again and for the last time, she looked and him next to her exactly the way she had pictured him from behind closed eyes: his hair tousled, his sleekly muscled, pale body impossibly tangled in the sheets. One eye was closed and the other fixed on her, dreamily, from a state between trance and waking.

Soon, she was drifting off herself, and in the midst of her slumber, she wondered: What was waking and what was dream?

But the question vanished with the dawn of newly awakened certainty that, as of this moment, it no longer seemed to matter.

Letter

Minerva awoke to the dim new light of dawn and turned over to look beside her.

Raven was gone.

Where he had been the night before lay a piece of paper on a sea of rumpled sheets. She turned toward it and picked it up, then pushed herself up into a sitting position against the headboard to read it.

Min,

I'm sorry I couldn't stay to see you wake up. If you look half as beautiful as you do when you're sleeping, I'm already kicking myself for missing out. I don't know what makes me happier, the fact that you're walking again—that you discovered your gift—or the fact we spent such an awesome night together. (If you can keep a secret, I do know, but I don't want to seem like a selfish ass by saying it straight up.) Anyway, I couldn't let your mom or her boyfriend find me here.

I don't know why that Carson guy is so interested in you, but I think it may have something to do with your gift. Whatever you do, don't let either one of them know you can walk. It's not safe. I'll explain more the next time I see you, and I think I'll know more by then, too. I don't want to chance going back to your house unless I know they're gone. I could come to you in your dreams, but somehow, that isn't the same, is it? Besides, I don't want you to doubt that it's really me you're talking to, not just some vision you've made up inside your head.

When they're out of the house, go down to the neighborhood park and meet me there. I'll be waiting. Until then, remember . . ."

Devotedly,

Raven

Minerva scowled. The whole note-on-the-bed thing without saying goodbye was like something out of a bad romance flick. But she had to admit it wouldn't have been good for her mother to find him here. And Carson . . . yeah, he had taken a kind of unhealthy interest in her. Raven was right. She'd keep her "miraculous" recovery a secret for now.

She wriggled her toes in delight. Yep, they still worked. She was still trying to figure out what had happened, but it was like Ryan had unleashed some power in her—her gift, as he called it—and now she was able to maintain it simply by remembering and focusing her mind to reproduce what she'd felt before.

Remembering. Raven used that word a lot, often in reference to himself. He wanted her to remember him . . . after last night, he hardly needed to ask; the memory of his arms around her and his lips pressed against her flesh was deeply ingrained in her consciousness now. There was no way in hell she was going to forget *that*.

But why was it so important that he kept saying it? And was he really just going to hang around the park all day waiting for Jessica and Carson to leave? The cops might pick him up as some kind of weirdo vagrant or stalker. It would have been easier for him to just pick her up in his car and take them someplace . . . except he didn't have a car. Apparently, he didn't have a cell phone, either. If he did, he hadn't bothered to give her his number. He seemed to prefer leaving notes, all nineteenth-century style, instead of actually making himself available for a call or a text. Was that too much to ask? Maybe he *was* a vagrant. He'd said his parents were dead, and he hadn't mentioned anything about having a job.

Gah! She was overthinking it all. She'd just have to go out to the park when Carson and Jessica left—and she knew they'd leave, because she knew her mother: She'd demand that he take her out somewhere just about every day. The theater. A concert. A fancy dinner. It was just a matter of time before they left, and when they did, what harm would it do to get some fresh air, to give her newly revitalized legs a greater test than just a couple of steps across the room? She'd meet Raven in the park and get some answers to these questions. He'd shared his body and the essence of who he was with her; now it was time for him to share these secrets.

"Hey, Minerva. You awake?"

It was Archer, his voice accompanied by three soft raps on the door.

Minerva pushed herself back down in the bed and covered herself. "Come on in."

"Hey, Mom wants to know if you want to go to the movies with her and Bradley and me. It's the new *Mutant League* movie! I've been waiting for it to come out forever, and they said they'd take me to it."

Minerva shook her head and flashed him a suspicious look. "Jessica's actually taking you to a movie *you* want to see? When's the last time that happened?"

Archer half-shrugged. "I think it was Bradley's idea, but what do I care? It's the *Mutant League*! Hey . . ." His eyes had moved from her face to the floor beside his feet. Minerva followed his gaze and saw that her Smurf pajamas were lying there. Oops. "How did those get there?" Archer asked.

"I was hot," Minerva answered, feigning annoyance. He was just getting to the age where he might suspect some other reason they were in a pile on the floor, but if he did, he didn't give off any hint of it.

Without missing a beat, he bent down and picked the pajamas up, then tossed them toward the clothes hamper by the closet. "Now you have to go with us," he announced, triumphant. "What do you want to wear?"

"Just bring me any old T-shirt and a pair of jeans. But I think I'll pass on the movie. Spending time with Jessica isn't at the top of my to-do list."

Archer frowned but did as she asked without arguing. He knew better than to try convincing her about something when her mind was made up. "I'll let you know when we're gonna leave in case you change your mind."

"You do that, Arch. And thanks. You're a great little brother."

"What's up with you? You've never said anything like *that* before!"

"Just in a good mood, I guess," she smiled. "Tell me if the movie's any good so I can rent it when it comes out on disc."

He nodded—"Yeah. OK."—and left the room.

Park

As promised, Archer knocked on her door to announce when they were leaving for the movies—a noontime matinee—and the moment she heard the car pulling out, Minerva jumped out of bed and threw on the clothes he'd laid out for her. She went to the kitchen and fixed herself a bowl of Jumbo Flakes, grabbed some milk out of the fridge and poured a light coating over them. The things got soggy too damn quickly. Not that she was going to wait around for them to wilt in the bowl; eating might be necessary, but she didn't want to waste any more time on it than she needed to.

After thinking things over, she'd decided not to walk to the park, after all, but to take her wheelchair instead. It wasn't that she thought she might not make it that far if she walked—she felt weirdly confident in her newfound ability—but she realized it would turn the neighbors' heads to see her up and about. Those neighbors would undoubtedly say something to Jessica, and if Raven's instincts about keeping her gift a secret were correct, it would be best not to take that chance.

As it was, Mrs. Peters from next door was surprised enough to see her out of the house at all, let alone waving as she passed by.

"I haven't seen you out of the house all summer, Minerva!" she said.

"Just needed some fresh air."

She wheeled herself down two blocks toward Bronkton Park, an expansive patch of greenspace thick with tall deodars and some eucalyptus trees. The city planners and set it aside for parkland when the neighborhood had first been developed, and that had been decades ago, so the trees had grown up high and thick. As a little girl, she'd always loved to play here, letting Raven push her as high as she could go on the swing set, clambering up the crayon-bright jungle gym, and hiding behind trees, pretending to be invisible. It was only natural he should want to meet her here.

She rounded the corner and headed down the curving concrete path toward the big pine tree where they used to hang out as kids, but when she reached it, there was no sign of him, so she kept going, deeper into the park, where the trees were thicker. It almost seemed like a forest pushing back against the sprawling suburban landscape, overgrown in places because the city didn't have enough money to maintain it properly.

Minerva came to two small picnic tables at the center of the park where families or young couples would often come with their picnic lunches, seeking refuge from the workaday world or the cares of home life. Perhaps, she thought, she might find Raven here. But the tables were deserted, except for a discarded, half-eaten bag of potato chips, now being attended to by a real raven who had flown down out of a branch overhead to chase away some sparrows.

Why would he have told her to meet him here and then not bothered to show up? Had she gotten the day wrong? It wasn't too late. She'd come as soon as she could, and he had said he would wait for her here. She sat there in her wheelchair, next to the picnic table, letting the filtered rays of sunlight fall across her face and wondering every few seconds how many minutes had passed.

Restless, she looked around to make sure no one was watching, then pushed down on the armrests and up with her feet until she was standing. Tentatively, as if she were doing something she wasn't supposed to be doing, she walked around the picnic tables, peering around the craggy corners of tree trunks to see if somehow Raven was playing the same kind of hide-and-seek game they'd played here together as children. Seeing her movement, the raven on the picnic table cocked its head and looked at her for a moment, then fastened its beak onto a potato chip and took flight with its prize, heading back up to the tree branch from which it had come.

The wind whistled at her softly, a midday lullaby, and she sat back down in her wheelchair, closing her eyes to the scattered sunbeams that drifted down upon her face.

"Hello, Minerva."

The voice startled her, jarring her from her reverie. It wasn't Raven's.

"What are *you* doing here?" She stared up at Carson.

"I could ask you the same thing." His tone was a little to condescending for her taste.

"I thought you were going to the movies with Archer and Jessica."

"I dropped them off there and came back to get you for our appointment."

"Appoint . . ." Oh, hell. That's right. She had agreed to go back and see that idiot Dr. Fitzgerald again. "I think I've changed my mind," she declared. "I don't think he can really do anything to help me."

"You said you were going to do this, Minerva." He was playing on her guilt. She hated to go back on something once she'd committed to it. . . . Did he somehow know that about her?

"I'll go next time," she said. "I have to meet someone here."

"Who?"

"Just a friend, Bradley, okay? Did it ever occur to you that my social life really isn't any of your business? Just because you're my mother's boyfriend . . ."

He moved around behind her, took hold of the handles on her wheelchair, and began pushing.

"What do you think you're doing?"

"Taking you to your appointment."

Minerva thought for a split second of jumping out of the wheelchair and slugging this guy in the gut. Or the jaw. She might be a woman, but years of relying solely on her arms to move around had made her upper body pretty damn strong. If she took him by surprise, she might be able to knock him down, start running and cry for help. But then her secret—the fact that she could walk—would be out of the bag. Instead of just taking her to a psychiatrist, they'd want to run a bunch of tests on her like some sort of freak to figure out what had happened.

Besides, she wasn't too happy with Raven for standing her up, especially after he'd been the one who suggested meeting here. If he did finally show up late, it would serve him right if she weren't there.

Lab

Carson had driven a couple of miles when Minerva noticed they weren't going in the same direction they'd gone the last time they went to Fitzgerald's office. Instead, they pulled up in front of a large, nondescript white office building off a side street in an area of town where Minerva hadn't been before.

"What's this place?" she asked as Carson brought the wheelchair around and helped her into it.

"A lab. Fitzgerald wanted to meet you here so he could run some tests."

The way he called it a lab, so matter-of-factly, reminded her of something out of Frankenstein. No Transylvania-esque Igor accent, but it didn't matter. There had been plenty of times in the past that she'd felt like a monster because of her paralysis, and she remembered how weird it had been, just after the accident, to see doctors poking and prodding her legs without feeling the least sensation there.

Minerva expected to be taken to a waiting room, but instead Carson wheeled her around the building and through a pair of doors in the back, then down a long corridor to what seemed like a large examination room. What kind of place was this? Why wasn't there a receptionist to at least ask about insurance and make you wait an hour past your appointment time before letting you see the doctor? Something about this felt very wrong. A lot of things, actually.

The growing anxiety she felt was making her legs twitch. She hoped Carson didn't see it, but he didn't stick around long enough to notice. Instead, he deposited her next to an examination table and just said, "Wait here"—then left.

The room was far larger than a typical doctor's office exam room and was equipped with a CT scan machine. It looked like a doorless laundromat dryer or an oversized white donut with its tongue sticking out—the place where patients lay during the scan. She didn't like something else she noticed there: straps that seemed intended to keep the patient tied down during the procedure. There were straps on the regular exam table, too.

Fitzgerald made his appearance scarcely a minute after Carson had left, breezing into the room like a man in a hurry, clad in a white hospital gown that matched the bleached look of everything else in this sterile wherever-it-was.

"How are we feeling today?" he asked, without bothering to look directly at her.

"I don't know about you, but I'm feeling like I don't want to be here," Minerva replied.

The doctor didn't say anything to that, but instead took out a bright, pencil-sized light and shined it into her eyes, one after the other.

"I thought you were a shrink, not a family doctor," Minerva said.

"Just relax, now. Psychiatrists have a license to practice medicine."

"I know that. I'm not stupid. But I have a family doctor. This is all just a big waste of time."

Fitzgerald clicked off the light and looked her in the eye. "I'm afraid I have to disagree, Minerva." His voice was too solemn for her to take seriously. Part of her felt like laughing in his face, but another part of her was apprehensive. "You're exhibiting behaviors that are consistent with extreme delusion. Manufactured memories. Imaginary friends. It could all be due to your prolonged isolation, but I can't overlook the possibility that there's a physiological component to your condition."

"Look, my condition's just fine and I'm not imagining anything, so you can call off this stupid exam right now. I agreed to therapy sessions—which was a mistake in the first place—but I never agreed to be anyone's guinea pig."

"I'm afraid it's too late for that," Fitzgerald said, and as he did, two large men in white gowns entered the room single-file and moved to stand next to him.

Minerva's anxiety had become full-fledged fear now, but she wasn't about to show it. "Who are these gorillas?" she snapped. "Didn't they make the cut with the Green Bay Packers?"

Fitzgerald smiled a mirthless smile. "They're just here to ensure that everything goes as planned. We're going to run a few tests, and hopefully we'll find out what's at the root of these false memories. Once we know that, we should be able to eradicate them." He turned to the two newcomers. "Gentlemen? Please help our patient onto the table over there. We'll need to start with a cranial CAT scan."

Minerva saw the two men nod, and at the same moment she felt a sensation wash over her that made it seem like all the blood was draining from her face. Her forced confidence was gone, and she opened her mouth, but nothing came out. She thought for a moment about standing up and bolting for the door, but she had a sickening feeling that, even with the element of surprise, she wouldn't get far.

The two men came around to either side of her and grabbed hold of her arms with clammy palms, then hoisted her up between them and carried her over to the CT scan machine. They deposited her on the table and secured her arms and chest in black restraints, placing her on the table so that her head lay back on a cradle.

The next thing she knew, the table on which they'd placed her was being moved into position, so that her head was inside the donut hole. Outwardly, she forced herself to remain calm, working not to give herself away by tensing her leg muscles. If they discovered her charade, she was sure, it would only make matters worse. But inside, she felt herself close to panic. Even when she'd been confined to her room as a paraplegic, that confinement had been on her terms, and though her useless legs might have restricted her movement these past twenty years, even they were a part of her. It wasn't like this; now, someone else was in control.

She closed her eyes.

"Try to relax and clear your mind, Minerva, and please remain completely still. This will only take a few minutes. If you move around too much, we'll have to administer a sedative."

Like hell.

Now that the gorillas had stepped away and she was on the table, she felt her panic start to recede a bit. There wasn't anything she could do to get out of here—at least not for the moment—so she'd just have to make the best of it. "I could relax a little better without these damned restraints."

"Please stay quiet, Minerva."

What on earth could he possibly hope to discover? "Clear your mind," he'd told her. *Well, then, you sonofabitch, I think I'll do just the opposite.* Despite her irritation at Raven for standing her up in the park, he was the supposedly false memory they were trying to get rid of. So it only seemed appropriate that she should hold on to that memory with the tenacity of a pit bull during this joke of a "procedure."

After a moment, she started to hear a series of clicking noises, followed by a whirring and light buzzing sound. It stopped after a while, then resumed and repeated itself again. None of it was particularly unpleasant, only mildly annoying.

She blocked it all out and focused on the vision of Raven's face, crystal clear against the black backdrop of her mind's eye.

That's it, Min. Just focus on me. I'm here.

But how . . .? Did I fall asleep inside this idiot's machine?

No, you're still awake. You've just managed to focus so intently on me that I was able to hear you, telepathically, and respond.

This is all too weird.

Yeah, Min, but isn't it cool? She could even "hear" him chuckle. *Actually, it works the same way the dreams did. In a dream, you naturally block every-thing else out to such an extent that the dream tricks you into thinking it's real. Not many people can achieve that level of focus in waking, but you have the gift. You're just now figuring out how to tap into it.*

Well it's nice of you to show up now, but where the hell were you earlier at the park? If you'd been there, I might not be playing the bride of Frankenstein to this whack job of a shrink.

Raven's expression darkened. Yes, she could even see that, too. It seemed to settle somewhere between hurt and guilt. *I couldn't, Min. I was there, waiting for you, for a couple of hours. But I was sitting there at the picnic table, eating a bag of chips, when someone came up from behind and hit me over the head. I blacked out, and the next thing I knew, I was here. I just don't know where 'here' is. It looks like a warehouse or something, but I'm tied up and whoever did the tying was no a slouch. I've tried getting loose, but I don't think I'll be going anywhere.*

Oh, great. Hey, I'm sorry for being mad at you.

His face brightened again. *I don't blame you. You didn't know what happened. I don't make a habit of breaking dates, though, especially with my favorite person.*

Minerva felt herself blushing and wondered if he could see that on the other end.

He continued: *And especially not when there's this much at stake.*

A frown replaced her blush. *What exactly is at stake? And why are all these people after us?*

Both our lives, to start with, he said, almost too casually, as if this was something he'd known for some time. *They're scared of your gift, Min. That's why I told you not to let anyone see you walking around. If they knew, they might try to lobotomize you. Or kill you.*

But why?

Before he could answer, though, the whirring stopped and she felt the table on which she was lying start to move. Her eyes opened instinctively, and Raven was gone.

"There. That wasn't so bad, was it? Now we'll just have to hook up an IV and inject you with some dye for a comparison. I promise it won't hurt, though."

Fitzgerald's goons hooked up the intravenous tube and pumped some colored dye through it, then they went through the procedure all over again. She closed her eyes again and focused on Raven just as intently, but this time, all she got was an image. He didn't seem to be aware of her presence, and this worried her. He'd said someone might be trying to kill him. What if . . .

She didn't want to allow herself to think about that. She'd just found him again after all these years, and she wasn't about to let him go because some lunatics wanted him dead.

After a little less than half an hour, they pulled her out of the scanner again; the gorillas picked her up and deposited her on the regular examination table, where she was again restrained.

"Am I some kind of prisoner here?" she demanded, ignoring the goons and staring at Fitzgerald. "Aren't you supposed to get a patient's clearance before you can do any of this? I never signed any forms or anything."

"Your mother provided the authorization, and Mr. Carson delivered the forms when he brought you in. I assure you . . ."

Minerva cut him off. "In case you haven't noticed, I'm of age. I make my own medical decisions, thank you. Jessica and Carson can both go straight to hell."

"Please, Minerva. They're trying to help you. You've been living in a severe state of delusion. I'm afraid you're not competent to make your own medical decisions at this point."

"Yeah? Well who says you're competent to be doing any of this? How do I even know you're a real doctor?"

"I could show you my credentials, if you like."

"To hell with your credentials."

Fitzgerald didn't say anything to that, and she fixed him with a self-satisfied glare. "Can I go now?"

"I'm afraid not. We're going to have to keep you here under observation at least until the tests come back. We've got a room prepared for you, though. Gentleman, if you would please escort Ms. Rus to the holding area."

The holding area. What a reassuring name. Minerva closed her eyes as their clammy fingers locked onto her arms again, and she kept them closed as they set her down in her wheelchair and rolled her out of the room and down the corridor. At the last moment, she looked over her shoulder at Fitzgerald, who had turned his attention to studying some chart on a clipboard, and called in the sweetest voice she could muster, "Have a nice day, Doc."

Then, under her breath, she added, "If I have anything to say about it, it'll be the last one you have in a long, long time."

Captivity

Raven opened his eyes and saw two other eyes staring back at him, mere inches away from his face. They belonged to a woman he hadn't seen before: a woman with pale skin, a few scattered freckles and a narrow face framed by dark, coppery, straight red hair.

"I see you're awake," she said, stating the obvious.

A throbbing ache in Raven's right eye socket fell just short of piercing pain. He tried to reach up to touch it, only to have the futility remind him that his arms were tied behind the back of the hard wooden chair he was sitting in.

"Who are you?" he said.

"My name's not important, but for the sake of convenience, you can call me Jules."

"Any chance I can get a glass of water?"

"Maybe. In good time, my Raven." She smiled a smile that he sensed was meant to hint at the freedom she withheld from him. It was a prospect she wanted to remind him of and, at the same moment, ensure he knew he couldn't have.

"I'm not 'your Raven,'"

"I think those ropes around your wrists might indicate otherwise," she said. "Of course, you're only mine as long as you remain alive—if that's what you call it. If I have my way with you, you'll be back in the grave, where you belong, before much longer."

"How do you know . . .?"

"Oh, it's not that hard to figure out, really. We've been tracking your kind—or, rather, the kind you feed off—for decades now. They always lead us to you, eventually. Sometimes, it just takes longer than others. Tell me, do you feel any guilt at all about how you're using that Rus girl for your own purposes? Or do the undead feel no remorse? You're not some sparkly vampire in a teen romance novel, you know. You're a pathetic corpse feeding off that poor girl's naïveté, her isolation, and a misplaced wistfulness for a childhood friend."

"That's not how it is . . ."

"Oh, isn't it? Then tell me, Raven, what happens if she stops thinking about you for more than a few days. What if she forgets you, Raven? What happens then? I'll tell you what happens: You fade right out of existence again, just like you did the first time all those years ago in that car crash. You might have convinced yourself you have some affection for poor Minerva in order to placate what's left of your conscience. But in the end, it all comes down to one thing: You need her to survive. It's all just self-preservation, isn't it? Everything's all about you."

"No, it's not that way. You don't understand."

"Oh, don't I? Can you honestly tell me you never resented your parents adopting you to keep themselves artificially 'alive,' because you had the gift? Mary Lou Corbet had managed to maintain the fiction of her son and daughter-in-law's continued life for years, but she was getting old and knew she wouldn't be around forever. So she encouraged them to seek you out and adopt you. Not because they loved you, but because they needed you. Because you had the 'gift.' You weren't their beloved child. You were only an insurance policy, and that's all Minerva is to you. Admit it. It's a classic case of an abuse victim turning around and abusing someone else, except you're abusing a living, breathing woman. You're still dead, and no matter what you try to tell yourself, you'll never be master of your own destiny again. You'll always depend on her. Can you look me in the eye, Raven, and tell me that's in any way fair? Can you?"

Raven's muscles strained against the ropes and he rocked back and forth in his chair. "How dare you lecture me about any of this? You say you care about Minerva, but you've taken her prisoner the same way you have me. You're the user here, not me."

"Keep telling yourself that, my pet. It makes no difference to me. I'm here to do a job, and that job—no matter what you might think—is to keep living people like Minerva Rus safe from the bloodsucking likes of you."

She spat on the floor at his feet and then, in a perverse turn of events, brought her still-moist lips up to his and kissed him passionately on the mouth.

His immediate instinct was to wipe the faint saliva away with the back of his hand, but he was still tied up.

"Now," she said. "Don't I kiss a whole lot better than your precious Minerva?"

Raven was so angry he actually bared his teeth at her. "Who the hell are you?"

"I told you, Raven, you can call me Jules. I'm Minerva's guardian angel, and I could be much more than that to you, if you'd let me."

Raven composed himself. "You know, I don't think much of your bad attempts at playing mind games," he said. "You tie me up and tell me you want to put me back in the grave . . . and now this? You're pathetic."

"Maybe. But you're the hostage, not me. I'm the one in control here. And if you cooperate, I could make it worth your while. All you have to do is help me persuade your paramour to forget you. We can do that from the other end, but it would be messier for everyone involved, so we thought we'd give you the chance to play the heroic boyfriend and sacrifice yourself for your lady love—to prove to me, once and for all, that it isn't all about you, after all."

"I don't have to prove anything to you."

"Quite true. And you don't have to save your girlfriend from some pretty nasty consequences if you don't comply."

"You said you were trying to protect her."

"I am. That's why I'm making you this offer. But there are others who'll need protecting from her if you decide to reject it. Think about it for a while. I'll be back to check on you in a little while, darling."

She leaned over and kissed him again, and this time, Raven was the one who spat on the floor. "In your dreams."

Doubts

Minerva had stopped wishing that her mother gave a damn about her years ago, but she found herself thinking about that again now. Unfortunately, Jessica wasn't the type to worry about her daughter if she failed to come home by nightfall, especially if Carson fed her some bogus story. What would he tell her? That he'd put her up with some friend of his to give Jessica a break from having to take care of her? That he'd put her in some looney bin asylum somewhere? That wouldn't be far from the truth. And Jessica wouldn't care anyway, as long as the government didn't come looking for her to blame her for neglecting a cripple.

The only person Minerva thought might worry about her was Archer, and he was just a kid. She'd grown so isolated from the outside world that no one else even knew her enough to care. She hadn't even been on her Facepage account in months. Heck, maybe Fitzgerald was right about the whole thing. Maybe she *was* crazy—and so desperate for human companionship that she'd made up an imaginary friend for herself at the age of 21. Her dreams had bled into her conscious life, and she'd accepted them as reality because they were so much better than her pathetic situation.

Of course, it was impossible that Raven had come back to her after so long. Of course, he was really dead. Of course, she couldn't really walk again; if she could, why was Raven telling her to keep it a secret? What if it wasn't really Raven but her own subconscious telling her that? It was awfully convenient. She could continue to delude herself about an ability she didn't really have by providing an excuse not to face the truth when she tried to stand up in front of Jessica or Carson or Fitzgerald . . . and nothing happened. Or worse yet, she fell flat on her face.

None of those doubts changed the fact that she could still feel her legs—or thought she could. She'd heard about phantom limbs in amputees. Maybe this was like that.

There was a knock at the door. "May I come in?" It was Fitzgerald. He'd kept her here for a day now—one of the gorillas had brought her beef stew for dinner and lukewarm oatmeal for breakfast—but it wasn't until now that he was finally coming to check on her.

"No one's stopping you. I'm the prisoner here, remember?"

The door opened and Fitzgerald entered, no longer dressed in a hospital gown, but instead in a gray dress shirt and casual suit. Not only had his dress changed, his demeanor seemed to have softened as well. "How's my favorite patient today?"

Minerva grimaced. He wanted something from her. "Oh, just about as well as you might expect, considering I've been cooped up here against my will for the past, what is it, eighteen hours?"

"I'm sorry, Minerva. Your mother thought this would be best for you."

That's right. Carson wouldn't have to provide some excuse to Jessica, because she was already in on the whole thing. She'd had her *committed*, for freak's sake!

"So you think I'm a nutcase. I'm surprised you didn't put me in a strait-jacket."

Fitzgerald smiled. "We only do that if we conclude you're a danger to yourself and others. I don't think you are. I think you're just confused. It's my hope that we can unconfuse you."

"Do you mean brainwash me?"

He shook his head, his brow furrowing slightly. "This may be hard for you to understand, be I believe you've brainwashed yourself. You've become so secluded and detached from the rest of the world, that you've created your own little world to live in. There's nothing wrong with that. Everyone likes to escape now and then. Take in a movie. Lose yourself in a book. But at the end of the day, the movie's over or the book's done and you return to reality . . . except you haven't. You're refusing to leave because you feel safe there."

Minerva just stared at him. He might have a point, but she wasn't about to admit it.

He retrieved a plastic chair from the corner and sat down opposite her. "What is it about your life that you hate so much?"

"You're a psychiatrist, right? Are you really that dense? Let's see. I've spent the past fifteen years as a cripple—yes, I know that's not the P.C. term for it, but when you get right down to it, that's how people see me. Then there's Jessica, who cares more about her flavor-of-the-month boy toys than she does her only daughter. I've never had a job, never had a boyfriend, never had much of anything in my miserable life."

He didn't answer right away. She could tell he was thinking. *Yes, you could get a job*, he might tell her. *Lots of companies hire the disabled and make accommodations for them, and there are dial-a-ride programs for transportation.* He was probably also thinking she wouldn't have any trouble finding a boyfriend. Yes, she was attractive enough, but to be honest, she didn't really care for the few guys she'd met. Most of them were idiots, and the few who weren't either wanted to take pity on her or take advantage of her—"take" being the thing they had in common.

"Look, Doc, I know I wallow in self-pity sometimes, but that doesn't make me crazy. You've got no reason to hold me here."

"Please, stop being defensive for a moment and believe me: No one's calling you crazy. I'm just trying to help you here."

"Okay, but you just called me defensive. News flash, Doc: Accusing me of *anything* isn't exactly the best way to get past those defenses."

"You're right," he said, leaving it at that.

"So how long do you propose to keep me here? From what I've heard, you get a 72-hour hold, and then you have to let me go—unless, as you put it, I'm somehow 'a danger to myself and others,' which you've already said I'm not. So, I could just sit here for the next couple of days and wait you out, at which point I could simply waltz—or roll—right out of here, free as the crippled little bird I am."

Fitzgerald stood and started pacing. She could tell she'd rattled him a little.

"It's not quite that simple," he said. "We need to keep you here until you're ready to go home—until we've gotten rid of these delusions."

"And just how do you propose we do that?"

The question seemed to alleviate some of his anxiety, and he sat back down in the chair. Maybe if she put things back on him, she could get him to drop his guard and find out what this was really all about. Despite her own nagging doubts about Raven and the nature of her new reality, she couldn't help but think there was more to this ridiculous exercise than some benevolent concern for her sanity.

"I've got the results of your brain scan, and it shows some abnormal activity in your amygdala, the center of your brain that controls long-term memory."

"You're saying my neurons got crossed somehow?"

"In a manner of speaking. It's more complicated than that, but the results aren't conclusive and I'm hoping it's not a physiological problem."

"And if it is?"

"Let's cross that bridge when we come to it, shall we? I don't want to do anything invasive if we don't have to. I'd like to try something else first."

He was good. If he was trying to scare her by implying that he might lobotomize her if she didn't go along with whatever else he had up his sleeve, it was working.

"I'd like to try a course in hypnotherapy," he continued. "If you respond favorably, it should indicate that your delusion is psychologically based, and there won't be any need to go further. Of course, we'd have to see you back here for periodic treatments, but we don't want to get ahead of ourselves here. Let's see how the hypnotherapy goes. It's painless and noninvasive. But I do need one thing from you: your cooperation. It can't work unless you're open to it, and unless you consent, we'll have to look at other approaches."

Other approaches. The implicit threat was becoming more explicit.

"Who's going to perform this hypnosis? If I agree to it, do I get to go home?"

"I'm a trained hypnotherapist," Fitzgerald replied, "so I'll be conducting your sessions. I've developed some new techniques that I believe will be more effective in not just dimming, but eradicating your delusions. Let's see how they go on an inpatient basis. Then we'll be able to determine how long it's best to keep you here."

"You say 'we' like I have some choice in the matter," she muttered under her breath.

"You do." It was as if the softness had drained out of his voice and had been supplanted by a steely warning. He wasn't playing around.

Minerva was silent for a moment as she looked him up and down, sizing him up.

"When do we start?" she said finally.

"Now."

Revelation

A day had passed, and Raven felt weaker. He hadn't been able to find Minerva with his mind, and he sensed that she was somehow preoccupied. It would be okay, he told himself. She'd come back to him. She wouldn't abandon him—not now, when everything had become so crazy. Still, without the ability to feel her presence, he worried. What would happen if, somehow, the same people who had abducted him managed to somehow convince her everything was just in her head? What if they were able to make her forget about him?

"You fade right out of existence again, just like you did the first time." That's what the Jules woman had said. And she was right. He could survive for a short time without her attention, but in the long run, he'd just fade away like a ghost consigned to oblivion. *Stop feeling sorry for yourself!* he chided. But then, in the very next thought, *You can't help her if you're dead again, can you?*

It was dark all around him, then the door to the room opened and a bright sliver of light pierced the blackness, framing a woman's silhouette in the doorway.

"Hello, my pet. Feeling a little down today?"

She walked up to him and knelt down in front of him, her lips pursed in an exaggerated pout and her eyes feigning compassion.

"I'm fine."

She reached up and traced a long, red fingernail along a line underneath his left eye socket. "Oh, I don't think so, love. You look quite tired to me. What's wrong? Is your girlfriend too preoccupied to keep you in her thoughts these days? Maybe she's found another lover, Raven. Maybe she wants a real man she knows won't leave her if she turns her back on him for a few moments."

"I'm still here," he growled through gritted teeth.

"But for how long? I'm worried about you, Raven, truly I am. If you knew what I know, you'd be worried, too."

She paused, waiting for him to take the bait, but he stayed silent.

"Oh, come now, don't tell me you're not the least bit curious about what's happening to Minerva? I know you haven't been able to reach her these past few hours, and I also know why. Wouldn't you like me to tell you?"

He wrinkled his nose slightly, but nodded.

"Don't worry. Curiosity kills cats, not ravens . . . at least not right away." She laughed. "Here's the scoop, darling: A colleague of mine has your beloved under observation, and he's begun using hypnosis to treat her 'condition.' As a matter of fact, he's reporting very good progress. In a few days, he'll have Minerva realizing that you were nothing more than a figment of her imagination, a phantom lover she concocted to fill a void in her pathetic little life."

"You're lying," he seethed.

"Oh, am I? Then why are you feeling so drained, my dear? You can't tell me it's for lack of food. I know you devoured that steak dinner I served you last night. Oh, that's right. You revived ones don't actually *need* food, do you? But I bet it still tasted good. Too bad you wouldn't let me join you. It could have been heavenly."

Raven's mind raced. What if she was right?

"Want a little piece of friendly advice?" the woman continued. "Forget about her. She'll forget about you soon enough one way or the other, and you'll have no choice but to rejoin your parents in that eternal sleep. Unless, of course . . ."

"Yes?"

She stood up and leaned over him, accentuating her sense of control. She smiled a smile that was nearly a smirk, then parted her lips and leaned in closer. She could feel the warmth of her breath on his neck, the breaths quickening slightly as she drew closer. Then, she said it: "Raven, I have the gift."

She pulled away from him and stood back up, leaning back and crossing her arms in front of her. "Let that sink in."

He did. Then: "How do I know you're telling the truth?"

"Let me into your mind, and you'll know soon enough."

Raven looked at her, and for a split-second he let down his guard. In that same moment, he felt her essence come flooding into him, warm but tainted, yet all the same, exhilarating. Sometimes, you don't realize how hungry you are until someone puts a piping hot meal in front of you. This was like that. He'd been slowly losing strength since he'd lost his connection with Minerva, and this woman, Jules, had poured that strength back into him like a tidal wave.

"You see?" she said, a self-satisfied look spreading across her face. "I'm not playing games with you, Raven. I really like you. I had to scare you a little earlier so you knew what was at stake here, but really, it's better this way. Minerva can live her life without pining over some long-dead romance that never really was, you can preserve your own life and I . . . well, I get you."

"How did you do that" he asked "if you don't remember me from before?"

"It's simple," she said. "I know you now. With the gift, that's all it takes."

Raven shook his head, dizzy from the sudden infusion of vitality she'd provided. "But what do you want with me?" he asked finally.

"All in good time, darling."

Turnabout

Fitzgerald's first hypnotherapy session had been painless—at least as far as Minerva could tell. She emerged feeling none the worse for wear; she had the sense that she was forgetting something, but as is normal with forgetting, she had no idea what it was. It felt as if a name were on the tip of her tongue, but she couldn't quite bring it farther forward to her lips. Some kind of a bird. A crow, perhaps. Or a mockingbird. It certainly seemed to be mocking her.

"You said I'm supposed to be feeling better, so why does it feel like I've lost something?" she asked.

"That's to be expected," Fitzgerald said. "You came to rely heavily on your delusion, and now that you're releasing it, you're going to feel a sense of loss. But it isn't a loss if it never really existed, is it? Just keep telling yourself that and stop trying to remember. Let it go and move forward."

Sure, it's just that easy, isn't it? Maybe for you. You're not the one who feels like you're losing a part of yourself.

"Shall we try something a little different now?"

Minerva nodded, "Okay."

"Give me a moment."

He left the room and returned a moment later carrying a large, blue pillar candle on a porcelain stand. Setting it on the table he'd placed between them, he struck a match and touched it to the wick; when it was alight, he turned and flicked the light switch by the door, then returned to sit across from her.

"Now, I want you to stare directly into the flame. Let it dance in the corners of your mind, and imagine it expanding slowly inward, until it fills your entire consciousness. Until there is nothing but that flame. I want you to let go of everything else in your mind and see in that flame the essence of who you are, burning brighter and brighter, its glow warming and reassuring you. Relax and feel it surrounding you in its embrace . . ."

Minerva allowed his voice to slowly recede into the back of her mind, letting the amber glow transport her. Soon, indeed, there was only the flame. It felt so familiar to her, as if it had been there with her all along. It had been there beside her when no one else stood near, there on the bedstand in her room, the only light in a truly dark existence for so many years . . . . Until one night, when its light had shown upon a face too long hidden in shadow: a childhood friend she had all but forgotten until the flame of memory had sparked something to bring him back to her. His name, a dark avatar, stood in contrast to the glow of the candle, yet somehow in harmony with it, associated with it in the depths of buried memory.

Raven.

She remembered.

Had she really been imagining everything? Even with Fitzgerald right there in front of her, she still felt sensations in her legs that she hadn't felt for fifteen years, and she couldn't shake the feeling that, if she chose to, she could use them to stand up right in front of him. She was tempted to do just that, but something inside warned her to maintain the pretense—not just the pretense of her paralysis, but the pretense that she was in a state of hypnosis. She wasn't—not anymore. But she kept her eyes fixed on the flame to preserve the illusion.

"Now," Fitzgerald was saying, "I want you to make the flame your refuge. You need no other comfort. The flame alone is sufficient. All else fades away like a dream forgotten in the first moments of waking. Keep the flame in your mind and turn now to look at me. Look into my eyes and see the trust I have there for you. Share your trust with me. Open yourself to me and relax. Know that you can depend on me, just as you depend upon the flame—to keep you safe, to guide you toward the truth. The light of truth that dances in the candle."

Minerva turned toward him and fixed her eyes on his, just as he had asked her to do. Those eyes were dull and gray, almost like clouds passing before the face of the sun, obscuring it. For all his learning, for all his supposed expertise, it struck her that he seemed all but blind to anything that wasn't directly in front of him. He was unaware that she had shaken off his trance; perhaps he had been told she was gifted, but if so, he didn't know what that meant.

For the first time, as she gazed at him, she realized the depth of its meaning herself. It went beyond the ability to heal her paralysis, the ability to contact Raven with her mind and summon him not only to her dream world but even into her waking life. Her gift could take energy, any sort of energy, and mold it into the shape of whatever memory she might call to mind. This was why they'd abducted her. They were afraid of her, as if she were a mountain lion that had come down out of the foothills into some suburban neighborhood, throwing its residents into such a panic that they rushed to hunt her down, tranquilize her, capture and declaw her.

Her pupils froze as she stared into Fitzgerald's eyes, and she felt a sudden rush of anger, even loathing, toward him for what he had been trying to do to her. He had been trying to take a portion of her identity from her, to turn her from a wild animal into some docile pet or lab rat to be kept here indefinitely as part of some collection. He'd never intended to let her go, she felt sure, no matter how much she cooperated with him. She was too dangerous, too valuable.

He had tried to take the past away from her, so she would grant him his wish and yield it up to him . . . just not in the way he had intended.

As he tried to impress his will upon her, she drew upon her own energy to meet his and reversed the flow, turning it back upon him. She summoned the most horrible memory she could think of and released it directly across the link that bound them together. She relived in her mind every excruciating moment of the car crash that had left her paralyzed. The feeling of being thrown up against the roof of the car. The panic of being so completely out of control that only one thing could make it worse—the fact that it was happening to a powerless six-year-old child. The pain of something like a broadsword slicing muscle, nerve and tendon in both your legs and the vacant, maddening numbness that followed it when she awoke in the hospital.

Fitzgerald's eyes widened as he experienced it, just as she had. She saw him try to turn away as she held him there, a prisoner as surely as he'd taken her prisoner himself. Captivated by the fear, the terror and the agonizing pain that only she had felt on that day. She shared it with him now. All of it.

His face blanched. She was dimly aware of him trying to shut his eyes against the anguish of it, and in some distant place beyond her reverie, she heard him scream, just as she herself had screamed on that awful day. Now she, too, was reliving it, and the images, sounds, and feelings were as vivid to her as they had been when she'd first experienced them. Her mind felt numb from the pain of it. And when it was more than she could endure any longer, the pain of it shredded the link between them and she slumped back in her wheelchair, exhausted.

The next thing she knew, Fitzgerald was staring up at her from the floor, looking out from half-dead gray eyes that seemed to be pleading with her like a lost puppy.

"What have you done to me?" he wailed. "I can't feel my legs!"

He had obviously tried to get up out of his chair, only to have the now useless appendages fail him. He was paralyzed, just as she had been.

Minerva looked down at him. What *had* she done? She could feel herself shaking, whether from the effort of what she'd done or the cruelty of it, she couldn't be sure. She just knew that she had to get out of there, away from that laboratory.

So she stood up from her wheelchair and staggered into the corridor, looking for someplace to run . . . only to be met by two very large men who looked like they had once tried out for the Green Bay Packers.

~

Jules' secure communication device blinked suddenly, the screen lighting up.

She looked over at Raven, who had fallen asleep even amid the obvious discomfort of being tied up in that uncomfortable chair.

He was getting weaker.

The screen started to flash. That meant one thing: a high-priority message. Only a handful of people had access to this line, and only a handful of that handful had ever used it to send her a flashing signal.

She tapped the screen to stop it from flashing, entered a secure access code and watched as a very short message, written in red letters, appeared:

"Operation Mind Wipe compromised. Target Minerva Rus no longer secure."

The sender's ID code followed: Sigmund7r3Ud.

Fitzgerald.

She didn't bother to return the message but instead deleted it and typed in a new destination for the next message she would compose.

It consisted of two words: "Operation compromised."

She pressed send, then typed five more letters and sent that, too: "Abort."

She looked over at Raven again. He wasn't even moving. Things were spiraling out of control, and she didn't have much time.

Tapping the screen again, she typed in another destination, then sent another one-word message: "Terminate."

Outranked

Biltmore was waiting in the parking lot outside the facility when he got the text: "Operation compromised."

That was all. Nothing on who had sent it and nothing on how the mission had been "compromised." He hoped it meant he didn't have to go back to spend another night with that Jessica woman. Her expensive tastes were rapidly depleting his expense account. And she was becoming combative, demanding that he take her here or there at a moment's notice. It had been hard enough to get her to sign Minerva's commitment papers (even if they were bogus, it was a necessary ruse). She'd begun to ask more and more questions—not, as far as he could tell, out of any concern for Minerva, but instead because she wanted to cover her ass in case the government came snooping around.

He *was* the government, but he couldn't tell her that. Undercover operations could be a major pain that way.

Now, it seemed, she didn't like the fact that he'd gone off on his own without telling her where he was going. It wasn't as if he had any choice in the matter. He had to station himself near the lab in case something went wrong with Fitzgerald. The doctor had been reliable in the past (and why shouldn't he be, considering what he was being paid?), but he'd always struck Biltmore as a little too arrogant for his own good. Arrogance could translate into carelessness, and he couldn't afford any margin for error in this operation.

Then the second part of the message came through.

"Abort."

The order puzzled him. If something had gone wrong in the operation, he'd expected to receive another order: "Terminate." That had been the fallback position from the beginning. If the mission went off the rails, he had standing orders to eliminate the subject at the center of it: Minerva Rus. His contact at the agency had been explicit about that. But now, someone was changing his orders. The question was, who? And why?

The next text he received answered the first question.

"Authorization: JulesB6s4R."

Despite his years of training and mental conditioning, Biltmore felt his heart beating faster. Something had obviously gone very far wrong if his contact were countermanding her own orders.

His fingers sped across the keyboard of his securely linked cell phone: "Rationale?"

Nothing came back.

Damn that woman. He didn't know whether he was talking about Jules or Minerva—yet. He had to find out. He holstered his Baby Glock, opened the door to his blue 2015 Nissan 370Z and strode around the large rectangular garbage bin he'd used to hide his presence. The parking lot was quiet, which wasn't surprising, considering this was a classified government facility, off-limits to public or commercial use. The sun had baked the asphalt hot enough that he could feel it through the soles of his black running shoes, a deviation from the Oxfords that were more typical of male agents operating undercover. Whenever he had a sense he might need an extra step, comfort and performance were paramount—and the muffled footfalls helped, too. If anyone ever questioned him about it, he merely told them he had early-stage diabetes and his doctor had ordered him to wear flexible shoes as a hedge against neuropathy. No one ever questioned that excuse.

He crept around the side of the building, staying close to the wall, then deactivated the electronic lock on a service door and let himself in. If the agency knew he could do that, they'd have a fit—and change the code. But he couldn't risk using his passkey and tripping security if something had gone wrong inside.

The corridor that greeted him was as empty as the parking lot had been. Fluorescent light bathed it in the sort of glow you might think of when you envision the famed "white light" of near-death experiences. Biltmore himself didn't believe that was any more than the last-gasp hallucination of a dying person's wishful thought, but then, if someone had told him a few days ago that people could use memory-activated telekinesis, or whatever it was, to bring their loved ones back from the dead, he'd have laughed in their faces. He still wasn't sure he believed it.

Rounding a corner into a wider corridor, he saw it was empty as well. But he heard footfalls in the distance. He hesitated for a second: Should he move toward them even though it might mean exposing himself, or should he move away from them and risk losing Minerva? He knew the layout of the facility well, and he had a good idea where Fitzgerald was holding her, so it made sense to head in that direction, away from the footsteps. But if she were in that room, she'd likely still be there when he got back, and the footsteps were getting fainter, moving away.

He followed, shadowing them, creeping closer until it seemed they were right around the next corner. He'd been listening intently for the sound of Minerva's wheelchair, which made an intermittent squeaking noise as it moved forward, but he'd heard no sound of it and was starting to second-guess himself about not checking the room first.

Then, the footsteps stopped.

Biltmore heard a voice. "In there." It was a command.

"Like hell!" A woman's voice. Minerva's. Biltmore drew a mental blue-print of where they were inside the facility. If he remembered correctly, they were near the refrigeration unit, where some organic samples were kept on ice.

In an instant, he rounded the corner and was met with the sight of two large men who would have seemed more at home on a professional wres-tling telecast than in a medical facility. He recognized them, and he trusted they'd recognize him, as well. If he was lucky, he wouldn't have to use his Baby Glock.

The pair turned to face him. Each had a tight grip on one of Minerva's arms as she was standing between them.

Standing.

Biltmore contained his shock at the sight of that and addressed the pair: "That's enough," he declared. "I'm here to take custody of the subject. You can turn her over to me."

"Sorry, Boss," the larger of the two men answered. "We're under orders to terminate her."

Biltmore blinked. "I'm under orders to abort the operation. Who gave the order to terminate? Fitzgerald? I authorized his involvement in this to begin with. I outrank him. Release her to me, and . . . "

Biltmore's attention suddenly swung from the two men to Minerva, who was struggling as hard as she could against their grip and had lost her patience for a conversation that seemed, to her, like some debate between an angel and a demon over her ultimate fate. She couldn't tell at the moment which was which, but she knew she wanted a say in it.

"What is this, Carson?" she shouted at him. "What the hell *is* all of this?"

Biltmore froze. Despite his training and mental conditioning, he felt his heart beating faster. He'd never made a mistake like this before. It was fundamental: Never blow your cover to a subject for the sake of a fellow agent. He'd been so intent on trying to defuse the situation with these two operatives (who were low-level operatives, at that), that instead of taking them out efficiently with a pair of well-aimed shots, he'd blown his cover six ways from Sunday. That would have been difficult to explain, too, but he could always have said he'd been a trained security guard before he became a stockbroker and just happened along at the right time. It would have been a stretch, but a lot more plausible than finding a way to brush aside words like "terminate" and "authorized" and "operation."

As it turned out, he might have to use the gun anyway.

"Shut up!" one of the musclemen said, squeezing Minerva's arm too tightly.

"Or what? You'll kill me? Seems like you're going to do that anyway. Or try to. That's what terminate means, last time I looked."

Biltmore was impressed with her courage. She obviously knew what she was facing, but she seemed more angry than scared.

She had turned her attention from Biltmore to the man who was holding her right arm. "You want to kill me, don't you?" What was she doing? She was goading him. "I want you to look me in the eye and say that. I don't think you have the balls."

The man squeezed her arm even tighter, twisting it, and she let out a half-scream in pain. But even in the midst of it, she held his gaze when, like any good he-man (and bad agent), he decided he couldn't ignore a challenge and squared his face to meet hers.

Slowly, Biltmore saw his expression begin to change from one of bravado to one of questioning, and then the look of pain that had appeared on Minerva's face just a moment before began transferring itself to his countenance. The anger he'd heard in the young woman's voice a few moments earlier was spreading like a storm across her face, etching itself into the her brow in deep furrows and into lips pursed together in concentration. Biltmore could have sworn he heard her whisper an old children's taunt in clipped staccato under her breath, "I am rubber. You are glue. . ."

It was surreal.

Biltmore had seen enough. Whatever was happening, it wasn't good, and he couldn't allow things to spin any further out of control. Raising his pistol, he fired it at the ceiling, sending small bits of plaster cascading down on them. The muscleman Minerva had been focused on released his hold on her and fell to one knee, clearly dazed, but his companion kept a firm grip on her left arm.

Biltmore, maintaining his composure with some difficulty, even given his training, addressed himself to the man. He had already compromised his cover, so there was no use in trying to tiptoe around the issues at hand.

"I'm going to ask you again," he said. "Who gave the order to terminate?"

"JulesB6s4R. And *she* outranks *you*."

That doesn't make sense, Biltmore thought. *She's the one who gave me the order to abort.* But then, not much that had happened in the past half-hour made any sense to him.

The muscleman began pushing the still struggling Minerva toward the open door to the main refrigeration unit. They were going to lock her in there and freeze her to death. Biltmore wasn't about to let that happen.

"And this outranks you," he said, holding up his Baby Glock. "Let her go. Now."

The man glared at him but let go of Minerva, and Biltmore watched as she slowly walked toward him, clearly apprehensive but just as clearly preferring his company to the alternative.

"Jules won't like this," the man warned as his companion got to his feet.

"Jules obviously knows a lot better than you do that there are more efficient ways to terminate a subject," Biltmore said. "Allow me to demonstrate."

In one swift motion, he raised the pistol and saw Minerva flinch as he deftly brought it to bear, then fired.

Once.

Twice.

The two musclemen lay dead on the floor.

Damn, he said to himself. *I should have done that in the first place.*

Retreat

"Just who are you, really?"

Minerva stared at the man in the driver's seat of the Nissan as they moved at 70 miles per hour down U.S. Highway 101.

"It's complicated."

"That's a Facepage status, not an answer."

"I'm the guy who just saved your life and probably lost his job for his trouble."

She chuckled and glared at him. "I had the situation under control until you decided to go all Liam Neeson on those two jerks."

"Two. That's the point. Whatever you were doing to that one guy, I'll admit, was impressive. But somehow I don't think you could've brought down the other one too. And, speaking of questions to be answered, how *did* you do that? And how did you wind up out of that wheelchair and standing on your own two feet?"

Minerva said nothing.

"You don't have to answer me," he said finally. "I can figure it out myself."

"I can figure some things out for myself, too," she responded. "Let's see. You're not really Jessica's boyfriend, or you're just pretending in order to get to me. Don't worry about that offending me. I really do hate her. She's had it coming for a long time. And I'm flattered, really. No one really cared enough about me to kidnap me and then save my life, all in just a couple of days. But I don't think I'll trust you just yet. You seem pretty conflicted."

"You don't know the half of it."

Concrete barriers whizzed by them as they sped along in the car-pool lane. It wasn't long, however, before traffic slowed—as it always seems to in Southern California—and the freeway rush slowed to a crawl.

"Where are we going?"

"Someplace safe."

"Like that last place you put me where they wanted to put me on ice? Isn't that a mafia thing? Are you with the mob or something?"

"No."

"The CIA?"

"At the moment, it appears, I'm working on my own, thanks to you. Something's not right about any of this."

"You're just now figuring that out? Score one for Mr. Smartypants!"

The truth was, Biltmore hadn't figured out where they were going next. He was too busy trying to figure out what had just happened. Jules had issued a "terminate" order to those two goons at the same time she'd instructed him to abort the mission. That either meant she didn't trust him to follow through with her real orders or there was more to this operation than he'd been told. She'd been the source of his information, but now she seemed to have severed contact with him. This could be because she believed he had followed her "abort" order, or there could be something more to it. But if so, he had no way of knowing what it was, and he wasn't about to act without something more to go on.

"Gas."

"What?"

Minerva pointed to the gas gauge. "Wherever you're going, you'll need gas to get there, won't you?"

He nodded. He was missing details that he usually picked up. Maybe the same thing that had made him the agency's choice for this operation—the hit on Mary Lou Corbet all those years ago—had compromised his effectiveness in carrying it out. Maybe that's why he'd been given the "abort" signal. But maybes wouldn't take him very far. He needed firm answers.

Biltmore eased his way across the freeway through the heavy traffic, lane by lane, and got off at the next exit, turning right at the end of the off-ramp and then right again into a service station. They were greeted by a large green plaster brontosaurus and a line of two cars before they could even get to the pump island.

"I'm going into the store for an energy drink," Minerva announced. "Want anything?"

Biltmore could feel her eyes on him, but he wasn't about to meet her gaze. He'd seen what she could do.

"That can wait," he said simply. "Stay here while I pump the gas."

"Or what?" she said. "You'll shoot me? Tie me up? If you try it, I can scream so loud the whole neighborhood will hear me and you'll be spending the night in jail for assault. Do you really want that, or do you want to let me go get that energy drink?"

Biltmore hesitated a moment, then nodded. She was angry enough that she just might follow through on her threats, but despite her bluster, she didn't have anywhere else to go. He was betting she'd be back, and if she did try to make a run for it, he had a car—and confidence enough in his own ability as a tracker to bet he could find her before she got very far.

"Thanks," she said, and disappeared inside the convenience store while he slipped a twenty into the remote-pay station and started pumping the gas. The sun was starting its descent, which was a good thing. Nightfall would give him cover to carry out what he had to do next . . . once he'd figured out what that was.

When Minerva re-emerged from the station a moment later, she was carrying a Rock God energy drink and had a rather large individual in tow: a man in his late twenties wearing a gray mechanic's shirt with his name— Ron—embroidered on one side and that same green brontosaurus on the other. Did mechanics still wear those things? Apparently this one did. He strode up to Biltmore, his chest self-confidently puffed out like a rooster without the feathers.

"Can I help you?" Biltmore asked.

"This young lady tells me you've been harassing her," he said in a slight Southern accent. Tennessee, Biltmore guessed. "I don't allow that kind of behavior at this establishment."

"There's been no trouble," Biltmore said as the pump clicked, indicating the tank was full.

"That's not what the young lady says. According to her, you've been transporting her against her will."

"That's right," Minerva said, a self-satisfied smirk on her face.

Biltmore replaced the gas pump on its cradle, reached into his pocket and produced his wallet, then flipped it open to reveal a badge bearing the letters LAPD, a serial number and the name Aaron Welker.

Ron backed up a step. "Sorry, Officer," he said. "I didn't realize . . ."

"No harm done." Biltmore's lips curled upward in a genial smile. "It's a rough part of town. Better safe than sorry. Now, we'll just be on our way."

"Of course, Officer. Have a nice day."

Biltmore nodded, moved around the pump to put his arm behind Minerva's back and escorted her into the car.

"So you're a cop?" she said when they were inside again and pulling out of the lot. "Aaron Welker, huh? I didn't think you looked much like a Bradley."

"That was stupid, Minerva. Really stupid."

She ignored his attempt at a menacing tone. "So what should I call you? Carson? Welker? Mr. Potato Head?"

"Carson will do," he said. "It's not my real name, but that doesn't really matter."

She grunted, then fell silent as he pulled around the corner into a back alley behind a discount grocery store.

He shut off the engine, reached into the glove compartment and produced a black strip of material.

"Hey!"

He wrapped the material around her head, covering her eyes, as she struggled against him. "Do you want me to tie your hands, too?"

"You're only doing this because you saw what I did to that goon of Fitzgerald's back there."

"No, I think I've figured out it's not a good idea to look you in the eye, Minerva. I don't need a blindfold to protect me from you. It's there because I can't let you see where I'm taking you. I've compromised too much already; I can't compromise that."

She stopped struggling and fell silent; the traffic finally started to break up, and they began moving more swiftly toward their destination: the abandoned motel he had used as a base. He had the equipment he needed there to investigate what was happening and to make contact with others within the organization. At the very least, he needed to confirm the "abort" order with someone other than Jules—someone who, he hoped, could tell him why she'd ordered him to abandon the mission on the one hand and issued a "terminate" order on the other.

A little more than an hour later, he pulled the car off the freeway and onto the abandoned stretch of old highway that led to his haven.

In the passenger's seat, Minerva sat quietly, eyes closed behind the blindfold. Not only did her mind feel as though it had been fractured into a hundred pieces by everything that had happened, her body felt nearly limp from exhaustion. She felt the car come to a stop, and Carson/Biltmore come around the side and open the door for her. She let him help her out of the car and made no move to be free of the blindfold or struggle against him as he put his arm lightly around her waist and led her forward. What did it matter? What did any of it matter now? Her existence had been so pointless for years now that it was scarcely worth the struggle to reclaim it. What was there to reclaim, anyway? Yes, she could walk, but she still had no friends, a sociopathic mother and, when it came right down to it, no life.

"You can sit here," she heard Carson say, and she felt herself sit down on a well-cushioned couch covered in material that felt a little like velvet.

She sat back and exhaled, and she realized that, with everything that had happened, she'd barely thought of Raven in the past two days. Just about the same time she remembered him, though, he faded from her mind's eye as she fell inexorably into a deep, relaxing slumber.

Proposition

When Raven awoke, his surroundings had changed. He appeared to have been taken to an apartment several stories up in a building overlooking a Los Angeles suburb. Glendale, maybe. In contrast to the dark warehouse where he'd been caged up before, this place was bathed in light—albeit the fading light of a day all but concluded. Broken clouds, like orange and yellow streamers, their colors deepening moment by moment, hung suspended in the darkening sky. The smog that typically hung over the area was mercifully absent, and he gazed out an expansive bank of windows from a long, light tan sectional couch on which he lay.

Raven sat up and rubbed his eyes. His restraints had been removed, as well, and he could move freely, but despite his recent slumber, he felt tired. More than tired, really: listless and virtually without energy.

"I thought it was the least I could do, to make your last few days—or hours—among the living as comfortable as possible." The woman who called herself Jules walked toward him from behind a large potted fern that partially obscured a kitchenette across the room. Her green skirt flared outward as she sat down on an ottoman barely two feet away from him.

"How did I get here?"

"Don't you remember? You fell asleep. You've lost a lot of energy, darling. It just didn't feel right to leave you in that dingy old warehouse in your condition."

"No . . .," he mumbled. "I don't remember any of it . . ."

She shook her head and frowned in an attempted gesture of sympathy. "I'm not surprised, really. The memory's one of the first things to go when you start losing consciousness. That's how it's worked with the others we've dealt with. We like to say you've got 'the fades.' You'll feel a little light-headed, and you'll end up nodding off more and more frequently—until finally, you just don't wake up. There's no pain to it really. You just . . . fade away. Here. Maybe this will help a little."

She handed him a cup of warm broth, which he hadn't even noticed she'd been holding. She was right: He really was losing it.

He put it to his lips, but it was nearly tasteless.

"I'm sorry it's not better," she apologized, "but the senses become duller as your deterioration progresses. I'm afraid nothing will taste too strong, even if it's steeped in jalapeno juice." She laughed at her own cruel joke. "You'll experience blurred vision, tinnitus, a loss of sensation in your extremities. Don't worry. This is all normal."

"I'm dying and you want me to believe it's normal?" Raven said. He realized upon hearing his own voice that his speech had grown slurred, as if he'd been drinking heavily.

"You're not dying, Raven. You're already dead. You're just reverting to your natural form. Now, it is still possible to prevent this, but the longer you wait, the harder it will be. It's easy to bring someone back the first time, but each time after that, it gets a little harder. It's kind of like cloning. You degrade a little with each attempt, until finally there's nothing left to retrieve."

"Minerva will remember," he said, more to himself than to her.

"I'm afraid that's not too likely," Jules said, the sympathetic frown returning to her face as her voice took on a syrupy sweet tone. "Be honest: You haven't felt her in a couple of days now. That's why you're like this."

Raven said nothing.

"She's forgotten you, Raven. She's moved on. Can you really blame her? What kind of future would she have with a phantom from the past?"

He shook his head.

"That's right, none. But you could still have a future, Raven. Remember that flood of energy I sent you before? You could feel like that all the time. All you have to do is promise me you won't try to contact Minerva anymore. Allow me to be the one who keeps you alive. There's more power in my gift than Minerva could ever hope to channel, and it could all be there for you if you agree to work with me."

Raven took his eyes off her and stared out the window. The sky was growing darker now, and the color was draining from the clouds. Had it ever really been there in the first place? Or was it just a trick of the fading light, a product of the sunlight's trajectory as it reflected off bits of water suspended in the sky? Maybe he himself was no more real than those colors, just the product of some bizarre trickery that made him seem more than he was.

He looked back at her, barely able to keep his eyes open.

She moved closer and cradled his cheek in the palm of her hand. It felt soft and soothing, welcoming.

"Imagine what we could do together, my pet? Together we could harness the power we share between us and bring back so many others who have passed beyond. Think of it! We could retrieve the greatest minds of the Renaissance and the Enlightenment. Da Vinci. Rembrandt. Bacon. Newton. Shakespeare. We could bring back Einstein and Jung and Picasso. All this is within our grasp if we only combine our talents."

He raised his head slightly, a questioning look on his face.

She smiled at him, white teeth revealed behind lips painted bright in ruby red. "We'll speak more of this when you're feeling better. Let us just say that you are special. Never before has one with the gift died and been returned to this life by another. You have within you the potential to access your gift in a way no one else ever has. I can teach you how to do that, and together, we can change the world."

He couldn't keep his eyes open any longer, and sleep took him once again.

Epiphany

"I need your help."

Minerva awoke to the feeling of a pair of hands up by her ears, loosening the blindfold that had been tied around her head.

She sat up straight, disoriented, then remembered where she was: wherever it was Carson had taken her.

"Minerva, I need your help," he said again.

"With what?"

"I need you to contact Raven. Something's gone terribly wrong."

Things had gotten so muddled and confused, Carson couldn't possibly explain it to her even if he wanted to. He'd spent the past few weeks trying to persuade her *not* to contact Raven, even setting up the sessions with Fitzgerald in an effort to make her forget him—to convince her that she was crazy and it all had been an illusion. It had been cruel, but necessary to avoid the alternative: If he failed to sever the link between Minerva and Raven, his only possible recourse would have been to terminate her.

Or so he thought.

But he'd been able to reach the agency and, to his surprise, had found his former contact there, TaniaX3iFY. He'd assumed she'd left the agency when Jules took over his assignments, but that hadn't been the case. In fact, she had protested the reassignment at the time, but Jules had obtained the backing of some higher-ups in facilitating the change.

When he asked Tania about Operation Death Trap, she seemed surprised. "We closed the book on that one after your initial termination job," she told him. "I've got the record of the file right here on my screen. It says, 'Closed.'"

"Then what's this all about with Minerva?"

"Minerva who?"

"Minerva Rus."

"Sorry, Triage. She's not in our database."

Biltmore's mind reeled. "Then what's *she* been up to?" he half-whispered, as much to himself as to Tania.

"What's who been up to?"

"Jules. JulesB6s4R. She's the one who gave me this assignment."

"Triage, I hate to tell you this, but there *is* no assignment. According to our records, you've been offline for the past three months. You're supposed to be taking a sabbatical. Sounds to me like maybe you need a little more time off."

"Thanks. I just might." He ended the conversation.

Based on what Tania had said, one of two things was going on. Either Jules had put him on a deep-cover assignment—and he'd just revealed the details to someone who was never supposed to know—or else she'd gone rogue and had concocted a bogus operation from the ground up to accomplish who knew what. The more he thought about it, the more his suspicions leaned toward the second option. First, Jules had pulled him into an operation no one seemed to know anything about, and then she'd tried to lock him out with an "abort" order just when things seemed to be coming to a head. It looked to him like he'd served his purpose by delivering Minerva to her and become more of a threat than an asset.

So she'd cut him loose.

It might have been that she just didn't trust him to terminate Minerva, so she'd given the order to someone else. In point of fact, she would have had good reason for such doubts.

Or maybe Minerva hadn't been her real objective, and maybe she'd wanted him out of the way before he figured that out. If Tania was to be believed, Minerva hadn't been on the agency's radar. She hadn't even been aware of her gift until very recently, and the agency had no reason to believe she'd be able to use it . . . if the agency even knew about it in the first place.

Come to think of it, all the information he'd received about Minerva and her gift had come from Jules. From what he could tell so far, it had turned out to be accurate. But what if the agency didn't have a clue about any of it—beyond the original Operation Death Trap, that is? What if Jules had information no one else even knew existed, and she was exploiting it in some way to fulfill her own agenda?

If she'd been ready to kill Minerva, there must have been a bigger prize involved in all this, one she'd be interested in preserving.

What could it be?

Or who?

"You want me to contact Raven?" Minerva was still half-asleep, and the thought that she might be dreaming crossed her mind. Had Carson just done a complete 180 and asked her to do the very thing he'd been trying to keep her from doing?

"Yes."

She shook her head slowly. She'd just awakened from a sound sleep, but she didn't remember seeing him in any of her dreams. It had been as if he hadn't been there—like he'd been hidden from her or walled off somehow.

"Why should I do this for you?" she asked. "Who's to say you won't try to find him and kill him?"

"I'm won't do that. Look. Whoever was trying to kill you might have somehow gotten to Raven, as well. I need your help to find him so we can protect him."

We?

A wave of guilt rushed over her. The last time she's been in contact with Raven, he'd told her he was being held prisoner somewhere. That was why he hadn't met her in the park. But things had turned so bad so quickly for her, she'd all but forgotten about his predicament. Fitzgerald and his cronies had taken all her attention; she'd been so intent on just surviving and getting the hell out of there that everything else had receded into the background. Now it came surging to the forefront again at full force.

"Raven is in trouble," she declared. "How did you know?"

"Just a hunch. I'm good at those."

She decided to trust him, at least for the moment. She had no way of knowing where Raven was, and if Carson could help her find him, she could cross the next bridge when she came to it.

"I'll try to contact him," she said. "But no guarantees. And if I do manage to reach him and he tells me not to trust you, it's done right there. Do you understand?"

"Perfectly. And thank you."

He seemed sincere.

She gestured toward the window. "Close the shades there. If I'm gonna do this, I'll need as little distraction as possible."

Her abductor nodded and did as she indicated.

Minerva closed her eyes and listened to the ticking of a cuckoo clock in the background, lulling her into a trance as she focused her thoughts, her heart, her entire being on the task of reaching Raven. She realized as she concentrated how much she had missed him; even though her conscious mind had been occupied by the need to stay alive, her subconscious mind hadn't forgotten their first kiss, the night they'd shared, and his words of encouragement to her when no one else had seemed to care.

As she focused on those things, brought them vivid to her mind's eye and lingered on them, another image began to form beyond them in the distance. She heightened her focus, pushing her mindsight forward to meet it there. She rushed ahead, ready to embrace the man she knew would meet her there as she delved deeper into her own need, her own desire.

"Raven!" she called out.

But the image that formed in front of her, when at long last it became clear, wasn't that of the young man with dark wavy hair and the smile that had taken her heart. It was . . . a woman. With long, straight red hair and pale skin. She was smiling an almost demonic smile from between a pair of too-red lips.

"You're . . . not Raven."

"Sorry to disappoint you," the woman answered, spreading her arms out before her. "Those images in your mind were quite . . . touching. But I'm afraid he's otherwise engaged. Oh, and that friend of yours there with you? He's working for me."

"Who the hell are you?"

"Raven's new mistress, in a manner of speaking. You'll have to come through me to get to him, and I seriously doubt you're up to the task. Actually, I know you're not. This is the only warning I'll give you: If you try to contact him again, your friend Mr. Carson or Biltmore or whatever name you know him by will be sweeping the shards of your mind up off the floor with a whisk broom."

She thrust her hand forward suddenly toward Minerva, and Minerva felt herself tumbling backward as if she'd been hit by a tornado. Her focus frayed at the edges, then came apart at the seams as the vision melted away into nothingness and she opened her eyes involuntarily.

"What happened?" Biltmore ask her.

But she was shaking too much to answer him.

Phantom

"I need to talk to Phantom."

Jules paced back and forth across the apartment's plush white carpeting, staring at the sleeping form of Raven with one eye as she talked into the secure communications device the agency had provided her.

"Phantom27iR5 is not available at the present time."

"Goddammit, *make* him available. This is important. JulesB6s4R."

There was a brief silence on the other end, and she waited for a few seconds before another voice came on the line.

"This is Phantom. Make it quick. I've got a meeting with some idiot senator in half an hour." It was a golf game, actually, but there was a senator involved, and Phantom didn't like to give out details to subordinates.

"Your senator can nurse a tequila sunrise in the clubhouse till you get there," Jules scoffed.

How had she known?

"I need to know if you've heard anything about Operation Death Trap," she spat into the phone.

"You know we're not using that anymore, Jules. It's Operation Reanimate."

"Yes. Yes. I know. That's not the point. I want to know if anyone inside the agency's been snooping around about ODT. That's still what Triage thinks we're calling it, so that's what would come up on the radar if . . ."

"As a matter of fact . . ."

"Yes?"

"One of our lower-level contacts, TaniaX3iFy, searched our database for those keywords just yesterday."

Jules made a motion as if to hurl the phone at the apartment's plate-glass windows, then, balling her other hand into a fist, she brought the device back to her ear. "And you didn't bother to *brief* me on this, Phantom? Do you understand what this means? Tania was Triage's contact before I replaced her. If someone's asking her about ODT, it had to be him. And if she told him"—she switched to an artificially dumb, high-pitched voice—" 'Gee, Mr. Triage, sir, we don't have anything in our files about that . . .'" She switched back to her own, deep voice with its hint of a European accent. "Do you get what's just happened here?"

She had to wait for a moment before he answered. "Okay, I get you, Jules. But this isn't the end of the world. You cut him out of the operation anyway. He'd served his purpose—now he's done. If Tania told him there's nothing to find, what's the issue?"

"The issue is he's not stupid enough to let it drop. He's been with the agency 22 years, Phantom. He's not some dumb kid who just fell off the garbage truck yesterday. He'll keep asking questions. About me."

Phantom's tone brightened a little. "That's a good thing, Jules. There's no record of ODT at the agency, so he probably thinks you're some rogue agent working alone on this. That's exactly what we hoped he'd think if it got to this point."

"You mean that you'd hang me out to dry," she said under her breath, away from the phone, but he heard it all the same.

"To the contrary. If he thinks you're operating alone, he's more likely to get careless. If something goes wrong, we've got your back, Jules. Don't worry."

She kept her voice low, not wanting to wake Raven. "Something's already gone wrong," she said. "A lot of things, really. For one thing, the prime subject hasn't let me into his mind yet except for one brief moment. I'm starting to worry he'd rather die a second time than betray his stupid prima donna girlfriend."

"But she's . . ."

"Dead? Oh, no, she's very much alive. It seems those goons you assigned to Fitzgerald botched the termination order, so guess who's still obstacle number one in Operation Reanimate. That's right, sweetheart: Minerva Rus."

There was another brief silence. "She's a neophyte. You can handle her."

A slithery smile spread across Jules' face. "Yes, I can. And thank you for the vote of confidence." Her voice lowered to a husky near-growl. "Pity I can't *return* it!"

She touched the screen and cut the connection.

Raven stirred slightly on the couch, but it seemed to be an effort for him even to shift position in his sleep. If she didn't get to him soon, she'd lose him. Or, nearly as bad, she'd have to remove the block she'd placed on Minerva to revive him . . . which would undo everything she'd been trying to accomplish to this point. There had to be a third option—one that would allow her to maintain the upper hand against Minerva and give her more time to gain Raven's trust. Scratch that. No matter how seductive she was or how compelling her arguments were, he wasn't going to go along with her on this. Too bad, really. He would have been fun in bed. But at the moment, fringe benefits like that were about as low on her priority list as you could get.

There was only one way to ground this Raven. If her feminine wiles didn't work and threats didn't do the job, she'd just have to trick him.

The question was: How?

Confessions

Minerva felt like she'd just been hit by a some combination of a runaway diesel truck and a case of the Russian flu—or at least what she imagined those things might feel like. She'd never actually experienced either one. But she was shivering all over and sweating, as though she'd had a fever, and her muscles ached, even the newly awakened ones in her legs.

"What happened?" Carson was asking her again, a look of concern spread across his face. She realized she must look pretty bad; she'd never seen that expression on him before. "Did you contact him?"

She shook her head rapidly from side to side, the anxiety affecting her movements. "Someone else . . .," she nearly stuttered. "Someone else was there."

"Who?"

". . . Never seen her before . . . said she was his 'new mistress' and warned me not to try contacting him again . . . or else."

Carson fetched a quilt and spread it across her shoulders, but it didn't stop the shaking. She wasn't cold exactly. She just felt overwhelmed, her body seemingly brimming with anxiety. Some of it was her own, but some of it felt like it had been forced upon her by someone else—by whoever it was who had confronted her in her mind.

"Can you describe this person?"

She nodded. Her own anxiety was beginning to subside, but the other's was still there, like some parasite. How was that possible?

"Red hair . . . down past her shoulders . . . pale skin . . . piercing blue eyes . . ." Those eyes had been the worst of it. They'd held her there as if in some kind of trance state, and it had been some massive force from behind them that had flung her backward, shattered her focus.

A frown that mixed concern with recognition settled on Carson's face. "I know that woman," he said, as much to himself as to Minerva. "But how did she get to you like that? How could she have . . .?"

He knew the answer almost immediately, though he didn't care for it.

"She has the gift," he said.

Minerva sat up straight, a look of steely resolution in her eyes as she pushed back against what had been inflicted on her.

"You mentioned her eyes," Carson continued. "Did she look you directly in the eye?"

"Yes."

"You see what she's done, don't you? Exactly what you did to that buffoon back at the lab."

Minerva nodded. She'd realized it at almost the same moment. But what she'd done was worse than Carson could know. He still didn't know what she, Minerva, had done to Fitzgerald. She'd turned his hypnotic assault back on itself, like reversing polarity on a magnet, and flooded him with not only his own weak energy but with her memories of the accident. He hadn't been gifted, yet she'd been able to inflict horrific damage with just her own power. If this woman she'd just met in her mind were gifted, and had executed the same kind of reversal on her, she was lucky to be alive. Perhaps if it had happened in person, she wouldn't be.

"How do you know this woman?" she asked, pushing the last of her own anxiety aside as if she were a snake wriggling out of its skin. The other woman's induced panic still clawed at her, but she fought to ignore it.

Carson thought for a moment, considering how much to reveal. There was no help for it now, though. The operation, whatever it had been, had been hopelessly compromised, and he was entirely on his own in this, facing someone who was clearly very dangerous—not only a masterful liar, but extremely powerful on top of it. Minerva was alone, though, too. His best option, and perhaps his only good one, was to repair the distrust he'd created between them and persuade her that they should work together. That wouldn't be easy.

"The woman was my contact, the person who gave me this assignment."

"Assignment?"

"Yes. I was supposed to keep you from accessing your gift—and keep you away from Raven."

Minerva's fingers dug into the velvety cushions on the sofa. That was exactly what this woman had just tried to do.

He continued: "If I failed, I was supposed to kill you, but she aborted the assignment and gave those orders to the goons at the lab." His voice was direct, unapologetic, as it seemed to be most of the time. It was as though he were reciting the results from the latest horse race over a loudspeaker at the track.

"And now I suppose you want me to trust you."

He nodded.

Dude, you need to work on your people skills. "Do you think I'm crazy?"

"No, but I hope you're desperate. You should be after what just happened, and I'm in a position to help you if you're willing to let me."

Her fingers relaxed a little, leaving indentations in the cushion.

"Why do you care? You could just walk away from this. You just said she aborted the assignment . . . what kind of 'assignment' is this, anyway? Just who are you working for."

"At this point, no one. I know you don't want to trust me, but I will tell you this: I think the reason she pulled me off this was because she sensed I didn't have it in me to go through with that 'terminate' order. I wasn't going to kill you."

"Then why did you take me to that torture chamber?" Her fingers dug deeper into the cushion again. "Was that supposed to make me trust you?"

Carson leaned back, allowing a rare look of frustration to cross his face. It was gone almost as soon as it appeared. "Jules set that up; I went along with it because she told me she planned to keep you alive by erasing your memory. If the alternative was to kill you, I figured it was best to go along. But then something—I don't know what—must have gone wrong, and she decided she would have to kill you. She must have known I wouldn't have gone through with that because enlisted those goons to do it and took me off the case."

Minerva stood to her feet, but he stayed seated. "You don't make a very convincing argument."

"Sorry. It's the only one I've got—the only one that's not B.S., anyway. I'm trusting you with it in the hope that you'll trust me, but if you don't, I have a question for you: Who *are* you going to trust?"

Minerva didn't hesitate: "Raven."

"And how are you going to find him? I may be able to help you with that, but if you go back into that mind tunnel of yours again you might just get yourself killed."

"I can handle myself."

"So can I. I just think we could handle what we're up against better if we work together."

She stared at him, but he averted his eyes.

"So much for trust," she scoffed. "You're afraid to even look me in the eye."

"Fair enough," Carson said, tilting his head slightly to one side and standing to face her. He realized as he did that she was as tall as he was—he had never considered her height when she was in her wheelchair—and that her eyes were roiling with determination. Whatever Jules had done to her, she'd obviously shaken it off, or at least brought it under control.

He looked at her, waiting for her to do her worst. But he didn't flinch. He was trained not to, and besides, whatever happened, he figured he probably deserved it.

Confiscated

Jessica Meyer lay in bed with an old quilt balled up at her feet because it was too hot, clad only in orange frill panties and a T-shirt that read "Stop the World, I Wanna Get OFF!" She'd thought it was funny when she got it at Cold Burn in the mall, but no one else seemed to laugh when they saw it. There was no accounting for some people's tastes. A bowl of soggy Grain Flakes sat in her lap, while an old episode of some bad 1960s sitcom droned on in front of her.

It was eleven in the morning, but she didn't see any reason to get out of bed. No one was here except Archer, and he could occupy himself on the computer all day. He got his own meals, did the dishes, and took out the trash. He was in every way the opposite of his delinquent sister, who insisted that she be waited on hand and foot, always blaming the accident for her condition—and her mother for the accident. Ingrate. It was nice to have Minerva gone for a while, so she could enjoy some peace and quiet.

What wasn't so nice was Brad being gone. As much as she chafed at having to deal with Minerva's bad attitude, she'd enjoyed having a man around the house—or, more importantly, to take her *out* of the house. She hadn't even heard from him for a couple of days, and she hoped she hadn't scared him away. He was nice to her, and even if it was just for the sex, that was better treatment than she got from most men. You took what you could get in her situation, and what she'd gotten from him was the best she'd ever had.

The one thing he hadn't given her was his phone number, which she thought was strange, but she hadn't questioned it until now. She found herself hoping he was okay, but more than that, hoping he hadn't dumped her like the others had.

She jumped a little when the doorbell rang, and some of the milk from her cereal bowl slopped out onto the bed.

"Godammit!" Who the hell could that be? More of those religious freaks trying to sell her some timeshare in heaven for a few thousand dollars in their offering plate? No, thank you. She might look like white trash, but she wasn't *that* stupid. She didn't need anyone else to tell her about God. She'd been to church a few times, and she had that Bible she'd swiped from the Seven Slumbers Inn sitting beside her bed. That was good enough.

She got up and threw on some pink sweatpants, then grabbed a brush and ran it hurriedly through her hair as she headed toward the front door. Maybe it was Brad, she thought. She'd considered giving him the key, but she had told herself it was too soon. Good thing, too. She wouldn't have wanted him to walk in on her looking like some freak refugee from the city zoo. As it was, she didn't have time to put on any makeup, but it would have to do.

"Agh!" The brush snagged in her knotted hair, and she forced it through.

The doorbell rang again.

"Hold your horses. I'm coming!"

She opened the door to the sight of someone she didn't know: a red-haired woman in a gray pantsuit, accompanied by two larger, official looking men in dark dress suits and matching fedoras.

"Men in black, eh?" she joked, her eyes on the two men.

No one seemed amused, though—least of all the woman. "Talk to me, ma'am. Eyes here, please."

"Who the . . .?"

Before she could finish, the woman had reached inside her jacket lining and produced a small case containing identification. It bore the name Leticia Renard and the words "Adult Protective Services."

"We've received a complaint about your daughter from one of the neighbors. There's some concern that her guardian may be neglecting her. They haven't seen her from quite some time, and they asked us to check in on her."

"Who? Which neighbors."

"I'm afraid that's confidential. If you'd just let us in so we can check on her well-being, we can log our report and be on our way."

Jessica didn't move. "Look, sister, this is my home. You can't just come barging in."

"I'm afraid we can," Ms. Meyer. "Would you like to see the judge's warrant?"

Jessica glared at her but stepped aside. "You can come in," she said. "But Minerva's not here."

"Oh?" The redhead cocked an eyebrow. "And where would she be."

"We had to commit her—just for a few days. She was acting weird. It was for her own good."

The redhead, now safely inside, squared her shoulders and looked Jessica in the eye. They were about the same height, though Jessica might have been an inch or two taller. "We?"

"Well, I did. . . . It was my decision . . . Brad suggested it might be a good idea."

"Brad?"

"My boyfriend."

"So you have an unattached stranger living in the same home with your daughter?"

Jessica blinked. The questions were coming in rapid-fire succession, and she wasn't used to being put on the defensive like this. "He's *not* living here," she replied. "Not that it's any of your business, *Mizz* Renard."

"I'm afraid the court says it is, *Mizz* Meyer. Or do you prefer "miss?" You're not married, are you, or do you have a boyfriend on the side?"

Jessica glared at her, but she knew better than to get on the wrong side of the government. She'd applied for federal relief once and lost her patience with the woman behind the counter who had asked her to fill out yet another form. She'd let loose with a choice four-letter word, after which her application had been "put on indefinite hold" then and there.

She took a deep breath to calm herself, but the other woman spoke first. Her voice was friendlier now, but with an undertone that still seemed threatening. "Of course, we know you're not married, Ms. Meyer," she said. "That's in our files. Just a little humor. Now, if your daughter isn't here, if you'll just allow us to have a look around to confirm that."

Jessica nodded.

"Good, then. We'll check her room, if you don't mind."

The woman tilted her head as a signal to her two companions and started off down the hall. *How did she know where Minerva's room was?* Jessica wondered. There was something not quite right about any of this, but she wasn't in any position to argue.

The three of them re-emerged from the room about ten minutes later, carrying a box full of Minerva's things—clothes, mostly, along with a stuffed white bear she'd had since she was little, a bottle of Adore Moi perfume and a few other odds and ends. The drapes, too, had been removed from the window and placed in the box.

"What are you doing?" Jessica objected. "You can't take those. They belong to me."

The redhead stopped emphatically where she was and directed a piercing stare at Jessica. "Minerva isn't here. That's the point. These things are evidence, and they'll be returned to *her* when we're done with them. Now, if you'll step aside Ms. Meyer, we'll be on our way . . . unless, that is, you want us to take you into custody for obstruction. We are empowered to do that, just so you know."

Jessica took one step sideways, and the woman pushed past her with the force, it seemed, of a small tornado.

The two men followed.

"Do you have a card or something?" Jessica stammered. "Some way to get in touch with you."

The woman turned and looked back at her, smiling, and paused briefly as the two men left the residence.

"Surely, you're familiar with the old saying, Ms. Meyer: Don't call us . . ."

Her words trailed off as she turned and left, closing the door hard behind her. Jessica wondered whether she'd left out the second half of that saying on purpose. It only took her a second to conclude that she probably had.

Trust

"We have to get out of here."

"Why?" Minerva looked at Carson askance. "I thought you said you were taking me to someplace safe."

Carson shook his head slightly, considering. "She's been here—the woman who confronted you in your vision, and she'll be back if she knows you're here. From what you said about your encounter with her, she probably does. Did she say anything to you about this place, anything at all?"

Minerva thought for a moment. "She said something about a friend of mine who was working with her. I assume she was talking about you."

Carson started pacing. "Then she does know you're here. But if she still thinks I'm working with her . . ."

"Are you?"

He stopped pacing just long enough to scowl at her, then started up again. "I thought we trusted each other."

"Because I didn't go all Medusa on you and turn you to stone when you stared into my eyes?" She chuckled, but it was a laugh all but devoid of humor. "Maybe I just don't like what I'm capable of, okay? Maybe I don't do that to people unless I know for sure they're trying to screw me over. I don't know that for sure about you, but that doesn't mean I can trust you as far as I could throw your 400-pound mother."

"My mother's not . . ."

"Don't take me so literally."

". . . alive anymore."

Minerva stopped and bit the left side of her lower lip. "Sorry," she said, sincerely yet grudgingly. She was being honest: She didn't trust him. She was here because he'd brought her here, and she was staying because, for now anyway, it seemed like her best option. "If I'm going to trust you, you're going to need to tell me everything about who you are and who you're working for."

Carson pulled up a stark wooden kitchen chair that looked like it had been around since the 1950s and sat down directly across from her, looking her directly in the eyes once again.

He came right out with it. "I'm a spy. And an assassin. And a hacker. And a whole lot of other things. I can go down the list if you want."

"You're CIA?"

He shook his head. "Used to be. Ever hear of something called FIN?"

"What's that? Some kind of scuba diving rental place."

"Stands for Federal Intelligence Network. It's part of Homeland Security. If you *had* heard of it, I'd be worried. It's about as far undercover as you can get."

Her eyes told him she wasn't going to buy it that easily—even if it were the truth. "Before 9/11, al-Qaida built up a loose network of terrorist cells throughout the Middle East. Bin Laden was the focus of it, but most of them operated all but autonomously from one another. There was very little in the way of central command structure, which might sound disorganized, but it had a key advantage: It wasn't a true hierarchy that you could disable by cutting off the head. It was like a cancer. If you killed one cell, it didn't matter, because there were always others to take its place."

"So, you worked for al-Qaida?"

"No, no. I'm not a terrorist—well, I guess some people might call me that, but I'm not al-Qaida. What I'm getting at is that FIN is built on the same idea: small, autonomous units operating with almost no connection to each other or even to any central base. Field agents get assignments from a single contact; beyond that, we don't have much contact with headquarters."

Minerva leaned back. "And let me guess: Your contact was demon girl from my vision."

"Yes."

"When she called off the operation, I contacted HQ, and they said there was no record of it in the database. No record of you, either." *Which could mean anything*, he thought to himself. *Either Jules is operating on her own or they want me to think she is.* He wasn't going to tell Minerva that, though.

Either she was smart enough to figure it out on her own, or she didn't need to know. It wouldn't make any difference to her anyway.

Carson went to the kitchen, opened the fridge, and pulled out some mustard, mayo, and sandwich meat. He reached into a plastic bag with half a loaf of bread inside and pulled out a couple of slices, slathering them with mayonnaise and tossing a heap of pastrami on top. No cheese or lettuce or anything, just the pastrami.

"Want some?" he offered.

"I think I'll pass," Minerva replied, her stomach churning at the thought of that much mayo. Jessica made sandwiches the same way, though at least she bothered to put pickles on them and a wilting lettuce leaf (which Minerva usually removed and threw in the trash). These days, Jessica told her to make her own sandwiches, for which Minerva was grateful.

Carson shrugged. "Suit yourself."

"Okay, then," she said as he returned to sit down in front of her and shoved a corner of the sandwich in his mouth. "Say I believe everything you're telling me. What do we do now?"

"We've got to get out of here," he said. "There's no telling whether she'll show up here looking for me—more likely, for you, and from what you told me about what happened in your vision, I don't want to see what might happen in real life."

Minerva's response surprised him. Just after her encounter with Jules, she'd been a quivering mess, barely able to speak. Now, she leaned forward and looked him straight in the eye—it wasn't the kind of look she'd had when she confronted that guard back in the lab; it was the same kind of look a boxer has entering the ring.

"I can take care of myself," she said. "It's what I've been doing all my life. Has this friend of yours had to deal with not being able to walk since she was six years old? Or people saying things about her behind her back—or to her face? What about those looks of contempt they pass off as pity?"

He thought it was a rhetorical question, but when she paused, he realized she was waiting for an answer.

"No."

"I didn't think so. Sometimes people who look the weakest on the outside are really the strongest on the inside because of everything we've been through. Demon girl doesn't know this about me. She took me by surprise before. That won't happen again."

"Good."

She laughed. "See? I can be pretty convincing when I wanna be. I think you're right, though, we ought to get out of here. I don't want to risk seeing her again if I don't have to."

Carson polished off the last bite of his sandwich and put the plate in the sink. He wondered idly when he'd get around to washing it—if he ever would. With Jules out there, it might never be safe to come back. What he didn't want to say out loud is that he was pretty sure he and Minerva *would* have to deal with her again. He just hoped it would be on their terms.

Minerva put up a brave front, but she had no clue what it was like to deal with someone from the agency. And if that person happened to have a supernatural gift at her disposal. . . . The conversation ended the way it had begun.

"Yeah," he said. "Let's get out of here. Now."

Reunion

Colored lights swirled across Raven's field of vision and disappeared at the fringes of his awareness, then flickered back in front of him like fireflies against the backdrop of a primeval forest. Tropical vines draped themselves across Scotch pines and cedars in an unnatural array of trees that seemed to be dancing or swaying to some unheard, cacophonous melody.

In fact, this landscape was soundless, but not quiet. Too much was happening for that. A lion padded out from behind a baobab tree, stopped there in the clearing and turned to look at him. It opened its mouth, and Raven saw its chest shaking in a thunderous but unheard roar. Its teeth glistened in the tainted silver glow that seemed like moonlight except there was no moon that he could see. On second thought, it wasn't silver, but coppery-gold, and the lion's teeth weren't teeth but daggers dripping with blood.

Its mouth curled up at the sides, mocking him, then it disappeared—not behind some tree, but simply disappeared, blinking out like a star in sudden morning.

But there was no morning here.

A crew of workmen in hard hats rushed in to the place where it had been and stationed themselves at the foot of the baobab tree, which looked impossibly big around, perhaps as far across as a football field. Each of the workmen pulled out a Swiss Army knife and chose a different implement with which to assail the tree: a corkscrew, a file, a blunt pair of scissors. The tree shuddered as though possessed or in some great agony, and green fluid began to pour from wherever the workmen pierced its bark. But when he looked closely, Raven realized that the workmen weren't human at all, but had the faces, bodies, and appendages of red ants. They seemed to be shouting at him, but still he heard no sound as they motioned toward him, animated, to move back or go away.

MEMORTALITY

The baobab's limbs seemed to morph into human arms, reaching out to him in desperation. A knothole appeared to undulate, like lips forming the words, "Help me!"

He ran forward toward the ants, which continued to yell and gesticulate even more wildly before finally scattering as he was nearly upon them. Not scattering, actually, but vanishing into nothingness, just as the lion had.

Then one of the tree's human arms grabbed him and wrapped itself around him, only now it was slick and covered with tentacles, like an octopus'. He could feel the tentacles constricting around his torso, cutting off the flow of air to his lungs, and he struggled against it. He clawed and gouged at it with his fingernails and then, when that proved to no avail, bit into it with his teeth, clamping down hard and setting his jaw like a pit bull.

It tasted the way he imagined maple syrup might taste if it had been suffused with blood dripping from a nearly raw steak.

The tentacle loosened its hold, and he spat violently on the ground as he half ran, half fell away from it. Stumbling and falling to his knees, he jumped up again almost at once and stared back at the baobab tree as he scampered away like a monkey across the forest floor. But the tree was no longer a baobab; rather, it was a series of vines hanging from nowhere he could see, swaying in a breeze he couldn't feel.

He turned and ran. His legs felt like they were churning against quicksand, and he could barely see anything in front of him save for a dense fog that appeared to supply its own dim glow. Beyond that lay only deep black shadows, nearly formless and oscillating at the edge of his vision, just as the colored lights had danced there a few moments ago.

Looking down, he saw the forest floor was still beneath him, covered in rotted leaves that appeared to have fallen a very long time ago. They were mostly tar-black now, barely recognizable against the small patches of brown earth that showed through at intervals from beneath them.

And then there was something else: crumbs.

Raven could see a trail of breadcrumbs had been scattered across the leaves, leading in roughly the same direction he had started to travel.

Having no other sense of place or direction, he decided to follow them. A memory tugged at the recesses of his mind—a memory of a fairytale he'd heard in his youth about two lost children trapped in a dark wood who had left a trail of breadcrumbs to find their way back. He remembered his parents reading it to him. Except those crumbs had been eaten by ravens,

138

and they'd become impossibly lost. Was he meant to find them? Or was he the Raven meant to condemn them to some horrible fate? Or was he really even here at all?

The breadcrumbs led him onward, through the blanketing mist that felt oddly warm against his face. It had become impossibly humid here, like some swamp or bayou in the depths of summer, and streams of perspiration ran down his brow, stinging his eyes and blurring his vision as he struggled to keep moving forward. He heard what sounded like an engine from somewhere in the distance, but it seemed to cut out and disappear after a few moments. It was the first sound he'd heard here, and when its echo faded, he was engulfed in silence once again.

Then another sound came to him: "cuh-CAW! cuh-CAW!" It sounded like some tropical bird very close at hand.

He couldn't see it, though. He couldn't see anything through the mist.

"Cuh-CAW! cuh-CAW! cuh-CAW!" Its shrill voice seemed almost frantic, as though it were calling for help. Then, a final "cuh . . ." that was snuffed out in a sickly sounding gurgle that was replaced anew by silence.

Raven felt dizzy and looked down again, relieved to find the breadcrumbs were still there. They were the one thing that seemed to remain the same in this place. Where had he been before this? He tried to think, but he couldn't remember. He couldn't remember anything in the short term, just blurred and warped fragments of scenes he assumed were from his childhood. But he couldn't be sure. Perhaps they were from some earlier time in this fractured fairy tale where he found himself. Or perhaps he'd been here all along.

He focused on the breadcrumbs, but they seemed to shimmer and blur and dance in front of his eyes. There was no way of knowing where they were leading him because the dim luminescence seemed to come from all over and the fog kept him from discerning any sense of direction. Without realizing it, he'd started taking smaller steps to avoid somehow getting thrown off track. Who knew whether the next step might send him tumbling off some unseen precipice?

He had no idea how much time had passed. It might have been a few hours or even days, but the light never changed, so he had no way of knowing.

The sweat was growing worse, running almost in a torrent down across his forehead and dripping onto the ground in front of him. He blinked and wiped his brow, but it only returned worse than before. He rounded a bend—if it was, in fact, a bend and he wasn't just imagining a curve in the road—and came upon perhaps two dozen sparrows hopping about and bending their heads down to the earth, picking at what was left of the breadcrumbs on the path. He rushed at them, waving his arms wildly in a frantic attempt to shoo them away, but as he reached them, they disappeared, just the way the lion and the worker ants had before. The breadcrumbs, mercifully, remained . . . at least in sufficient number to keep him on track.

A little ways on, Raven became aware that the fog seemed to be lifting, or at least growing a little less dense. Shapes that had been nothing more than dim, shadowy outlines of uncertain objects now became deodar and palm trees, oak and maple. They didn't belong in the same forest, but nothing seemed to belong here, himself included.

Then, for the first time, he began to make out a sign that he wasn't alone, at least as far as human habitation was concerned. Not too far ahead, he was just beginning to make it out now, lay what looked like a modest cottage in a clearing. As he drew closer, he could tell it was well kept, but there was no sign that anyone was inside: The windows were dark, and the drapes were drawn. As the mists parted further, he noticed it had been painted in a wide array of bold colors, from turquoise to orange to royal purple, bright yellow and even hot pink.

No, not painted. The surface looked like . . . cake frosting.

He approached a white picket fence and put his hand on the gate, only to find his fingers sinking into the material the moment they took hold of it. Surprised, he removed them and found some of the gooey whatever-it-was sticking to his hand. Raising it to his face, he sniffed it, then touched it to the tip of his tongue and blinked at the distinctive taste of marshmallows.

A short front pathway led to a wrap-around porch with pillars colored and even shaped like candy canes. The doorknob looked like a butterscotch drop, and a huge slice of pumpkin pie had been wedged into the half-circle window space near the top of the door itself.

Raven tried the knob and found it turned easily, allowing him entrance into a room lit only by a hearth fire and a few scattered candles. More beams of yellow light drifted across the room from the kitchen area, where a huge stove stood propped slightly open; whoever lived here had apparently lit it and stepped out for a moment. He hoped the owner of the cottage wouldn't mind him stepping inside. He was so very tired and still sweating, even though he felt a persistent numbing chill across his entire body. It didn't feel cold so much as vacant, and moving closer to the hearth to warm himself didn't seem to have any effect on it.

A small, pink cat with a gumdrop for a nose was sleeping by the fire, and it lifted its head lazily when he bent down to stroke it. Its fur wasn't as soft as he expected; in fact, it was sticky—like cotton candy.

He was startled from considering this further by the faint sound of two children's voices, coming from behind a door off to the right.

"Help us, please!" came the plaintiff call of a young girl, perhaps about five years old.

"In here!" came the boy's voice, perhaps a little older, but not much.

Trying to shake off the numbness and fatigue, Raven hurried toward the sound of the voices. As he did, the childhood memory he'd been trying to access suddenly clicked into place and a pair of names came flashing into his head. *Hansel and Gretel.* It was a fairy tale his mother had read to him as a child, and now he seemed to have landed squarely in the middle of it. The story had always been a favorite of his. Of course, he had liked candy and birthday cake—what child didn't? But there was something more to it than that: These children had been able to find their way out of a scary predicament all on their own, without any help from the adults who were supposed to control their fate.

Raven went to the door through which he'd heard the children's muffled voices and tried the knob, which was shaped like a peppermint drop.

It stuck.

"Help us!" the girl called again.

"Hold on. I'll be there as soon as I can."

He tried to twist the knob and jar it loose through sheer force, but it held fast. Then an odd idea occurred to him. Kneeling down, he took the doorknob in his mouth and bit down as hard as he could. A loud crack greeted his ears, and he felt a large chunk of hard peppermint candy come off in his mouth. It didn't taste as good as he remembered it from childhood, but that might have been because he felt queasy in his weakened state. He was sweating even more now from the effort of trying to open the door, and his head was aching in that no-man's land that lies somewhere between throbbing and dizziness.

Thankfully, breaking the knob had also released the locking mechanism, and the door drifted open inward with no more than a gentle shove.

It was even darker inside this room than it was at the front of the house, but he immediately made out the outline of two figures lying prone on what looked like slabs of granite, their arms and legs fastened down so they could barely move. But the pair weren't the children he'd expected to see, but fully grown adults. Even now, as he watched them, the voices changed as they called out to him, deepening and becoming oddly familiar.

His mother's.

His father's.

"Please, Raven, don't leave us here," said the woman, for a woman she now was.

"How could you have left us behind?" asked the man, trying to raise his head as Raven moved over beside where he lay.

"I didn't mean to," Raven said, his voice tinged with sorrow. "But I couldn't do anything. I just couldn't."

"You could have saved us, dear Raven." His mother's tone held a mix of comfort and regret—the sort of regret meant to mask an accusation she was fighting not to make. "We've been here waiting for you all this time, and you've finally come back to us," she said. "Please don't let the witch get her hands on us. She's going to cook us and eat us so we can never come back again. But you can save us, Raven, I know you can. Just like you saved Gramma Mary Lou. You remember, don't you? Please."

Raven just stood there, unsure of what to say. How had this happened? There was no way he knew to explain it, but now, somehow, he was here with them again, and they needed his help.

He stared at his parents' pleading faces as he untied the cords that held them prisoner.

"Hurry!" his father urged him. "Before she comes back."

Even amid the excitement of seeing them again, Raven found himself fighting desperately against his growing fatigue.

"Don't worry," he said. "I won't let you down this time."

Between

"You can't take them out of here."

Raven started at the sound of the familiar voice that greeted him as he exited the room, one step ahead of his parents. What had begun as a place devoid of sound had gradually become normal, at least in that respect, although in almost every other way it still seemed more like a warped carnival funhouse than anything resembling reality.

"Minerva?"

"In the flesh." She stood at the far end of the room, and his eyes had a hard time focusing on her in the dim shadows of the firelight. Though she seemed strangely blurry, he could tell she was wearing the same Smurf pajamas she had worn on the night they had been together. It seemed like an odd choice of attire, but then everything about this place was odd.

"What are you doing here?" he asked.

"Looking for you, actually. I've *been* looking for you for the past three days, wandering around this weird place. I'm still not quite sure what you call it, but I think I'm getting an idea of what it is."

Raven took a step toward her, but she backed up a step.

"Please don't come too close," she said, sounding apologetic. "You're not well. I can't risk catching your sickness, or we both might get stuck here."

He stopped, reminded of how ill he did feel but also dimly aware that his condition wasn't contagious.

"I need your help," she said.

He turned to look over his shoulder at his parents. Both their faces were creased with worry, their eyes slightly wide with apprehension.

"Don't listen to her, son," his father whispered. "She's a witch. She was going to try to bake us in that oven in her kitchen."

Raven looked back at Minerva and then again to his father. "Dad, don't worry. That's Minerva. You remember her, from when we were kids? You used to take her out with us to the pier and the park on weekends. You just don't recognize her because she's all grown up now."

"No, Raven. Please, listen to your father," his mother said. "That's a witch. She's trying to trick you."

Minerva gave Raven a guarded yet determined smile. Despite their whispered tones, it was obvious she'd heard what they had been saying.

"This place confuses everyone," she said. "I don't blame them for not recognizing me. Everything here is fluid. Distorted. That's why I had such a hard time finding you."

Raven turned back to his parents, but when he saw them again, they seemed to be fading, becoming translucent before his eyes. It was like what had happened to the lion and the sparrows, only more gradual. He felt suddenly weaker, like he had to sit down or he was going to collapse, and he closed his eyelids tightly in an effort to keep himself upright. When he opened them again, however, he found himself sprawled out on the floor. His parents were gone, but Minerva was still there, staring at him from across the room.

"Where did they go?" he asked.

"That's one reason you can't take them out of here," she answered. "Raven, you're dying. You aren't strong enough. Even if you were, you wouldn't know how. That's why I need your help. To save them. This place—I call it 'Between'—is like a no-man's land between life and death. Like what the Catholics call purgatory or limbo."

"Then why were my parents here? They've been dead for . . ."

"You brought them back, Raven. Just the way I brought you back. But you didn't have enough strength to keep them here. Thank God I found you in time. If I'd taken any longer, you might be dead already."

"How do you know so much about this place?"

She smirked at him. "When you've been wandering around here for three days, you pick up on a few things."

Raven wiped his brow. He was sweating less now, but he barely had the strength to raise his hand. Lights danced in front of his eyes, just as they had in the forest when he'd arrived here. Minerva had said he was dying, and something inside was telling him she was right. But why hadn't he started to feel better when she'd found him? He remembered that much about how this was supposed to work. Just the fact that she had remembered him, was thinking about him, should have been enough to revive him. He wondered if she were right: Maybe he was sick—and contagious. But could a dead person get sick? It didn't make sense.

"Listen to me." Her voice was suddenly insistent, almost demanding. "You can save yourself. You can even save your parents, but you may have to do some things you don't like. I know there's a woman holding you there. She's very powerful. She almost destroyed me trying to get to you. You can use that power if you know how, but you have to find out what she wants. Find out how she operates. Then use it to your advantage."

Raven tried to nod, but his head was lolling against his chest and he could barely raise it.

"Help me," he said, his voice sounding weak and raspy in his own ears. He realized his pleas sounded just like those of his parents when they'd been trapped in that room. Who had locked them in there? Where was the witch they had been so afraid of—the person they'd for some reason thought was Minerva?

Minerva looked at him, her eyes piercing and insistent. "You have to open yourself to me, Raven. You're too sick for me to bring you back on my own, just by remembering. You have to help me. Can you do that, Raven? Can you look into my eyes? Help me help you. Please. Before it's too late."

Fatigued and desperate, he did as she asked. He looked into her eyes, searching for the love he'd seen there when they'd been together, hoping to latch on to what he knew she felt for him. But he was so weak, he couldn't seem to find it. He felt like a drowning man grasping for anything that might hold him up, above the waves, a moment longer—anything that might allow him just one more breath, one more chance to scramble again so he could find another.

And then, at the moment when he felt he might not have the strength for another attempt, he grabbed hold of something. Something solid behind her eyes. He held it tight and felt her holding on to him even more tightly, her strength making up for that which he lacked. It seemed like a vice grip around his upper torso, so strong that he couldn't have shaken free of it even if he'd wanted to—not that he wanted to. It was his lifeline, his connection to the living world and his ticket out of this strange house of horrors.

"I've got you, Raven," she said soothingly. "Everything's going to be okay now."

Persuasion

The woman who went by the code name JulesB6s4R (aka Leticia Renard, aka a dozen other aliases) scrambled to shed the pajamas she'd been wearing. They didn't fit her perfectly, but they'd done the job. Now she had to get out of them before Raven woke up again, which would be any minute now.

Her plan had worked perfectly. In his weakened state, she'd been able to convince him she was his beloved Minerva and had persuaded him to open himself to her. The contrived excuse about not wanting him to "infect" her—he wasn't really sick, of course, just fading—had been a gamble, but it had paid off, allowing her to put enough distance between herself and him that he hadn't recognized the flaws in her projected disguise.

She worried more about the fact that she would have *felt* different to him. All she could do was hope that he'd been too weak to notice anything but the fact that she was saving him from a second death—which she was— and that she wouldn't have to go through it all again. The stage of her plan she'd just completed had been a challenge, but she'd pulled it off. The next step would be even tougher: getting him to trust her as Jules, not Minerva. She'd bought herself some time for that, but if she failed, she might have to go back to the place called Between all over again.

She practically tripped in her hurry to shed the Smurf pajama bottoms. Who wore Smurf pajamas, anyway? Hell, who wore pajamas at all? Whatever. They had served their purpose. Gathering those things from Minerva's home had helped her to focus more on who she was, had made her act more convincing. It had helped that Raven was halfway out of it at the time; now she just hoped that the half of him paying attention had taken her . . . er . . . Minerva's advice to heart.

Hurriedly, she tossed on a burgundy tank top and slipped into a pair of jeans—not her usual style, but sometimes, casual was better. More comfortable for one thing, but also less intimidating. She needed to be that now.

As she stumbled out into the living area, still pulling up her pants, she saw that Raven had, in fact, awakened. He was sitting up on the couch, blinking as his eyes adjusted to the light while staring out the bank of windows across toward the hazy horizon.

He turned as she entered the room, his eyes stopping when he caught sight of her. They sparkled, fully alert, without a trace of the lethargy and confusion that had filled them before. She smiled inwardly at his restoration and that inward smile broadened at the knowledge that she was responsible for it.

"You look better," she said, putting her hands on her hips as she looked him up and down.

He nodded. "Thank you," he said curtly.

"I was worried about you, Raven," she said. "You didn't look good there."

"I didn't feel good."

"I'd offer you some tea, but I don't have any. I do have some whiskey, though."

Raven shook his head.

"Suit yourself."

Raven watched her as she went to the kitchen and opened a cupboard. Reaching up, she took down a bottle filled with amber-colored liquid and poured some of it into a clear crystal glass. "Hope you don't mind if I have some myself."

"No."

Raven kept his eyes on her, wary. She was behaving less like an abductor and more like . . . he couldn't quite put his finger on it. Not a friend, exactly, but not an adversary, either. Part of him wanted to take advantage of it and try to get the hell out of there. Maybe if he could get her drunk, he could find a way out. Or he could just try to overpower her physically, now that his strength had returned and she no longer had him tied up. But he remembered what Minerva had told him in that place—what had she called it? Between?—and he remembered how it had felt seeing his parents again after so long. Was she right? Could he really free them? And was this woman's power the key to doing so?

Everything he had been taught made him doubt it. Those who had been brought back couldn't bring back anyone themselves. That's what he'd been told from the beginning. But what if the one who'd been brought back *had the gift*, like he did? That might make a difference. And what if that person had help from someone else who was gifted? If what Minerva had told him in Between was right, he might be able to harness this woman's power to find his parents again and bring them back. Even if it were only a slim chance, it was worth exploring.

Still, he didn't want her to think he was staying here willingly.

"How long are you going to keep me here?" he demanded.

She laughed a hearty laugh, and with that glass of whiskey in her hand, it occurred to Raven that she seemed a little like a pirate. She half-walked, half-sauntered over to a plush chair set at an angle to the sofa, then plopped herself down with an air of confident carelessness. "You can leave now, if you want. I'm not stopping you."

It was a gamble, and she knew it. He might just take her up on it. If she'd done her job in Between, he'd stay voluntarily and this bluff might earn her a small measure of trust. On the other hand, if she hadn't done her job, it was better that she know now so she could come up with a Plan B.

Raven made no move for the door. "Then you're done with me?"

"I didn't say that. I still think you and I could do great things together, Raven." She ran her index finger from her chin to halfway down her neck. "But if you don't want that, I can't force it, and there's really no other reason for me to keep you here. If you don't work with me willingly, nothing can really happen here. You can go back to your little girlfriend and we can both pretend nothing ever happened here."

"You're acting like we slept together or something."

One side of her mouth curled up in a half-smile. "Well, not exactly. But you did open yourself to me and we shared . . . the essence of who we are." The moment it was out of her mouth, she regretted saying it. Sometimes, her confidence spilled over into arrogance, and she let her guard down. If he grasped the implication of what she'd just said, everything might come unraveled then and there.

Sure enough, he seemed to catch his breath for a moment.

"I opened myself to you?" he said slowly. "She used those words, too. That's what I did with her."

"With whom?" She was careful not to let any hint of the concern she felt seep into her tone.

"Minerva."

"When? What happened?"

Raven hesitated. He didn't want to tell her; he was fiercely protective of any time he spent with Minerva and considered it theirs alone. Yet Minerva herself had suggested that he might somehow be able to use this woman's power to free his parents.

Still, why had Minerva used the same words this woman had used just now? She'd never told him to "open himself to her" before; it had just happened, naturally, and nothing like that had ever been necessary for him to gain strength from her.

"You saw her when you were unconscious, didn't you?"

"Yes, but she wasn't quite acting like herself."

Jules leaned toward him and put the palm of her hand against his left cheek. He forced himself not to flinch.

"I know I've tried to keep her from you before, but I'm very glad she found you this time," she said. "If she hadn't, I don't think you'd be here now. Her connection with you must have been what saved you. Before you came out of it, you were tossing and turning, sweating like crazy. You seemed to be in a state of delirium, like you were having some terrible nightmare."

"Nothing seemed quite real there," he said. "It was all distorted."

Jules kept her hand beside his face and brushed his hair back. "I know. That's what happens. You were being pulled back to the other side; your reality was rippling and disintegrating."

"My parents were there, too."

Jules pulled back suddenly, her eyes wide. "Your parents?"

"Yes. They were tied up there and I was trying to get them out, but then Minerva was there and a moment later, I almost passed out and they were gone."

"Of course!" Jules clasped her hands together. "Think about it, Raven. If they were there, it was because *you* brought them there." She was talking faster, her voice more excited than he'd ever heard it. "They disappeared because you didn't have the strength to hold them there, but now that your strength has returned, who knows what could happen! It's possible you could bring them all the way back!"

"How? I've always thought that couldn't happen."

She put her hand on his, grasping it firmly and fixing him with an intense stare. "How often has one of the gifted been brought back? It's always the other way around: We use our gift to bring back our loved ones. But here you are."

Raven pursed his lips together. "Unfortunately, I don't know how I did it, and I've only done it in that half-dead state. Minerva called it 'Between.' After they died, I tried to bring them back a few times just by focusing on their memories, but nothing ever worked. Who knows? Maybe I was just so far gone I was hallucinating before Minerva brought me back."

"Maybe," she drew out the word, as if considering. "But I don't think so. I think you might just need some help. I've been with people when they've gone through the fades before. I've guided them back to the other side— made it easier on them."

Raven's back stiffened and he leaned back, away from her. "What do you mean, 'guided' them back?"

"When they lost their connection here." Her tone was calm, patient. "It's like being at someone's bedside when they die, the first time, I mean. It makes it easier if someone's there. I have the ability to visit this place Minerva called the Between without being on the point of death, because I haven't died in the first place. At least not yet." She winked, but her attempt at humor made no impression on Raven.

"I'm not going back there," he said. "Especially not with you."

"Even if it means saving your parents?"

Raven said nothing, but the silence in his head was filled by the advice he remembered Minerva giving him before: *Find out how she operates. Then use it to your advantage.*

After a moment, he nodded. "What is it I have to do."

Fatality

Minerva counted the trees that lined the center median on the highway as Carson drove southeast at a steady pace.

"We need to figure out where she is," he said absently.

"And just how do you propose to do that, Mr. Spy Guy? The last time I contacted Raven, he had no idea where he was. Just some black room that looked like a warehouse."

"She wouldn't have kept him there for long," Carson said. "Standard procedure is to keep moving. Frequently. So no one can get a fix on you."

"And you're sure she's following 'standard procedure'?"

She had a point. Nothing about this operation had been conventional, and if Jules were a rogue agent, she wouldn't be going by the book. What was she up to?

A few light drops landed on the windshield, scattershot, dancing down out of a stone-gray sky. It wasn't normal to get a storm like this in late summer, but a change in the jet stream had driven a tropical storm up out of Baja, and it was wreaking havoc with the traffic.

"Can you put some feelers out again? Try to get a feel for where they might be?"

He could feel her eyes upon her, and when he looked out of the corner of his eye, her expression said it all.

"You don't think I haven't tried?" she answered, her tone clearly frustrated. "She's got me blocked. It's like she put up the Great Wall of China in there."

The raindrops began to multiply, hitting the glass and pooling together insistently. Carson clicked on the windshield wipers, which began slowly whap-whapping back and forth in front of them. He slowed the car slightly with the flow of traffic as headlights flickered on to combat the darkening skies.

"You know her," Minerva said. "Where do you think she might be?"

Red taillights blinked on and then held steady ahead of them; traffic slowed to a crawl.

"That's just it. I don't know her. FIN agents know as little about one another as possible. Coordinators—the ones who hand out the mission assignments . . ."

"Like the redhead?"

"Jules. Yes. People like her know other agents' skill sets so they can choose the best person for each job. But beyond that, it's all a blank slate. We don't socialize. We don't share the details of our lives. It's all for our own protection—and so missions won't be compromised."

They were stopped now. A siren broke through the patter of rain, falling harder now, and the sound of the windshield wipers, growing louder as an ambulance raced up from behind them in the access lane.

"I have an idea," Carson said suddenly. "You might not be able to get through to Raven, but maybe you could get through to *her*."

Minerva gave him the kind of look that said, *What are you on?* But instead she said, "I'm listening."

The ambulance screamed by them, followed by a fire truck.

"Think about it," Carson said. "She's expecting you to keep trying to reach Raven; she's not expecting you to come after her. When you tried to find Raven before and she blocked you, were you able to pick up on her . . . what would you call it? Frequency? Vibration? Scent?"

"What do I look like, a bloodhound?"

"You know what I mean."

The traffic had started moving again, but slowly, in fits and starts. The rain fell less insistently now, turning into a mist, but the rearview mirror showed the darkest clouds still behind them, to the west.

Minerva ran a hand through her hair, considering. "I might be able to find her again," she said. "After our last meeting, I don't really want to. I think she could have killed me."

"I can understand that," Carson said, glancing over at her. "But this time, you'll have the element of surprise on your side. She won't be expecting you."

The car crept up beside the place where the ambulance and fire truck had pulled over. It looked bad. An 18-wheeler had pulled off to the side and didn't seem too badly damaged, but a teal-colored compact car—which looked like it had hit the rig from behind—was crumpled up so badly that it was hard to see where the front of the car had been. It appeared to have run up under the rig's trailer and had been reduced to a pile of twisted metal debris. The ambulance had pulled in right behind it, and two paramedics were unloading a gurney and wheeling it toward the car.

"Stop the car," Minerva said. "Pull over here."

"What?"

"You heard me. Stop it now or I'm getting out anyway."

They were going maybe five miles per hour, and Carson could tell she wasn't kidding.

He pulled ahead and off the highway right in front of the fire truck. Before he could even shut off the engine, Minerva had opened the door and stepped out onto the edge of the freeway. The traffic was moving slowly enough that she wasn't at risk of being hit, but the questioning looks some of the people gave her as they passed by made her wonder, for a second, whether she was doing the right thing. It was impulsive, to be sure, but she had felt something as they drew closer: She thought she'd sensed the life draining out of the person who'd been in that crash, and she felt she had to investigate.

"You can't go over there, Miss," a firefighter said to her stepping into her path.

The hell I can't. She fixed him with a steely look that would have fit perfectly on the face of a Valkyrie.

The man blinked but couldn't avoid her eyes; a moment later, he felt his legs giving way beneath him and he tumbled to the ground.

Minerva shot him a rueful smile. He'd regain the use of his legs after a few hours; she hadn't hit him with the full force of her memories, the way she had that mad scientist, Dr. Fitzgerald. She was learning to control this ability of hers, to measure it out. But she knew that if she did, in fact, make contact with this Jules person again, she'd need every ounce of what she possessed and probably a lot more.

Right now, though, she had to get to the injured woman—it was a woman, she could sense now—before her life slipped away.

"Let me through!" she shouted.

A man in a paramedic uniform turned at the sound of her voice. "Hey, who are you? You're not supposed to be . . ."

"I'm a doctor," she snapped, realizing that, at 21, it was a bit of a stretch.

The paramedic grabbed hold of her wrist. "You don't look like a doctor," he said. "Besides, we've got this."

"Oh, you do, do you? Then why is that woman over there about to die? And what do you think a doctor's supposed to look like when she's off duty and just got out of her car in the middle of a rainstorm? The woman on *Grey's Anatomy*?"

The man let loose of her wrist, and she was relieved she wouldn't have to repeat what she'd done to the firefighter.

"Thank you," she said curtly. "Your friend over there needs some help. Looks like he collapsed. I would have stopped to treat him, but I think she"—she nodded her head toward the gurney in front of her—"needs my help a little more. Now if you'll excuse me."

"Wait. How did you know it was a woman who needed help? And how did you know she was dying?"

Minerva stormed ahead without answering. *She'll be dead before I get there if I stick around here to answer your questions*, she thought. *And you wouldn't believe the answers if I told you.*

When she got to the gurney, they'd nearly wheeled it into the ambulance. "I'm a doctor," she said again. "Let me see the patient."

"I'm afraid . . ."

Minerva ignored him. She could see the woman's breathing was very shallow, and she pushed her way past to get a closer look. There was a gash along the woman's temple, and her arm was twisted at an odd angle. It appeared to be broken. But the worst of it was the wound in her lower chest. Blood had poured out to such an extent that the white sheet they'd placed over her was stained on an area the size of a teacup saucer.

"Get out of the way! We've got to get her on the ambulance!" yelled an ambulance man.

"If you don't get out of *my* way, she'll be dead before she gets there!" Minerva yelled back.

Someone nearby whispered, "She's already as good as dead."

The woman's eyelids fluttered open, and Minerva stepped up beside her and put a hand on her shoulder. She was young—maybe 28 or 30. Her short-cropped brown hair was matted against a forehead free of wrinkles, and the severe trembling in her upper body seemed almost to the point of convulsions.

"Who are you?" she rasped, her expression confused.

"A friend," Minerva said, fixing her gaze intently on the woman. If she could glean enough from her in these final moments—enough to remember . . . Gingerly, she sought to find her way inside the woman's mind, past the waves of pain that met her at the gateway, to find out who she really was. But because of that pain, everything was fragmented and jumbled. Images that seemed to be from childhood—the front gate of a grammar school, a kite flying away and getting tangled in a tree—where interspersed with more recent fragments: a man in a black cape at what looked like a wedding reception and a small Siamese cat lunging at a feather play-toy. There was even what appeared to be the woman's own view of jumping out of an airplane.

The visions were shattered—along with Minerva's concentration—as she felt an arm on her shoulder pulling her backward, almost violently.

"I don't care who you are, you need to get the hell out of here and let us do our job!"

Minerva stumbled backward and slipped on the wet asphalt, turning her ankle as she fell to one knee. As she did, the woman's convulsions became worse, and her entire body seemed to be contorting itself, thrusting itself up off the gurney like a fish flopping around on the deck of a boat. The paramedics moved frantically to attend her, but the bleeding in her abdomen was becoming worse, and there was nothing they could do for her. The convulsions became light tremors, then stopped.

Her eyes fluttered closed again . . .

"I can't find a pulse," one of the paramedics said.

"Get her into the ambulance! Now!" He flashed a worried look at the first paramedic, who shook his head.

"Still nothing!"

They wheeled the gurney up the ramp into the back of the ambulance, then worked feverishly to get her hooked up to monitors and an IV.

"She's not breathing."

"Dammit!"

One of the paramedics put his head down next to her face, then started trying to perform CPR, but the blood was still leaking out of her abdominal wound and she wasn't moving at all.

A moment later, they stepped away from the gurney.

"She's gone."

One of the paramedics pulled a sheet up over her. His companion stormed out of the back of the ambulance, heading directly for Minerva, a look of fury in his eyes.

"This is all your fault. If you hadn't gotten in the way, we might have saved her. If you're a doctor, I'll make sure you're charged with malpractice. If you're not, I'll do my best to see that you're locked up for manslaughter!"

Minerva backed up a step. Her ankle stung, but it didn't feel like it was broken. Sprained, maybe . . . Ouch! It hurt to put any weight on it.

"And maybe I should have *you* charged with assault." It was Carson. Minerva had been so involved in reaching the dying woman that she'd forgotten he was even there.

"And you are?" the paramedic asked.

"Rory Despain, attorney," Carson said. Was there no end to his string of aliases? He pulled out a wallet, rifled through it and produced a business card with the name he'd mentioned and a law license number.

"Heh. So there really are ambulance chasers. This is the first time I've actually run into one. Well, you can get the hell out of here, too. Sue me later if you want."

"I'm not an ambulance chaser. I'm the doctor's gentleman friend."

Minerva barely caught herself before she shot him a *what the hell* look.

"Doesn't make a difference to me," the paramedic barked. "If I'm trying to do my job, and you get in my way . . . hell, that woman just died because of her." He pointed at Minerva.

But Minerva wasn't paying attention. She'd withdrawn back into herself and was focusing on the memories she's seen and felt inside the woman's mind, trying to piece everything together. There was a passport with the name Amber Hardin-Torres—she could tell now that had been the woman's name. The other things she'd picked up were starting to come into focus. She thought she might just have enough.

Minerva came out of her reverie.

"Amber's not dead," she said, glaring at the paramedic.

"Amber?"

"The woman in your ambulance. That's her name—you can check her ID if you don't believe me. And she's not dead."

"Of course she is! I . . ."

"Dan, you'd better come have a look at this."

The paramedic turned to face his companion, who was standing beside the woman in the ambulance: the woman who was now sitting straight up on the gurney as though nothing had ever happened. She was breathing again, the tremors were gone and the bleeding had stopped. Forgetting all about Minerva and Carson, the man dashed up the ramp to see what was happening.

Carson leaned over and whispered to Minerva: "Good work."

"Thank you," she said, allowing a self-satisfied half-smile to spread across her face.

He pulled her aside, farther away from the paramedics and back toward his car. "But now what are you going to do?"

She hadn't thought about that. She'd been so intent on trying to bring the woman back—on testing herself to see whether she even *could* bring her back—that she hadn't even thought about the long-term implications of what would happen if she succeeded. Now, however, it dawned on her: Someone with the gift would have to keep this woman in his or her thoughts, or she would simply fade away.

"I guess we'll have to take her with us." It was a half-statement, half-question, born of the fact that she didn't have any other ideas. She couldn't just let Amber die again.

"Oh, no. I'm not bringing her along. How are you going to get her out of that ambulance?"

Minerva steeled her voice, banishing any trace of the questioning tone. "You may not be, but I am. And I'll get her out of there the same way I brought her back. Watch me."

Carson just stood there, watching her, as she strode back toward the ambulance, fists balled up in determination, limping only slightly from the twisted ankle. He'd seen her like this before at the lab with Fitzgerald, and he knew better than to get in her way.

She walked up to the paramedic who had pushed her to the ground. "Excuse me."

He turned around. "What? You again? Listen . . ."

"No, you listen. As the attending physician here, I'm taking custody of the patient to make sure she gets some proper care. *You're* the one who almost killed her."

"I can't release her to you without . . ."

"Without the patient's consent, right?" The paramedic was startled at the sound of the woman's voice.

"Uh, well, we still need to make sure you're okay, and . . ."

Amber stood up beside the gurney and did a pirouette worthy of a trained ballerina. (Minerva racked her brain but couldn't find any evidence of a performing career in the memories she'd accessed.) Minerva found the sight of the woman, still covered in her own blood, dancing about like that almost comical. "You yourself just said there was nothing wrong with me," Amber said. "What did you call it? A 'miraculous recovery?'"

"Yes, but . . ."

"Save it, Boy Scout. This woman here's the one who saved my life. Don't ask me how I know, but I know. I'd rather go with her than put my life in *your* incompetent hands again."

The paramedic was speechless. "You'll have to sign a release form."

"Keep your damned paperwork. This isn't a hospital, and I'm not your patient."

And with that, she turned around, nodded slightly toward Minerva, and the pair walked together back toward the car. Minerva winced a little with each step she took on her bad ankle, but it was so good to actually feel something—anything—there after so many years of paralysis that the pain almost felt good to her.

She was surprised to feel Amber move up alongside her and slip an arm around her waist. "Put your weight on me," she said. "It's the least I can do."

"Thanks." Minerva forced an awkward smile. She wasn't used to people offering to help her.

"That ankle's swelling up quite a bit. Looks like a nasty sprain, but I don't think anything's broken."

"Yeah, I didn't think so, either. How can you tell."

Amber smiled an ironic smile. "I'm a doctor, honey. And yes, I know you aren't one. But I'll keep your secret if you tell me one thing: How in the world did you pull off whatever it is you did to me back there?"

Back at the ambulance, the paramedics were wondering the same thing. They were wondering something else, as well: whether they'd imagined everything that seemed to have just happened . . . because there on the gurney, when they looked again, lay the dead body of Amber Hardin-Torres. This was the same woman they'd seen, just a moment before, walking away from them down the emergency lane of the freeway.

Yes, they might have imagined it, except for the fact that every one of them had seen exactly the same thing.

Missing

"I'd like to file a missing person's report." Jessica stood at the front counter of the police station, staring into the eyes of a skinny, balding man with ghostly blue eyes who looked to be in his late thirties.

"Name?"

"Mine or hers?"

The man was thumping the eraser end of a pencil against his desk behind the counter. Who used pencils anymore?

"The name of the missing person, Ma'am."

"Mi-ner-va Jane Rus." She drew out each syllable to make sure he got it. She didn't like cops—never had. Not since the time she'd been pulled over for doing 45 in a 35 zone and the officer hadn't fallen for her damsel-in-distress routine. She'd made the mistake of cussing him out under her breath when she thought he was out of earshot, filling out the ticket. He hadn't been out of earshot, unfortunately for her, and that four-letter-word had earned her a trip down to the station. She hadn't been back since then, and she wouldn't have been here now if it weren't for the fact that she was worried. And pissed as hell.

Not worried about Minerva. Frankly, she didn't care if she ever saw her again. But she didn't want to be held responsible for her disappearance, and she figured it would be better to report it herself than keep quiet and have the cops blame her. If anyone should get the blame, it ought to be that loser, Carson. Sure, he talked a good game, but when it came right down to it, he'd skipped out on her just like all the rest. He'd probably sweet-talked Minerva just the way he'd done with her, and the poor cripple had been desperate enough to fall for it . . .

She laughed at herself. *I guess that just means she's as stupid as I am.*

The point was, she wanted to make Carson pay for the way he'd treated her, and if she had to involve the cops, well so be it.

"Can you describe her?"

"Let's see. Twenty-four. About 5-foot-10—or she would be if she wasn't in a wheelchair." She laughed aloud.

The cop stopped thumping his pencil and looked up at her. "What's funny about that? My son's in a wheelchair."

Jessica bit her lip. "Damn. Sorry. No offense, Officer."

The man just glared at her, his weird ghostly blue eyes staring through the transparent bulletproof barrier between them like ovals of ice.

"What else?" he said finally.

"Dark hair. Almost black, like mine. Pale skin. She doesn't get out much."

The man scribbled something with his pencil on a notepad.

"Any birthmarks or other distinguishing features?"

"Not that I know of."

"She's your daughter and you don't know whether she has any birthmarks?"

Look, asshole, are you going to help me or waste my time telling me what a bad mother I am?

She managed a wan smile. "There's a scar behind her right ear from when she got cut by some glass in the accident."

"Accident?"

Yes. Don't you know what an accident is? Maybe you should have one, smart ass. Then maybe you'd figure it out.

"She was injured in a crash when she was six. That's why she's in a wheelchair."

"Oh. Sorry, Ma'am."

She smiled, more convincingly this time, feeling like they were back on equal footing—as much as anyone could ever be on equal footing with a cop.

"Are you going to be able to find her?"

The man set down his pencil and laced the fingers of his hands together in front of him. He didn't smile back. "She's been gone more than 24 hours, so we'll put out a description of her. But to be honest, since she's an adult and you haven't offered any reason to think she's mentally confused, we can't make it a high priority."

Of course she's mentally confused, you idiot. Does anyone stay in their room all day doing nothing but reading and feeling sorry for themselves if they're not mentally confused?

"What if she's been abducted?"

"Do you have any evidence of that?"

"She and my boyfriend—at least I thought he was my boyfriend—both disappeared at the same time. I think he might have something to do with it."

"Fine. Give me his name and description, too. We'll run him through our database and see if anything turns up."

Jessica told him everything she knew about Brad, which she had to admit wasn't much. He hadn't told her a whole lot about himself. But she hadn't cared as long as he was paying for dinner and meeting her . . . other . . . needs.

"Okay, Ma'am," he said when she was finished. "Like I said, we'll do what we can."

She scrawled her number on the back of a losing lottery ticket stub, slipped it into the tray under the glass and pushed it toward him. "Just call me if you find them, Officer. Please." *I want to see you put that loser in handcuffs and cart him off.*

He nodded. "Next in line, please."

She turned and headed for the front door, barely paying attention to the suddenly excited tones around her.

"Hey, guess what just came on the news?" one of the cops was saying. "Major accident on the 101."

"Yeah, I heard it on the scanner earlier. Some poor woman killed herself smashing into the back of a furniture truck."

"That's the thing. She was dead. The paramedics saw it. She coded out and everything. But some woman came along out of nowhere and brought her back to life."

"Bull."

"Yeah, you're dreamin', Joe. It's just the news tryin' to make it sound like some miracle."

"Maybe, but they say the dead woman just got up and walked away with the other one like nothin' happened. But then—now get this—after they disappeared, they looked back at the gurney and the body was still there. Dead as a doornail like nothing ever happened."

Blah, blah, blah. They canceled All My Children *and now they're giving us this on the evening news? What a joke.*

Jessica stepped out of the station into the humid breeze that announced the next wave of the storm was about to hit. She'd forgotten her umbrella, too. *Dammit, I should have known this would all be a waste of time. Cops. Don't know their badge from a free toy in a cereal box.*

Back inside, the officer with the pale blue eyes filed the notes he'd taken in a manila folder. One of these days, the department would make it into the 21st century and give him a damned computer terminal at his station so he wouldn't have to go to the back office and retype everything in. Sixth-graders at his kid's school got new tablet computers, but the Seventeenth Precinct? They had to share nine-year-old desktops.

He glanced down at the description the woman had given him just as another description came over the scanner.

"Woman. Caucasian. Early to mid-twenties. Standing 5-foot-9 to 5-foot-11. Dark hair. Slight scar near right temple. Sought for questioning. Last seen eastbound 101 with unidentified male, early forties. Be on the lookout. Over."

The officer with the pale blue eyes did a double-take, then shook his head. Couldn't be the same person. Minerva Jane Rus was in a wheelchair.

He put the folder aside.

"I said, NEXT!"

Cantina

"So I'm afraid you're stuck with me," Minerva said, finishing her long and rather hard-to-swallow explanation of what had just happened to Amber.

At least it had been the truth. Mostly. Minerva had left out the part about what she'd done to the first paramedic who'd gotten in her way. The rest of it was hard enough to believe without her throwing that into the mix. Amber was a doctor, after all, and they had that motto, "Do no harm."

"Stuck with us," Carson said from the front seat.

"Don't listen to him," Minerva quipped. "He's Jessica's ex-boyfriend, and he can't get over the fact that she dumped him."

"Jessica?"

"My . . . er . . . mother."

"*She* dumped *me*?" Carson interjected.

"Men and their egos," Amber chuckled. "They never can admit when they just don't measure up."

Minerva didn't laugh, but breathed a barely audible sigh of relief instead. If Amber was up to making jokes, that meant she wasn't too upset at the news of her undead status—either that or she didn't believe a word of it.

"You're taking this all really well," Minerva said.

"Not really. I'm still not sure what to make of this. All I know is I've been looking for an excuse to take some time off from my practice, and I guess this is as good as any. I do need to get back to my apartment and get out of these awful clothes, though. I'm used to the sight of blood, but my own? Not so much." She lifted her bloodstained shirt and looked at what now appeared to be unbroken flesh underneath. "I guess I can't argue with results. Whatever you did, and however you did it, thank you."

Minerva just nodded and offered a barely perceptible smile. She wasn't used to compliments and didn't know how to take them.

They got to Amber's apartment, a two-bedroom townhouse in Studio City, and waited as she packed a suitcase. She lived alone there with a single tuxedo cat named Trapper (after a TV doctor, of course) and enough house plants, it seemed, to fill an atrium. Minerva had learned that she'd divorced after being married for a couple of years: The hyphenated name came from her parents, not from that brief union.

She showered quickly, threw some makeup, toothpaste, and toiletries into a smaller case and said, "Okay, I'm up for it. Let's go."

"What about your cat?" Carson asked.

"I'm not going to be gone *that* long, am I?"

Minerva and Carson just looked at each other, then back at her. Their expressions left no doubt about the answer to her question.

"Oh." The disappointment on her face lasted only a couple of seconds, though, before it was replaced by a look of resolve. "I'll just text Bailey to look after her for however long I'm gone," she said. "Now what do you say we find someplace to eat. I'd offer you something here, but I'm a doctor, not a chef. Besides, after what I've been through, I think I deserve a nice meal out. What do you say? Know any good Mexican where we're going?"

Minerva laughed. It seemed weird to her that people who were technically dead still wanted to eat. But she had to admit she still didn't know a whole lot about their condition. Raven had been the first "undead" person she'd met, and he certainly seemed to function just fine in other . . . physical . . . respects as well.

"You're blushing," Amber noted.

Minerva turned her head slightly away.

"Who is he?"

She looked back at Amber, embarrassed about being embarrassed. "Someone . . . like you. He used to be dead, but now he's not. You'll get to meet him, I'm sure." *I hope.*

Carson shook his head. "I don't think it's a good idea to eat in public. There are people out looking for us. For all I know, they're following us already."

"You would have noticed them," Minerva said, appealing to his ego. "I'm famished, too, and Mexican sounds great."

165

She thought she saw Carson wince. He was outnumbered and, while he was probably right, it was hard to argue with an empty stomach—in this case, two empty stomachs, and probably a third since Carson hadn't eaten anything since that gross excuse for a sandwich he'd made himself.

"Okay," he said at last, grudgingly. "How about Nacho Tacos? They've got a drive-through and we can grab a quick bite without . . ."

"No drive-throughs," Amber said flatly. "Sit-down. And *nice* sit-down. I plan to take my time and actually enjoy this meal. If it weren't for Minerva, I wouldn't even be having it."

Carson shot a look at Minerva that said, *Please back me up.*

Not a chance. "You heard the doctor. Take us someplace *nice*. Your treat."

To her surprise, Carson smiled at this. "Money is not an object." The smile disappeared. "Your safety is."

Despite his objections, however, he drove them a few miles up the highway, exited on Laurel Canyon to Ventura Boulevard and pulled into a driveway under a sign that read "Cabo Fantastico Grill and Cantina." The name sounded cheesy, but the place looked nice enough, with a couple of palm trees bent inward toward each other across an entryway set back from the parking lot and a small artificial waterfall running through a fern garden beside the front door. There was even a valet who insisted on parking your car for ten dollars. Carson gave him a twenty and told him to keep the change.

The parking lot seemed pretty much deserted except for a panhandler sitting on the curb with a silver bucket and a harmonica. It was too early for most people to think about an evening meal, and the place had just opened up for dinner, having closed for a few hours after the lunch rush.

They stepped inside and found themselves in a dark wood interior that looked more like a steakhouse or a seafood restaurant than a Mexican place. No sombreros on the walls and none of that annoying piped-in mariachi music. They'd actually put cloth napkins out on the tables, set up on plates in a pyramid fold. No wine glasses, but the place was known for margaritas, so that wasn't a surprise.

"Nice," Amber said, nodding her head in approval.

Minerva raised her eyebrows. "Whadda ya know. Maybe he does have taste."

"Thank you. I think," Carson replied.

"You're welcome," Minerva said with mock sincerity. "Now, if you two will excuse me for a sec, I need to visit the ladies' room."

"Wait," Carson said. "Maybe I should go with you."

"To the *ladies' room?*"

"Not inside, of course, but just to make sure . . ."

This time, it was Amber who spoke up. "What does she look like? A two-year-old? Or didn't you see the way she handled herself back there on the freeway? She's got this."

Carson realized she was probably right. Minerva wasn't his prisoner anymore, and she *could* take care of herself. He nodded.

As Minerva began walking in toward a sign that pointed to the restrooms, a hostess clad in a sunflower yellow skirt approached carrying a handful of menus. "Have you been helped?"

"We'd like someplace secluded, please," Carson said.

She nodded. "Of course, Sir. Right this way."

"I don't think so."

It was a man's voice, with a barely perceptible Texas accent, and it came from very close behind them.

The hostess, looking past Carson and Amber, saw the owner of the voice and started backing away slowly.

"I wouldn't turn around if I were you," the man said. "Eyes forward."

Amber felt something hard in the small of her back.

"Yes, that's a gun," the voice said. "And if you so much as move an inch, Miss Rus, I'll put a bullet through your back."

Amber's body stiffened, her shoulders tensing and her back arching. *They think I'm her.*

Carson stood completely still. When Amber cast a sidelong glance at him, it almost seemed like he wasn't even breathing. *All right, Mr. Self-Appointed Knight in Shining Armor, let's see you get us out of this one.*

"Here's how it's going to work." That Texas drawl seemed to get more pronounced the more he spoke. "You." He indicated the hostess, who stopped in her tracks. "Lock the front door and get over there." He nodded his head toward a dark leather bench set up for patrons to wait while tables were cleared. "If you try to run out, I'll shoot her." He nodded toward Amber-who-he-thought-was-Minerva.

The woman, a diminutive brunette with her hair in a bun, sixties-style, crept around him like a mouse trying not to wake a sleeping cat. When she got to the door, Carson spoke up. "He won't shoot her. He needs her alive."

"You're sure about that?" the man said.

The woman clearly wasn't; instead of taking the opportunity to run out the front door, she obediently bolted it and went to take a seat on the leather bench, as the gunman had demanded.

"That's a good girl. Now, I want you to . . . Wait. Who's that?"

"Hey, guys, the restroom's out of order," Minerva said as she walked toward them, then froze when she saw the Texan.

Amber spoke up. "That's my sister. She doesn't have anything to do with this." Then, frowning toward Minerva, she mouthed the words in exaggerated fashion, "He's got a gun."

Minerva didn't react but kept walking toward them. "Who's your friend, Sis? He's not bad. I didn't realize you had a date meeting us here."

A confused look appeared on the gunman's face. The file on Minerva Rus had mentioned a little brother but nothing about a sister. "Hold on right there," he warned, but Minerva kept coming.

"Not bad at all," she said, looking the man up and down. "You know how I like to steal them from you, Sis. And this one looks like he's really worth stealing." She batted her eyes at him suggestively; she had a feeling she was laying it on too thick, but she wasn't used to flirting, and it felt more than a little awkward. Solitude and sarcasm were more her speed. But if he could just get him to look her in the eye, she'd be able to. . .

"Enough of this!" The man shouted. "Stop right there. Now!"

Minerva did as he demanded. So much for her seductress alter ego.

"Now, here's what's going to happen: You three"—he indicated Minerva, Carson and the hostess—"are going to stay here while I take Minerva (he nodded toward Amber) for a little drive. You're going to stay here for at least half an hour, and if you try to leave, my friend by the front door will make sure you don't. Got it?"

The real Minerva nodded, still trying to make eye contact but unable to get more than the man's divided attention from the corner of his eye. It wasn't enough.

If the man wasn't bluffing and he really did have a partner outside the door, Carson was glad the waitress had stayed put. He should have thought of that. He could have gotten the woman killed. Now he had to make sure he didn't let that happen to Minerva or—again—to Amber. It was just wasn't easy when he had his back to the guy.

It was Amber who spoke next. "I'm sorry, but I'm not going anywhere with you. I guess you'll just have to shoot me."

The man grabbed her arm and wrenched it up behind her back. "Oh, I won't have to go that far. I'll just break your arm. Then if that doesn't work, I'll break the other one. And your fingers, one at a time. How does that sound?"

Amber grunted and bit her tongue. Literally. She could feel the pressure building, then sustained as he bent her arm against its natural position and held it there. If he forced it any further, it would snap.

"Okay," she managed to say.

"Good. I thought you'd see things my way."

Just then, the sound of a pan dropping came from the kitchen. The hostess wasn't the only employee in the building; the gunman hadn't counted on the fact that, in a restaurant that had just opened for business, there would be a cook on duty, too.

"Hell!" the Texan said, startled by the sudden commotion. He'd been so intent on making sure he kept his three captives in line that the distraction jarred his focus loose momentarily and he relaxed his hold on Amber's arm—just enough for her to pull it free and wrench her elbow back into the man's gut.

He managed to step back just in time to avoid the brunt of the blow.

Actually, he half-stepped, half-stumbled backward, just as Carson whirled and rushed him, diving at his legs and knocking him onto his back. Seeing him now for the first time, Carson realized how big he was: several inches taller and maybe eighty pounds heavier than Carson. From the look of him, most of those eighty pounds were muscle.

Despite his bulk, the man was able to roll deftly sideways, away from Carson, and pop back up on his feet like one of those inflatable clown punching bags. He also managed to keep his hold on the gun.

Carson could see he wouldn't get another shot, and he stopped short when he saw the gun was pointed squarely at his chest.

"Turn around!" the man shouted.

Seeing no other choice, other than having his guts blown out, Carson complied.

The hostess looked hopefully toward the kitchen, but everything had gone silent there. Whoever had dropped that pan earlier had probably fled out the back door, and even if still in the building, that startled chef wasn't about to come rushing to their aid.

Then Amber said something that no one expected her to say. It wasn't as though they had known her long, but she'd seemed trustworthy.

Until now.

"Hey, Mister," she announced. "I'm not Minerva Rus. She is." She pointed at the real Minerva. "She's the one you want."

"What the hell?" Minerva heard herself say.

The man smiled and looked at her. The restaurant's lighting was dim, and he hadn't considered that he'd picked the wrong woman to begin with, but now that he looked at her, it was clear she was right: Her face matched the profile pictures that had come with the assignment. Now this other woman, whoever she was, was trying to save her skin by handing over the real Minerva.

So much for "I guess you'll have to shoot me," Minerva thought. A good twist of the arm could work wonders.

The Texan stepped away from Amber and toward Minerva, but before he could cover half of the approximately ten feet that separated them, Carson stepped in front of him.

"If you want to get her, I'm afraid you'll have to go through me," he said.

The Texan pointed his Ruger LCP directly at Carson. "You forget who's holding the gun," he smiled.

And I guess you forgot about me. Amber flew at the Texan from just off to his left, but he saw her in time to turn toward her.

In the same motion, he fired.

Amber felt searing pain rise with the echo of blast as the bullet sliced into her torso just below her heart. But it didn't stop her momentum from sending her airborne body into the Texan, who toppled over from the force of the impact and crumpled to the ground. Carson and Minerva leapt forward in unison, Carson rushing to slam a steel-toed shoe into the side of the fallen Texan's face, and Minerva rushing to try get Amber off of him.

Before she could get there, though, the Texan fired again, directly into Amber's chest, and the force of it sent her falling away.

Carson pulled his own weapon and trained it on their assailant.

"Whose orders?" he demanded.

The man smirked. "You know I won't tell you that."

Carson shook his head. "Never mind. I've got a pretty good idea who sent you. Maybe you should tell her how stupid it is to send one man on an assignment like this."

"Or maybe I'll tell her how stupid it was to assign you to this operation in the first place. The only reason I didn't secure the target is that your friend there had a death wish."

Carson shrugged. "I suppose you could tell her that, but I think I'll save you the trouble."

He pulled the trigger and put a hole in the Texan's head, then turned without a second thought and hurried over to where Minerva sat leaning over Amber's body.

Amber blinked and smiled an odd smile.

For the second time in the few hours he'd known her, Carson saw blood pouring out of her—this time from two wounds, one right above the other in her chest.

Minerva looked at him, an expression of fear, panic, and sorrow in her eyes. "I can't bring her back again—not a second time. I don't know how."

Amber's smile widened, and Carson thought he noticed the flow of blood start to slow.

"You don't have to, Sis," she said, propping herself up on her elbows. "I don't think he can kill me if I'm already dead."

She sat up all the way and the two of them watched as the blood stopped flowing. "I guess I really *will* have to believe you now," she said, shaking her head in mock regret. "It's just a good thing I brought a change of clothes this time."

Revived

Minerva had never had a sister, but having Amber around was like finding out what she'd been missing. Amber was a lot like Minerva wished she might have turned out herself if she'd come from a normal home. Self-confident. Successful. Driven. Sarcastic. Well, Minerva realized, she already had that last one down herself. She might even be able to teach Amber a thing or two there.

Between the two of them, they were able to piece together with a little more certainty just what the gift could do and what it meant to the Revived. That's what they decided to call those who had been brought back from death through the use of targeted memory (a phrase Amber had thought up). It seemed a lot nicer to say "the Revived" than "the Undead," which made them sound like zombies out of some B-movie from the '80s.

As a physician, Amber knew enough about her own physiology to tell the difference between who she was now and who she'd been before she'd been brought back. There wasn't much. The Revived weren't shades or reanimated corpses. They were more like self-aware, corporeal holographic projections—if such things existed.

"Well, I guess they exist now," Amber had said when they were hashing through the mechanics of it. "Or, should I say, *we* exist. You might even say we're a parasitic life form, since we depend on someone else for our continued existence."

"Sounds more like a vampire than a zombie to me," Minerva quipped.

"I suppose, in a way, we are."

The revived body wasn't the same as the body that had been buried or cremated when the person died. Those paramedics who'd seen Amber code out, then get up and walk away like she never had so much as a hangnail—

they must have freaked out to look back at the gurney and find a dead body still lying there underneath that sheet.

"What I wouldn't have given to see their faces!" she said.

Amber's revived body could do most of what her old body could have done. She didn't have to eat, but she still could—and a steak-and-eggs breakfast tasted just the same as it always had. Her stomach, intestines, and bowels still processed food in the same way, too.

Breathing? That was no longer necessary, either, but if something scared her, she still caught her breath, and if she got excited, she still started breathing more rapidly. Her lungs worked just as well as they ever had, but like an appendix, they were just no longer necessary.

Perhaps most importantly, nothing could really kill her . . . except being forgotten by her gifted host. She could still be captured (it wasn't as though she could walk through walls), and she could still be hurt. But her injuries would heal almost immediately, without any kind of treatment—as long as she remained connected to the gifted individual who sustained her—Minerva. She felt like a mutant character out of a comic book. All she needed to go with her regenerative powers were some long, vicious-looking claws made out of some fictional super-strong metal alloy. Sometimes, truth really *was* just about as strange as fiction.

"All I need is a snappy skin-tight uniform, and I'll be set," she joked.

One good thing about bringing Amber along, from Minerva's perspective, was that she no longer had to be content with Carson's company. He tended to speak in short, clipped sentences . . . unless he was worried about her. Then he switched into protective godfather mode and started lecturing her. She was learning to tune him out, but it was more fun to change the channel and listen to something interesting. That's where Amber came in. Not only was she a doctor, but she'd built up a clientele that included a fair number of Hollywood celebrities. There was Aaron Mintz, the talk-show host who arranged live, on-air boxing matches for guests who wanted to settle a score. There was Ermaline the Shoe Queen, who'd made millions off designer footwear. And there was Zen Reckless, the drummer for an up-and-coming metal act called Medusa Made Me Hard.

Amber seemed to have done nearly everything that was worth doing, even if she was only 31 years old. She'd skydived from 15,000 feet in Rio, gone backpacking in the Grand Canyon, been to the Oscars on the arm of a B-grade beefcake actor, and even written an e-book about relationships that had sold several thousand copies online.

"What do you know about relationships?" Minerva asked her. "You're divorced, right?"

"You know the old saying: Those who can, do, and those who can't, they write books pretending that they're smarter than they are."

The other good thing about having Amber around was she happened to have a convenient hiding place. That B-grade beefcake actor, stage name Rafe Alexis, hadn't been too happy when she'd dumped him after the Oscars (he didn't win; he wasn't even up for anything) and had started stalking her. He'd even hired a private investigator to follow her around and take pictures, so she'd bought herself a gray wig—she'd always thought the idea of going prematurely gray was somehow chic—rounded up a new wardrobe and bought herself a small, out-of-the-way bungalow back in Topanga Canyon.

She'd taken a month off work and holed up there until old Rafe had lost interest, but she'd kept the bungalow afterward because she liked the idea of having what she called a "refuge from the whackadoodles in the Valley."

Carson, who seemed to worry about everything, had agreed to use it as a base—grudgingly—for the simple reason that he couldn't think of a better alternative.

Amber popped the cork on a bottle of merlot.

"Want some?" she asked.

Carson shook his head. "I don't drink on the job, and she shouldn't. At all."

"Since when do you answer for me, Mr. Fullofhimself?" Minerva shot back. "Yeah, Amber, I'll have some."

Carson's eyes looked like daggers. Well, not really. Eyes don't look much like daggers, even when someone's really annoyed—and Carson was beyond annoyed. "You can't let your guard down," he warned her. "You have no idea what Jules might be capable of if she finds a way into your mind while you're intoxicated. She's been there before, and she probably knows how to get back."

Amber poured about one-third of the bottle into a wine glass, nearly filling it to the brim, and handed it to Minerva, then she did the same for herself. "I don't know who this Jules person is, but I wouldn't worry about her," the doctor said. "She's not here. She's not going to find us. And you're not driving or operating any heavy machinery, so why not?"

Minerva couldn't think of a decent answer and really didn't want to. It had been too long since she'd relaxed and, to be honest, she couldn't see how staying stressed out would help her deal with Jules or any other unpleasantness.

"I need a break from all this," she admitted.

You don't get a break. Haven't you figured that out yet? But Carson bit his tongue and kept his admonitions to himself. He was good at reading people, and he could tell there wasn't anything he could say that would get Minerva to listen. He'd just have to be prepared enough for the both of them—and hope they wouldn't need it.

A couple of hours and a couple of bottles of wine later, both women were passed out.

Carson stayed awake. His instincts told him something bad was about to happen.

Bus

Minerva's eyes flashed open, but what she saw wasn't the interior of Amber's bungalow. She was sitting at a bus stop somewhere in the middle of a city. She could tell it was a city by the buildings—skyscrapers that rose toward the sun. But the sun was a dull copper color instead of blazing yellow-white, and instead of blue, the sky was red, clear but churning as though filled with storm clouds.

The buildings themselves weren't quite right, either. They seemed to pulsate and waver as they stood there, twisting oddly between base and apex, more like strands of rope than anything solid.

I'm drunk, Minerva told herself, feeling her head pound and remembering the too-much merlot she'd had the night before.

But no matter how drunk she might have been, it didn't explain this. She might be just 21, but she'd had more alcohol than this before; it had made the room seem to spin in lazy circles around her, but it had never altered the character of what she was seeing. This was more like what she'd been told might happen if she ever tried LSD—not something she ever had done, or would do. Not before and especially not now.

She felt queasy. Was that the alcohol or the effect of being disoriented in this odd, new place? She had no way of knowing.

A bus pulled up and stopped, not in the way a normal, solid bus with a metal frame would have done, but more like a rubber band: its front stopping and its rear section contracting into it, then finally extending again as it came to a delayed stop a second or two later.

The door opened with the familiar compressed-air *whoosh* sound, and she stepped on board . . . only to notice that the bus had no driver. Before she could rethink her decision, the door closed behind her and the bus was underway. She half sat, half fell into a too-small seat that didn't leave enough room for her legs. She found she was sitting next to a man in a worn Brooklyn Dodgers cap and a dark, thick wool coat, who appeared at first glance to be sleeping. On closer inspection, though, it seemed to Minerva that he wasn't breathing. She nudged him, and to her surprise, he grunted and opened his eyes slowly.

"I see she's got another one," he said, in a voice that carried a muted accent she couldn't quite place.

"She?"

"The Red Queen. She runs this place."

Who is this guy? The mad hatter? Never imagined him in a baseball cap. "Where are we?"

The man shifted in his seat and sat up a little. "Beautiful downtown Glendale," he said. "Or at least what it would look like if she'd designed it."

The next thing you know, I'll see a white rabbit hopping across the street. "How did you get here?"

"Hmph. Not sure, really. Just woke up here one day, and I've been here ever since." Suddenly, the man started singing something about some guy who got stuck on a Boston subway and never came back. She'd never heard it before, and he broke off, seeing the confused look in her eyes. "Kingston Trio," he said. "Before your time."

She'd actually heard of the band, vaguely, though she had no idea where. They'd been popular in the 1950s. "You've been here *that* long?"

He shrugged. "At least I got a chance to see the Bums finally win the Series. She let me out to see that. Must've been feelin' charitable then— knew I'd been a fan from back before the war. The only nice thing she ever did for me."

"This Red Queen of yours must have been around a long time."

He harrumphed. "Yeah, she's old, but she doesn't look it. Looks after herself, she does. And she's no queen of *mine*, Missy. I'm more like a prisoner of war from the other side. She doesn't want me dead, because she needs me. But she doesn't want me rocking her boat, either, so she keeps me here."

"Needs you? For what?"

"Don't wanna talk about it," he snapped. "I'm not going to do it, but she keeps thinking I'll change my mind. That's okay, though." His voice softened. "I may be trapped, but it's better than her forgettin' about me."

Minerva realized then why he hadn't appeared to be breathing: He wasn't. "You're one of the Revived," she said.

"Oh, is that what you call us? Hmm. Well, I figure it's better than her word for it: half-life. Did you know she was trained as a physicist?"

"I don't even know who she is."

"You will soon enough. You're gifted, like me, aren't you?"

Minerva lied. "I don't know what you're talking about," she said. She didn't know that this man could be trusted, and until she did, she wasn't about to go around handing out free information about herself.

"Smart girl," he said, smiling to reveal a mouth with more than one missing tooth. He extended his right hand, and she took it grudgingly. "Hiram Granger at your service," he said, nodding once deferentially.

"Nice to meet you," she said without enthusiasm.

"Granger's not my real name, y'know."

"Oh?"

"It's Greenberg, but I changed it because I didn't want the Nazis to find me. Fat lot of good it did me." He rolled up his sleeve, revealing a six-digit number and a triangle tattooed on his forearm.

Minerva just stared at him, not understanding.

"That's why they say 'never forget.' And you with such a keen memory. It's a shame." He shook his head slowly. "Some of us *can't* forget because we were there."

Minerva looked away, feeling guilty that she didn't know what this Granger—or Greenberg—felt should have been obvious to her.

"Auschwitz," he said finally. "I was there."

Minerva knew that name: the notorious concentration camp in Nazi Germany during World War II. Extermination camp was more like it. More than a million people had died there, mostly Jews, but Poles, too, and Romani and even some prisoners of war. Some by firing squad, others after being intentionally poisoned using pesticides, others still in gas chambers, their bodies burned by the thousands in crematory ovens. Minerva had heard about that in school, and she hadn't forgotten; tattoos like the one Greenberg wore hadn't been part of the lessons.

"At least you survived," she said.

He frowned and pursed his lips, and for a moment, Minerva thought he was going to spit on her.

178

"Does it look like I survived?!" he nearly shouted. "They killed me. And my wife, Sharon. We'd only been married six years, but we already had three children. Jacob. Aryeh. Little Elizabeth." His voice quavered as he spoke the names. "They were too young to work, so they killed them first. But they gassed all of us eventually. I was the last one—and the only one they revived. I wish they'd left me dead." He paused. "Except for the Dodgers winning the Series. That was the only thing worthwhile about this miserable life, if you can even call it that."

Minerva couldn't think of anything to say. Somehow, "I'm sorry" seemed almost a mockery.

The bus slowed and came to a stop underneath a tall apartment building that looked more solid than the others Minerva had seen.

"All out!" came the announcement from a disembodied voice.

Granger's smile disappeared, and he started to tremble, as if it had suddenly gotten very cold, but Minerva hadn't noticed any change in the temperature. It had been warm and muggy ever since she'd arrived, like she'd been deposited on the bayou in the middle of summer.

"What's wrong?"

Granger shook his head rapidly, as if he'd caught a fever. "This isn't right," he said. "This isn't right."

"I don't understand."

"All out!" the voice said again, more insistent this time.

"She never lets me off the bus. Never. This isn't right at all."

The next thing Minerva knew, the bus itself had disappeared altogether, and they were standing in the lobby of a building—presumably, the one the bus had pulled up in front of.

"Hey!" Minerva said. "What . . .?"

"Move along!" came another disembodied voice that sounded like it belonged to an invisible police officer.

Minerva felt something pressing against her back and tried to push back against it, but she was unable to resist. From the way Granger's body seemed to be contorting, his back arching and his feet moving forward in staggered steps, the same thing was happening to him. The two of them were being propelled forward toward two gold-colored elevator doors that opened with a *ding!* as if on cue as they came within a few feet of them.

They were thrust inside, and the doors closed behind them, and immediately the elevator began zipping upward at an impossible speed that left Minerva feeling like her stomach had been thrust down into her bowels. She remembered again the wine she'd drunk a few hours earlier and began to regret that she hadn't listened to Carson. Sometimes, being a spoilsport had its advantages.

Seconds later, they stopped, and her stomach was launched back upward toward her mouth. The doors separated, and they stepped—or rather, were pushed by that same unseen force—out into a small foyer that stood outside a single door bearing the number "1801."

"Penthouse," Granger mumbled. He was still shivering, even worse now than before.

They stood there for a moment, then the door opened to reveal the occupant of the suite.

"Hiram," she said. "What a nice surprise. Well, not a surprise really, since I summoned you. The least you could have done was bring me flowers. I know how much you've always fancied me, dear. No need to hide it. . . . But wait? Who do we have here? Did you actually have the audacity to bring a *date* to our little rendezvous?" Her eyes flashed, but the anger seemed cold and forced, not hot and immediate. The hint of anger faded almost immediately. "No worries," she chirped, a smile crawling across her face. "All is forgiven. You see, I've found a new plaything to replace you. I won't be needing your services any longer. In fact, silly me, it seems I've *forgotten* who you are. Perhaps you could refresh my memory?"

"No," Granger whispered, shaking more than ever.

The penthouse resident ignored him, her eyes fixed intently on Minerva. But Minerva knew better than to meet that gaze. She forced herself to look past the woman and caught sight of a figure walking across the room a few feet behind her.

"Raven!" she shouted, but he didn't respond. He looked in her direction, but only for a moment, seeming to look through her instead of at her.

"Don't waste your breath," Jules told her. "He's not really here. Neither am I, technically speaking, but you are. And I plan to keep you here a very, very, very long time."

Staircase

Minerva didn't hesitate, not after the last time she'd squared off against Jules. A head-on confrontation? She wasn't about to do that again—at least not until she felt more confident in her ability to hold her own. And after what Granger had said about this Red Queen being around a very long time, she had a feeling it might take a while to match her in terms of experience.

She turned and ran.

Granger was gone. Whether he'd faded away or simply tried to run, she didn't know. She didn't have time to care. What she wanted, at this moment, was to get away from here.

Remembering how she'd been forced into the elevator before, she decided in an instant to go for the stairwell beside it instead. Flinging the door open, she started down them at what seemed like a gallop, jumping from the third step up at each landing, grabbing the railing and whipping herself around like a roller derby jammer as she turned to attack the next level.

She was mildly relieved that she didn't hear anyone behind her, but that realization also worried her. If Jules wasn't following her, it likely meant one of two things: She'd laid out a trap somewhere up ahead, or she didn't think there was anywhere Minerva could run.

How many floors?

That's right—it was 18. She looked at the next landing to see how far she'd come and was greeted by the number 12. That was progress, at least. She was starting to feel winded.

11.

10.

Still no one behind her. But now, oddly, she seemed to be going more slowly . . . and not because she'd gotten tired. The walls, like the buildings she'd seen and the bus, seemed to be turning rubbery as she watched them go by—in slow motion at first, then reversing course. She stumbled and fell as the stairs seemed to come out from underneath her . . . except that they weren't stairs. She felt hard metal with jagged ridges crash up into her knees and pull her back upward as she struggled not to fall any farther. Looking down, she realized she was on an escalator.

She tumbled down a short distance farther, her shoulders crashing into the moving conveyer-steps; she put out her hand to steady herself against them, only to pull it away quickly when she realized her skin was about to get pinched between them.

Minerva tried to stand up and start downward again, but the escalator seemed to be accelerating and, impossibly, whipping around the corners that had been landings at each floor level a few moments earlier. The walls heaved and buckled, as though they were some thick liquid, like half-frozen tapioca pudding, and each time she tried to stand, Minerva found herself thwarted not only by the escalator's quickening pace but by her own sense of vertigo.

When at last it slowed enough for her to take a breath, she looked up and her eyes were greeted by an approaching number.

18.

She was right back where she started. No wonder Jules hadn't bothered to follow her.

Realizing there was no point in trying to head down the stairs again, Minerva got to her feet, steadying herself against the dizziness she felt by bracing the palm of a hand against the wall to the stairwell.

Tentatively, she opened the door to the 18th floor and found herself staring face-to-face, once again, with Jules.

"Get out of my dream!" she shouted, still careful to avoid eye contact.

The other woman merely laughed. "Sorry, dear, but this isn't *your* dream. I can forgive you for thinking it is, since you're new at this. But let me assure you, this dream is all mine. My world. My rules. I pulled you into it when you were stupid enough to let down your guard. And as you can see, it's not going to be easy for you to escape. In fact, I intend to make it impossible."

Minerva was tired. And scared. Really scared. But for right now, she was focusing all the energy she could muster into not showing it.

"Still, I'm asleep. I'm not dead like poor Hiram. You can't keep me here forever. I've got to wake up sooner or later."

"Do you? Do you reaaaaalllly." Jules drew out the last word so it became a taunt. "Haven't you heard what happens when you die in your dreams?"

"That's a myth," Minerva snapped. "Besides, you said this was *your* dream."

"So it is. That's just a technicality, though. And what they say is no myth—I can vouch for that. I've killed people here before, and they've all stayed quite dead."

"You don't scare me."

Jules laughed again. "I'm not trying to scare you. To be honest, I don't care much whether you're afraid or not, although I will admit that makes it a little more fun. Not as much fun as taking your pathetic boyfriend away from you, but that's a conversation for a different time. I'm not trying to scare you, I'm trying to defeat you. No, trying is the wrong word. I've already succeeded."

"Don't bet on it . . ."

"I don't make bets. I only deal in sure things." As she spoke, her hand flashed forward at lightning speed, and Minerva felt a jarring pain thrust deep into her side just underneath her ribs. Nearly convulsing, she staggered backward, seeing the hilt of the dagger embedded in her flesh and watching, as if she were a passive observer, as Jules twisted it and bored the blade in as deep as it would go. Minerva was dimly aware of the warm flow cascading out of her, the sensation all but overwhelmed by the piercing, searing pain of the blade.

Minerva's eyes opened wide, and in a moment of panic, she forgot not to look into her enemy's eyes.

You might kill me. But you won't beat me.

It was a moment of defiance, bracketed by blinding pain and sheer panic at the realization of what was happening. In that moment, she saw something she'd never seen in Jules' eyes before: uncertainty. Maybe she'd imagined it, and she had neither the time nor the discipline to analyze it amid everything that was happening to her. She closed her eyes tightly against the pain and felt herself falling backward, dimly aware that she would likely go tumbling down the stairwell but powerless to stop it.

Blackness enveloped her, and a single moment stretched into eternity.

Pulse

"Wake up!"

Amber groaned and opened her eyes reluctantly, propping herself up on a throw pillow she kept on the sofa where she'd been sleeping. Her dry mouth and throbbing head told her she hadn't shaken off the effects of the wine she'd drunk last night. How was it that her revived body could recover more quickly from bullet holes than from too much merlot? "Wha . . .?"

"I said, wake up!" Carson's hand was still on her shoulder, shaking it, even after she'd sat partway up.

She shook it off. "Hey, Mister, watch the paws." Sitting up fully, she rubbed the sleep out of her eyes. "What time is it?"

"Four a.m., but never mind that." Carson's tone wasn't just insistent, it was nearly panicked. It wasn't like him. "Something's wrong with Minerva."

"What do you mean? She's probably just got a hangover. I know I . . ."

Amber stopped herself. She felt strangely weak, and she knew it wasn't the wine, which shouldn't be affecting her this way anyway in her current revived state—unless somehow the link to her host had been compromised. Something *was* wrong with Minerva. She didn't need Carson to tell her that; she could feel it. "What's happened."

Carson gestured toward Minerva, who was lying still on the floor in the middle of the room. "A few minutes ago, she went into some kind of seizure, but now it's stopped."

Despite her fatigue, Amber jumped off the couch and rushed to where Minerva was lying. Kneeling by her side, she put two fingers to her neck.

"Shit. I can't find a pulse."

She rolled Minerva over and sprang on top of her, then started pressing on her chest at regular intervals.

Still nothing.

"My med kit," she barked at Carson. "In the bathroom. Bottom cupboard. Now!"

Carson jumped up and ran to the bathroom, retrieving a white metal box with a red cross on the side. He was back within seconds.

"There's a pink syringe in there. Hand it to me."

Carson did as he was told.

Amber stopped pumping to grab the long-needled syringe, squeezed the bottom to expel a couple of drops of fluid, then thrust the needle into Minerva's chest and injected the contents into her heart.

"Adrenaline," she said. "And please, no lectures about the dangers of brain damage. If this doesn't work, she won't have a brain left to damage."

Almost immediately, Minerva's chest heaved upward in a nearly violent convulsion, then sank back down to the floor. Her eyes fluttered open as Amber checked her pulse again, then breathed a sigh of relief. "She's back."

Minerva sat up immediately, appearing none the worse for wear.

"Easy!" Amber said, placing a hand on her shoulder. "You've been through a lot here. Take it from someone who knows what it's like: You've just come back from the dead."

Minerva let her shoulders relax and lay back down on the hardwood floor. Her back ached. How had she wound up asleep down there in the first place? She didn't remember much of the previous evening (that was saying something for someone with an eidetic memory—she really *must* have had too much to drink), but everything that had happened since was vividly etched at the forefront of her mind.

"You were right, Carson," she said, shaking her head. She didn't usually enjoy admitting she'd messed up, but given all she'd just been through, it was more of a relief than anything else. It was comforting to know that, for once in her life, despite the circumstances, someone seemed to have her back. Two someones now, counting Amber. Raven would have her back, too, if she knew where he was. *If she knew where he was.*

She sat up again. "Glendale."

"Glendale?" Carson repeated. "What about it?"

"I think they're in Glendale. Raven and Jules. I could be wrong. It might have just been some weird illusion, but that's what Hiram said: 'Beautiful downtown Glendale.' I didn't see an address, but I know they were on the 18th floor—a penthouse suite."

"Who's Hiram?" Amber asked.

"Someone she—Jules—was trying to use for some reason. He was trapped there, in this 'other' Glendale she'd created in her mind. But now that she's got Raven, she doesn't need him anymore. We have to get there before she realizes she's exposed herself. She was counting on killing me and keeping me prisoner there the way she'd done with Hiram. She would have done it, too, if you two hadn't saved me."

"I'm a doctor," Amber said. "It's what I do."

She pulled a pen light out of the med kit. "Open your eyes wide," she instructed and shone a bright, white light onto Minerva's pupils, one at a time.

A moment later, she turned off the pen light and returned it to the box. "How many fingers am I holding up?"

"You've got two hands, so ten."

"Now's not the time to be a smartass. Seriously, how many?"

"Okay, four."

"Right. At least you've still got your sense of humor—such as it is." She turned to Carson. "We really should get her to the hospital for an exam. I don't think she was out more than a minute, but we need to be sure she hasn't suffered any brain damage. There's a pretty high risk that goes with using epinephrine to restart a patient's heart, and . . ."

"Didn't you hear what I just said? I *know* where Raven is—at least, I think I do. I'm not going to any freakin' hospital. I'm fine. We've got to get to Glendale."

Carson looked at Amber. "She's right," he said. "And not just for Raven's sake. Anytime she goes to sleep, she could be opening herself up to another attack. We don't have time for a hospital stop."

"Then it's settled," Minerva said. "We're going to Glendale. And I just won't sleep till we get there!"

Amber shook her head. Beyond the whole gifted-revived dependency, she was growing attached to Minerva, and the trained physician in her couldn't shake the fact that she was putting herself at risk if she didn't get herself checked out. But Carson might be right: If this Jules person could inflict this kind of damage, she could pose the bigger danger.

"Did I ever tell you I've done some kickboxing in my day?" she said. "When we get there, point this Jules bitch out to me. I think she's due for a can of M.D. whoopass."

Photograph

Jules attacked the bowl of Wheat Flakes as though it had done her a personal injustice.

Raven stared at her across the table, letting his own cereal go soggy. He wasn't hungry and he didn't need the nourishment.

"Something wrong?"

He felt refreshed. At some point, he felt sure, Minerva had been thinking about him, and those thoughts had energized him.

It seemed like the opposite had happened to his captor.

Jules glared at him, then forced herself to soften the look. "Nothing you need to concern yourself with," she said. "I get migraines. Just had a bad night. Even we kidnappers have them, I guess."

She winced at her own feeble attempt at humor. Her usual poise had gone out the window after her latest encounter with Minerva. She'd had the woman dead to rights, but the little shrew had somehow managed to wriggle out of the trap she had set. Worse, Jules had been so sure of herself that she'd allowed Minerva to see the "world" she—Jules—had manufactured in her mind: a world that was too much like the real thing for comfort. If Minerva had recognized Glendale, their location could be compromised.

"We're going to have to leave," she said sharply.

Raven looked at her. "Why? Where to?"

"Has anyone ever told you it's not attractive when a man asks his female companion too many questions?"

You're not my companion. I'm only here because I'm using you—the way you're trying to use me. I'm only here because Minerva, for some reason, wants me here. And because I want to see my parents again.

"I've been thinking about what you said to me about going back and finding my parents. I'd like to do that."

Jules smiled. Those were the words she'd been waiting to hear, but not at this particular moment. Her priorities had changed after the botched attempt to contain Minerva. "That's good, darling, but not now. We have to get going, and . . ."

"Look," Raven said, setting down his spoon. (Not that he'd been using it anyway.) "You said you'd be able to help me bring my parents back. How do I know you're not just saying that to keep me here? You told me I was free to go, right?"

"I said I'd *let* you go." Her cooing tone held a hint of menace. "Maybe I've changed my mind."

"And maybe I don't want to help you do whatever it is you're trying to do," he countered. "You might be able to kill me, but correct me if I'm wrong on this: I don't think you can *force* me—or you would have done it already. In fact, you said so yourself."

Jules stood up. "We have to go."

Raven pushed the bowl of soggy cereal away from him but made no move to get up from the table.

"Not until you tell me what you want from me. If you can help me get to my parents, yes, I want to do that. But you wouldn't have gone to all this trouble unless you wanted something in return—something that's very important to you. I want to know what it is, or I'm not going anywhere with you."

Jules sat back down. Overconfidence in dealing with Minerva had put her in this pickle, but she remained sure of herself: Even if Minerva *had* figured out how to find her, she probably wasn't lurking right next door, waiting to pounce. Even if she were, the woman was still a neophyte. She didn't have anything close to the ability that she, Jules, had accumulated over decades of exploring her gift.

"Very well," she said, persuading herself to relax. "You're right. I do need your help. I want to bring back someone, too. You scratch my back, I scratch yours. That's the way it works, right?"

Raven nodded. "Go on. Who is this person?"

Jules got up and walked over to a wooden trunk in the corner, lifted the lid and pulled out a framed picture. It was a black and white photograph, yellowed some from age, of a man who looked to be in his thirties.

The subject smiled to reveal a slight gap in his two front teeth; an abundance of dark, black hair crowned his head, well-groomed but thick. His eyes appeared deep-set and his brow heavy, though it might have been the shadow.

"I don't know this man," Raven said after staring at it for a moment. "If I don't know him, I can't revive him."

"Maybe you can't do it directly, but you can do it." Jules sounded very sure of herself.

"How?"

"By bringing back your parents. That's the beauty of it. You get what you want, and I get what I want. Everybody's happy."

"What do my parents have to do with this?" he asked.

"Quite a lot, when you think about it," she smiled. "The man in that photograph is your grandfather."

Raven rolled his eyes. This was getting more confusing by the moment.

"They can't help you, either," he protested. "Even if I revive them. They couldn't bring my grandfather back if they wanted to because neither one of them was gifted."

"Ah, but their mother was. And *you* can bring *her* back. All you have to do is get inside your parents' minds, access their memories of her—and then use those memories to revive her. Then she can take care of things from there and do the same for your grandfather. It's like forming a chain, but taking a little detour along the way."

The proposal sounded so convoluted Raven felt like laughing. Going inside someone else's mind and using the information he found there to bring another person back? He'd never even considered that it might be possible. He'd only been inside one person's mind—Minerva's—and only then because her memories had drawn him there. He had no idea how he would go about doing the same thing with someone who hadn't invited him. The thought of it seemed invasive.

"Let me work out the details," Jules said. "Don't forget, I've been doing this sort of thing a long time. I know what it's like in Between. I can guide you so you don't get lost."

"Why are you so interested in this man—my grandfather—if that's really who he is?"

"What difference does it make, as long as you get your parents back? I would have thought you'd be happy to get your grandparents back in the bargain."

"I never knew them," Raven said almost wistfully, talking more to himself than to her. "My parents adopted me about the same time my grandmother died."

"So you'll finally have a chance to meet them," Jules said triumphantly. "Now, close your eyes and let's get started. We've got a lot of ground to cover, and the sooner we get started, the better it will be for everyone."

Raven had more questions—a lot more questions. But he brushed them aside out of eagerness to see his parents again.

He closed his eyes and quickly fell into a restless slumber.

Starlight

As much as Minerva had wanted to get started right away, her body just wasn't cooperating. Amber was right: Jules' attack had left her feeling weak and drained, even though there was no wound where the knife had entered her.

"Trauma is trauma," Amber told her. "Your heart stopped beating there, Sis. That's going to take a lot out of you, no matter how it happened."

Minerva nodded and took a sip of the herbal tea Amber had made for her. The two of them were sitting out on a redwood-deck back porch, underneath the a sky speckled with a hundred million stars. The sound of crickets chirping came from not too far away, but other than that, the evening was still. It was impossible to tell that, just a few miles from where they sat, a sprawling urban area of more than 18 million people stretched out over more than 1,500 square miles.

Carson opened the sliding glass door and came out onto the deck. Then, without saying anything, he reached into his pocket and pulled out a wallet, handing it to Minerva.

"What's this?" she said, inspecting the new leather.

She looked inside and saw a thick stash of new, crisp hundred-dollar bills.

"For living expenses," Carson said simply. "In case we get separated. I always keep an extra wallet or five lying around with different IDs in them. I think this one was for Pinky Linkletter, a fictional minor mob figure. Didn't think I'd need it on this assignment."

Minerva stifled a laugh as she looked at the Nevada driver's license with a photo of Carson wearing a fedora and a menacing look.

"It suits you," she said. "Though you could have kicked in for a woman's wallet."

"'Thank you' would have worked," he said.

She nodded. "I know." She was about as comfortable accepting gifts as she was accepting compliments—she'd had so few of either in her life. "Thanks."

"Don't mention it," Carson said, smiling at his own irony. Then he turned and went back inside.

Something padded through the bushes a few yards away from them. Opossum? Coyote? Or perhaps a feral cat.

"I know you want to rush off and rescue your friend. But the best thing you can do for him right now is remember him. That will give him the strength you lack—until you can recuperate."

Minerva didn't care for the sound of that, but she knew Amber was right. Having such a smart friend could be frustrating when she pointed out you were wrong, but there were worse things in the world than being wrong. Almost getting killed was one of them. She liked the fact that Amber called her "Sis." She felt like they had a good connection. But part of her couldn't help feeling sad that they'd discovered it because Amber *needed* her—the same way Raven needed her. Sometimes, she wondered whether the only people who actually wanted to be around her had their own agenda. Sure, it was nice to be needed, but it would be great if someone decided to stick around without the whole dependency factor.

She wasn't going to tell Amber any of that, though. She was glad for the company, even if Amber didn't have any other options.

"Tell me about this friend of yours," Amber prompted.

Minerva hesitated a moment before saying, "He's more than a friend."

Amber's chuckle was somewhere between a giggle and a full-fledged laugh. "I gathered that from your reaction the first time you mentioned him. You blushed about as red as a radish."

"I didn't."

"You did."

"Oh. Well, we go back a long way."

Amber, who was sitting beside her on a porch swing, turned to face her more squarely. "What is it about him?"

Minerva paused to consider a moment. "Have you ever known someone who you thought would always be there, then suddenly he wasn't—but then, somehow, like magic, he reappeared again years later? I was only a kid, but it was like something had been ripped out of me when Raven disappeared. When he died. I'd never had a friend like that, and I never did again. Now, all of a sudden, he's back. Can you imagine what that would feel like?"

Amber shook her head slightly from side to side. "I can't. I've never even had a best friend. Most of the guys I've dated either were intimidated by me or just wanted sex. The guy I married? I thought he was different. Brought me wine on our first date. Called me 'sweetheart.' Threw a surprise party for me when I graduated from med school. All the right things. Then we got married and it was like someone had flipped a switch. All of a sudden, everything was different about him. He wanted me to quit my job, stay home and have four kids! Yeah, he had the number picked out in his head already. I guess I never figured out that all that meticulous crap he did to make me feel special was because he was really a control freak."

"What happened?"

"I divorced his ass. I'm still paying spousal support because I make more than he does. A lot more. I wish he had been one of the guys who'd been intimidated. Would have saved me a lot of trouble—and money!" She laughed.

"At least you seem to have gotten over it," Minerva said.

"Trust me, Sis. You never get over it. It changes who you are. Do you think I'll ever get married again? Not a chance. I want to be myself, not someone else's idea of who I should be."

Minerva understood that. She realized as Amber was speaking that the accident had changed her the same way. She'd never trusted her mother after that—not that Jessica had ever given her a reason to trust her—and she'd withdrawn into herself, shutting out the world for the most part after that. She'd never become close to anyone again, except maybe for Archer, but he'd always been younger: a wide-eyed kid who hadn't learned enough yet to manipulate the people he loved and screw with their trust. Maybe he never would. He had a good heart, and she hoped it would stay that way.

"The accident changed me like that," she said. "But since Raven's come back, everything's starting to change back again."

Amber smiled one of those smiles that seemed full of regret and unspoken envy. "The person my ex was is never coming back. He never was that person. It was all an act."

"Maybe you just need to meet someone who's real in the first place," Minerva said.

"Fat chance of that now. Dead people don't get married or have babies or live happily ever after. I don't think it's possible to *die* happily ever after, is it?"

Minerva thought for a moment. "I don't know. Are you happy now?"

Amber took a moment before answering. "I guess so," she said finally. "I've found a friend I can talk to—that's more than what I had before. So, yeah. Maybe being revived isn't so bad after all. It sure as hell is better than the alternative."

"Yeah."

"But have you ever thought about it?" Amber continued. "You say you and Raven are more than friends, but it's the same with you: You could never get married, have kids, live a 'normal' life."

"You're a skydiving, kickboxing doctor, and you're talking about a 'normal' life? Sorry, but I don't think you're much of an expert there."

Amber laughed again, heartily this time. "Point."

Minerva sipped her tea again. "Look, I know it's not perfect, but he is— at least compared to everyone else I've met." She stopped, then hurriedly added. "No offense."

"Sis, I stopped being offended about the tenth time my ex called me a dirty whore. You want to know what's funny? He was the one sleeping around."

"I don't think Raven would sleep around on me," Minerva said. "I'm just *that* good." She laughed at her own false confidence.

"Well, it's not as though he has much choice. If he ticks you off and you decide to give him the cold shoulder, there's a lot more at stake than a night on the couch."

Minerva set the teacup down in her lap. She'd been happy with her decision to lay off the wine, but suddenly she felt the urge to have another glass. Amber had brought up the very thing that had been itching at the back of her mind for some time and she'd been trying to ignore. It had occurred to her just moments earlier, in the midst of this same conversation, and she'd struggled to force it back down. How dare she bring it up—and in such an offhand way, like it was some kind of a joke? Just because Amber's ex had been an abusive SOB, that didn't mean Raven was, too.

194

"Is that how *you* feel about me?" she shot back. "Better not tick me off, or I'll send you back to the grave where you belong?"

Amber didn't back down. Minerva got the impression that she seldom, if ever, did. "No, I like you. Honestly. But even if I didn't, do you think I'd be going around trying to make you angry? Hell no. There's a little thing called survival instinct involved. Ignore it at your own risk, Sis. I'm being up front with you *because* I like you—and because I don't want to see you get hurt."

"That's nice of you, but I can take care of myself." Minerva hesitated, waiting for Amber to come back at her with something like, *You'd be dead now if I hadn't stuck that needle into your heart,* but she didn't. Instead she put her teacup to her lips and took a long, slow sip.

"Thanks for saving my life," Minerva said at last, breaking the silence.

Amber chuckled. "Thanks for saving mine. I guess that means we're even. But that doesn't mean I'm going to stop worrying about you. You don't get off that easy."

Something skittered through the brush a few feet away from them, and Minerva started. She was still a little jumpy after all she'd been through, and her head didn't feel quite right. Her vision was a little fuzzy at times, and there were moments when the world seemed almost like that crazy place inside Jules' mind, swaying and pulsating at the edge of her awareness— like a little piece of that place had followed her back to the waking world, and she couldn't blame it on the wine this time.

"Something's wrong," Amber said.

Minerva had put her hand to her head in response to a mild spell of dizziness. Having grown up mostly alone, she'd never had much chance to practice hiding things in social situations.

"Just a little dizzy. I'm okay."

"No, you're not," Amber declared. "I was right in the first place. I need to get you somewhere I can examine you thoroughly. I didn't want to scare you, but shooting you up with adrenaline was a last resort. That's because it's not good for you. Really not good. When we do that to restart someone's heart, more than half the time, people end up with brain damage. I'm not kidding, Sis. This is serious."

"I just need a little more of this tea. I'll be fine," Minerva said, getting up and taking a step toward the sliding glass door that led to the kitchen inside the bungalow. But before she could take a second step, she felt her knees buckle—or almost didn't feel it before it happened. She suddenly realized she felt nearly numb below the waist, the way she had before she'd "fixed" her paralysis. She struggled to focus on strengthening them, but before she could concentrate, she found herself sprawled out on the redwood deck.

The world around her was growing more blurry, and her head pounded like a bass drum in a high school band at the Thanksgiving Day parade. The stars overhead whirled around like a pinwheel, and when she tried to focus on Amber, Amber seemed to stretch and contort as though she were made of rubber.

She was dimly aware of Carson opening the glass door and rushing out onto the patio.

Amber was bending over her now, and she felt her fingers at the side of her neck.

"Her pulse is strong, but we have to get her to a hospital. Now."

"We can't chance it," Carson said. "Everyone and their mother's looking for her."

"Would you rather she be dead?" Amber's tone was firm and measured, but furious, as if spoken through gritted teeth. "I know I wouldn't be."

The stars were still swirling, but they started to fade. So did everything else. Minerva tried to focus, but she felt like a drowning castaway who just couldn't hold on to the life preserver any longer.

Within seconds, everything was black.

Sleeping Beauty

Raven half-expected to step back into the world of Hansel and Gretel, but Between had changed a lot since he'd been there last. Maybe it was always changing, or maybe he'd just arrived at a different place than where he'd been last time.

He looked beside him, and there was Jules.

"Told you I'd be right there for you, darling." She grinned. He found it anything but reassuring.

They were on the edge of a small town he'd never seen before. It didn't look like anything he imagined existed in the U.S., except maybe in Vermont or someplace back East. There was an Old World feel to it, like it had been here a very, very long time . . . wherever "here" was. The town was actually more like a village, built across low, green, undulating hills that were also home to pasturelands where sheep and cattle grazed.

"What is this place?" he asked.

Jules shrugged. "I've never seen it before, but if you were thinking about your parents, my guess is you've taken us to wherever it is they are."

"The afterlife?"

"Not exactly. This is Between. The only reason it exists is that you're thinking of the kind of place where they might be—or maybe the kind of place where you'd want to see them."

"So it's just my imagination?"

"No. Not at all. It works here just like it does in the waking world when you revive someone. That person is real, but they depend on you for their existence. Except here, you can work with more than just memories and more than individual people. You can create whole new worlds from your imagination, and other people can visit them. Live in them, even. This is your handiwork, Raven. Invigorating, isn't it?"

They walked down a dirt path that gave way to cobblestones as they passed a few cottages on the outskirts of the village. A yellow Lab scampered out from behind a nearby house and bounded up to greet them.

"Hansel!" Raven exclaimed as the dog reared up on its hind legs and crashed into him with its two front paws, tongue out and straining to reach his face. He remembered naming the dog after a character in his favorite fairy tale—the one that had been re-created during his last visit to Between. It all seemed somehow connected by his own memories.

The dog jumped down and then back up again, dashing around in a circle, pawing at him and barking excitedly. His parents had brought home Hansel for Raven's seventh birthday, and he'd still been barely more than a puppy at the time of the accident. He must have died sometime between then and now—it *had* happened 15 years ago, after all.

Raven had so many questions about how it all worked. What had happened to those years he had missed? How had he emerged from 15 years of oblivion a grown man, with all the qualities of an adult male human, when the last thing he knew, he'd been an eight-year-old boy? It was as though all those years he'd missed had been somehow magically uploaded into his revived brain. As though he'd gone on his first date, graduated from high school, had his first job, gotten into college. . . . Except he had no concrete memories of any of that, just the sense that he'd wound up where he would have been if those things had actually happened.

"Were you remembering your dog just now?" Jules asked.

Raven shook his head. "No, not at all. I hadn't thought of him in ages."

Jules stopped where she was and grabbed hold of Raven's shoulders. "Are you sure?"

"Yeah. Positive. Why?"

Because he shouldn't have been able to revive someone, even a dog, even in Between, without thinking about it. He was a lot more powerful than she'd realized, and she'd have to tread carefully. Still, if he didn't realize the extent of his power, the fact that he *had* that power might make things even easier than she had hoped. She had to think quickly and tell him something that sounded believable but, at the same time, kept him in the dark.

"Remember I told you we're working with a chain?" she said. "Your dog is a link in that chain. He showed up because you were thinking about your parents. That could make our job here a lot simpler than I thought. Maybe we'll even be able to find your grandfather without rooting around inside your parents' minds."

That would be nice.

The Lab had turned away from Raven, scampered off down the road a ways, then stopped in his tracks and turned around to look expectantly at his master. Hansel barked three times, insistently.

"Looks like he wants you to follow him," Jules said.

"Looks like it," he said, then to Hansel: "Where you goin', boy?"

The dog barked twice more, and the moment Raven took a step toward him, he turned away again and started running over the cobblestones. Raven started running, too, with Jules alongside her. Hansel might have been almost twenty years old, but here in Between, he ran almost like a greyhound, skittering around one corner as they struggled to keep up.

The dog stopped finally at the door to a thatched-roof cottage that looked like it didn't have more than four rooms inside. Wagging his tail like a miniature whip, he jumped up and scratched at the door, barking loudly.

After a moment, a woman came to the door. She was scarcely more than five feet tall, her strawberry blond hair in a Dutch boy-style cut and a few freckles dotted her nose and a small section of both cheeks immediately to either side of it. She wore a blank expression at first, but the moment she saw Raven standing there in the doorway, a smile flashed across her face and she ran forward onto the front step, pulling him to her in a bear hug.

"Raven! I never thought I'd see you again!"

Raven squeezed her back, nearly as hard. He had to fight the tears pressing up against the inside of his eyelids as he squeezed them tight. "Mom," he barely more than whispered, relief and excitement mingling in his voice. After a long embrace, he pulled back from her. "I'm so glad you aren't trapped in that crazy house in the woods anymore. I tried to get you out, but . . ."

"No more talk of that," she said. "That wasn't your fault. Besides, we've got that witch right here with us now. She's locked up in the cellar, where she won't do any harm to anyone."

Jules masked the feeling of shock that flooded her like icy water cascading through her veins. She'd disguised herself as Minerva the last time she'd been here, which could only mean that the "witch" in the cellar was . . .

"Now, who have we here?" Sharon Corbet said, turning her attention to Jules. "Quite an attractive young woman you've brought to meet us, now, isn't she?"

"Mom, it's not what . . ."

"Oh, don't be modest, son, I can already see the way she's looking at you."

Jules stuck out her hand, but Sharon ignored it and instead gave her the same kind of hug she'd given Raven—just not quite as long. "Now, what am I to call you?"

"Jules . . . Cavanaugh," she improvised. Another alias to keep track of. Oh, well, it wasn't not like she planned to have any future contact with this insipid little creature.

"Come in, both of you! Your father's napping, but I'll have to go wake him. He won't want to miss this!"

She turned to hurry down the hall, but Raven grabbed her arm. "What do you mean, the witch is locked up in the cellar?"

His mother's face looked regretful but determined. "I'm sorry, dear. I know it sounds cruel, but you saw what she did to us. We couldn't have her just running around loose, could we? There's no telling what she might do if she gets free again."

"How did she wind up here?"

"Just kind of popped in. Literally. One minute, she wasn't here, and the next minute, she was. Looks like she's been through something really nasty, though. She showed up on our sofa just a few minutes before you got here, not even conscious, but tossing and turning like she was having some nightmare. We didn't know what it meant, but after what she did before, we decided not to take any chances. She's down in the cellar, but we're not heartless. There's a bed down there—a soft one, too!—and we put some blankets over her."

"Mom, I need to see her."

Jules put a hand on his shoulder. To anyone watching, like Sharon, it would have seemed like a loving gesture, but Raven felt the insistent warning in her grip. "I don't think that's such a good idea."

His mother quickly chimed in—in agreement. "She's right, dear. You saw what she did to us. We just can't risk it."

"You said she was asleep, Mom. And I told you before, she's not a witch."

His mother looked hurt. "But you *saw* how she had us caged up in there, like animals."

"And now you've got her caged up the same way. She's not the one who did that to you. I know her. She's not like that." He tried to pull free of Jules' grip, but instead she spun him around to face her. Before he knew it, he was staring into her eyes. Within seconds he heard her voice flooding his consciousness, though her lips weren't moving and she wasn't making a sound.

Listen, this wasn't part of our agreement.

I didn't know she would be here.

That doesn't matter. We came to get your parents, and I'll fulfill my end of it, but you have to help me get your grandfather back.

Or what?

You don't want to know the answer to that.

She's the only reason I'm even going along with any of this. I'm not leaving her here.

But I could leave you here. Without me, you can't get back. (She wasn't exactly sure of this, but neither was he.)

Then I'll stay. Minerva's here. My parents are here. It's not like the world back there has much to offer me.

Maybe. But if Minerva's unconscious, you'll fade—even here. And if you fade, all this—everything—disappears: you, your parents, your dog, every-thing. And Minerva will end up dead, too. Is that what you really want? I can keep you from fading if you open yourself to me. I've done it before.

If you open yourself to me. Something clicked inside Raven's brain at that moment, and he realized what had happened. There was a reason Minerva had used the same language Jules was using now—the same reason she had hung back at a distance instead of running up to him and embracing him, the way she would have if she had been . . . Minerva. The same reason his vision of her had been blurred. He had attributed that to his weakened state, but now he understood that hadn't been the problem at all.

Hadn't it been "Minerva" who had encouraged him to go along with whatever Jules proposed, on the pretext of finding out what she was up to? And wouldn't it have been Jules who benefitted most if he were to coop-erate with her plans?

He shut his eyes briefly and turned away from her, shutting off the voice inside his head.

"I'm sorry, Mom, but I have to see her." This time, he succeeded in tearing himself away from Jules' grip and rushed around a corner, where he hoped he would find the cellar door. The cottage was small, so he reasoned he wouldn't have to look far . . . except that the minute he rounded that corner, he came face-to-face with someone blocking his way.

His father.

"I can't let you go in there, son," he said, a look of concern etched on his face. Just beneath that concern, however, was an expression of just mildly suppressed joy. He stepped forward and wrapped his arms around his son, embracing him tightly. "It's great to see you, Raven. About time you came to visit your parents."

Raven pulled back. "It's great to see you, too, Dad, but if you don't let me get into that cellar, we won't have much time together. I need to get down there."

"Son, I . . ."

"Sorry, Dad, but I don't have time to argue this." Putting out his right hand, he thrust his way forward, wedging his way past his father with such force that the older man stumbled sideways.

"Raven!"

Pulling open the door to the stairwell, he pushed his way through and nearly tripped as the stairs started sooner than he could see in the dim light, which vanished altogether a couple of feet in. He groped for a light switch but found none and began feeling his way along the wall as he descended into the pitch black. It smelled stale down here. How could his parents have possibly confined Minerva to this place? Except they didn't know it was Minerva. They thought it was some witch—who was really Jules . . . who was right behind him.

"Raven, come back here!" she shouted, but she couldn't see any better than he could in the darkness and couldn't move any faster on the staircase, either. Which isn't to say she wasn't trying. Raven had taken just four or five more steps when he heard a commotion behind him: She'd tripped on the stairs and stumbled. Raven half expected her to come crashing down onto him, but instead he just heard a choice expletive, the sound of fabric ripping and a second expletive as he continued forward . . . slamming into a second door at the foot of the steps, which he hadn't seen in the darkness.

How the hell didn't I know there was a door here if I created this place?

He let go an expletive of his own, ignored the throbbing in the knee he'd banged into the hardwood door, and fumbled around in the darkness searching for the knob. Finding it, he turned, and the door opened easily inward. He slipped through and, in a single motion, turned and flung it shut behind him. There was a little light down here, filtering in from a small vent high on the rear wall, and he was able to see that the door was equipped with a wooden bolt that he slid quickly into place behind him.

A moment later, he heard Jules pounding on the door, then the sound of his parents' voices.

He ignored them as he saw Minerva curled up on a bed in the far corner of a surprisingly large cellar, her body still but her breathing labored.

"Minerva," he whispered, kneeling down beside her, but she didn't respond.

First Hansel and Gretel. Now Snow White. Or was it Sleeping Beauty? He always got those two confused. One thing that was clear in his mind is how beautiful Minerva was. It wasn't that he hadn't noticed before, but having been away from her these past few days, the impression she made was even stronger.

Well, if the prince awakened Sleeping Beauty with a kiss, I guess it can't hurt for me to try.

He bent over and kissed her gently on the lips, his mouth lingering on hers as much for the sweetness of being able to touch her again as in the hope that she might awaken. He drew back, then bent over and kissed her a second time for good measure, but when he looked again at her, nothing had changed. She remained still, her breaths slow and shallow, until . . ."

"Raven."

When she said his name, his heart quickened, but he could tell she wasn't responding to his presence. She was detached, as if in a dream. But if she'd spoken his name, that meant one thing: She was thinking about him. And if she was thinking about him, even in slumber, there was hope. Jules had been wrong: He didn't have to worry that she might forget him. Even in her present state, she was still remembering.

He leaned over and whispered in her ear. "I love you, Min," he said softly. "Please come back to me."

She didn't answer, so he put his head on her chest and listened to her heart. As long as it was still beating, he had hope.

Emergency

Amber all but ran into the emergency room at Serendipity Medical Center, pushing an unconscious Minerva on a wheelchair as Carson held the swinging door open.

An attendant at the main station looked up from her clipboard and demanded, "Who are you?"

"I'm a doctor, that's who I am. This is an emergency room, right? Well, here's an emergency for you!"

"I don't care who you are. You've still got to check in and wait for a bed. We don't have anything open just now, but . . . wait, I know you. You're Dr. Hardin . . . "

"Hardin-Torres. That's right." Amber stopped short of addressing the woman by name, because she honestly didn't remember it. She'd worked at West Hills on call several times and knew a lot of the staffers here, but not well. She looked at the name tag on the woman's white uniform and added, belatedly, "Shirley."

"They said you were dead," the woman named Shirley said. "Your face is all over the news."

"I don't care who's saying what about me or why," Amber snapped. "I have a patient here who needs attention now. Don't worry about alerting a physician. I can supervise. But I need access to some diagnostic equipment. I need to find out what's happening inside her head."

"Is she stable?"

"For now, but . . ."

"Then you'll have to wait in line, doctor. We're full up, and I've got a gunshot wound, a cardiac arrest, and a severe asthma attack here ahead of you."

Amber thought about arguing with her, but she knew it wouldn't do any good. She wheeled Minerva over beside a row of contoured plastic chairs connected to several others by a metal bar running underneath them. The lot of them looked like they'd been there since the 1960s. Fortunately, the one at the end was vacant—the others weren't. The attendant hadn't been kidding about the ER being busy. The sea of some forty people was producing a cacophony of noises from babies crying to feverish patients moaning to the swish-swish of a mop moving back and forth over the linoleum floor as an orderly cleaned up something just spilled there. Or dropped. Or . . .

It had been a good thing she kept a wheelchair at her bungalow. She'd taken her grandmother there once, years ago, after a stroke, and it had been left there after Grandma Grace had been taken to the hospital by ambulance that last time. Amber remembered Minerva telling her about how she'd been in a wheelchair for fifteen years before regaining the use of her legs; how sadly ironic that she was in a wheelchair again now.

A tall man with straight brown hair parted to one side and a boyish face breezed through the double doors at the end of the hallway.

Amber recognized him immediately and saw that he was heading straight for her.

Great. Henry Marshall. He'd been an intern when she was a visiting physician a couple of years back, and he'd always tried overly hard to impress her. He had even gone as far as to ask her out once. She'd turned him down—even though he had one of those infectious British accents and even though he had invited her to a paintball tournament. It was something she had always wanted to try. Just not with a guy who had a crush on her, no matter how cute he might be. She simply wasn't interested in getting involved with a guy again. Not now. Maybe not ever.

"Dr. Hardin-Torres." His greeting was formal, as was his bearing, but there was just a hint of hopeful familiarity in his tone. "I didn't expect to see you here. Do you know that everyone's been saying . . .?"

She put an index finger to her lips and looked around furtively, then flashed him a cautionary glare. "Yes. I know. And I would appreciate you *not* drawing attention to me. I have a patient here who needs help."

Marshall's eyes shifted quickly from her to Minerva, and Amber saw his eyes widen just perceptibly in recognition. She waited for him to blurt out something about Minerva's face being all over the news—and that everyone was out looking for her. But he didn't. Instead, he pursed his lips for a moment, then relaxed and knelt down in front of Minerva. "Do you have a diagnosis?"

"No," Amber said. "She's stable, but she won't wake up."

Marshall looked over at her. "Is she catatonic?"

Amber shook her head. "Look closer. At her eyes."

He did—and noticed they were moving back and forth underneath her eyelids. She was in the midst of a REM sleep cycle. He snapped his fingers in front of her face but got no response, then placed two fingers on her wrist to check her pulse. Her heart rate was slower than he would have liked.

"I'd like to run some tests."

That's what we're here for, Sherlock. But Amber didn't say that. She needed his help, and that British accent nearly made up for him stating the obvious. "Thank you, Henry. I'm really worried about her."

"I don't blame you." The doctor stood up and called for an orderly. "We need to take her upstairs," he told a short blond woman who arrived with a gurney. She was accompanied by a man in a white nurse's uniform with a gaunt face and short-cropped hair that was graying at the temples. "I want a private room for her, and we need to get her set up in imaging as soon as possible."

Amber mouthed the words "thank you" again. Private rooms were always at a premium here, and she knew he had called for one to reduce the chances that someone might recognize Minerva. If someone did, all hell would probably break loose, and with all the publicity recently, chances are someone would. He was on her side.

"We need to admit her first," the nurse said.

But Marshall shook his head. "There isn't time. I need to get her tested immediately; until then, she's under my personal care."

The nurse hesitated, then nodded and helped Marshall transfer Minerva to the gurney.

"I'll go with you," Amber said. And when the nurse responded with a questioning look, Marshall replied, "Don't worry. She's a doctor."

The nurse nodded again, and they made their way to an elevator that took them to the third floor.

It was then that Amber realized Carson hadn't followed them. In fact, she didn't recall having seen him since they'd entered the hospital.

"Did you see where my friend went?" she asked Marshall.

"No." He shook his head. "The minute you arrived, he went right back out the door."

Cellar

The heavy, dank air of the cellar seemed to press in on Raven. His parents and Jules had stopped banging on the door, but that offered him little comfort: Who knew what sort of lies she might be telling them out there? Now that he knew what she'd done—somehow getting him to believe she was Minerva—he had no idea what she was capable of doing. He only knew that she needed him, or thought she did, to bring back his grandfather. Why she wanted him to do so was a mystery; he'd never known the man and wasn't even related to him by blood (he was adopted, after all). What use could he possibly be to her?

Looking around, he noticed the cellar was littered with a peculiar array of items. There was an old Parka Cola lamp with a grinning, politically incorrect Inuit face that looked like something from the 1960s. A few cardboard boxes had been stacked against the wall in a small recess just the right size to contain them; a layer of dust had settled over them, as though they had been undisturbed for years. But if Raven himself had just created this place . . . nothing quite made sense here. Perhaps it was just the way he imagined his parents' home might be in the afterlife, and the dust, like everything else, was a projection of his own subconscious.

On the other hand, perhaps it was real. What if he'd summoned it here from the afterlife along with his parents?

It was confusing, this Between.

Light from the tiny vent up near the ceiling filtered its way down through the heavy air and fell on an old, nearly antique desk just below it. Raven walked over to it and tested the rolltop, which stuck at first, then yielded as he pulled at it more insistently, almost flying up amid a swirling cascade of dust that made him cough.

Inside he found an array of papers that appeared to have been shoved inside almost randomly by someone who couldn't be bothered to organize them.

Raven smiled. He remembered his father's impatience with that sort of thing. The receipt for an old stereo. A bank statement. He picked up a scrap of paper with a scrawled phone number he didn't recognize, almost discarded it, then at the last minute decided to put it in his pocket. Then he saw an envelope lying half-propped up against the back of the compartment. Reaching in, he slipped his index finger beneath the creased fold and opened it. Inside was a card, red like the envelope, embossed with gold lettering that read, "For my wife on our wedding day." Before he could look inside, a folded piece of paper fell out.

Raven set the card aside and opened the paper.

On it were written these words:

> I love you as a friend
> I cherish you, my lover
> I love the treasures found
> In every secret I discover
>
> Of your heart and of your essence
> Of your spirit and your dreams
> Crashing in on me like thunder
> From a desert storm that seems
>
> A raging, swirling, mesmerizing
> Echo of your soul
> That, whene'er I find the source of it,
> I know will make me whole
>
> I loved you from a distance
> I love you as a child
> Loves all things when first he sees them
> Wholly innocent and wild
>
> A miracle believed in
> Is a miracle come true
> A moment out of timelessness
> A moment spent with you

Raven looked at the card again, but could find no signature. A wedding day gift to his mother? But the words on the paper inside didn't seem like something his father would have written. He'd always been a romantic, but he had never been comfortable writing things down. Perhaps he'd copied them from some poem he'd found in an old book somewhere. Wherever they'd come from, Raven didn't want to risk losing them if this place went up in smoke once he left; he folded the paper and put it in his pocket, alongside the piece with the phone number.

Then he walked back over to where Minerva was sleeping and sat down on the foot of her bed. Her breathing was shallow but regular, and her eyes were moving rapidly in dream state.

What could those dreams be?

"You can't stay in there forever, darling."

Raven's head snapped around and he looked up to see Jules' face staring down at him through the vent.

She was the last person he wanted to see right now.

In that moment, a curtain he hadn't noticed before fell across the vent, and what light there was in the room vanished.

Traffic

"Damn traffic!"

Carson slammed his fists against the steering wheel—not that it did any good. Traffic on eastbound 134 was total gridlock, and this time there wasn't any accident on the freeway. It was just your typical L.A. area congestion, amped up a few notches.

Something had occurred to him when he'd been standing at the doorway to the emergency room at Serendipity Medical Center. It hadn't clicked right away when Minerva had mentioned Glendale, but memory was a funny thing. Sometimes, something could slip right by you and then, out of the blue, come back like a boomerang and smack you in the face. At least that's how it worked if you didn't have a photographic memory like Minerva's. There were times Carson wished he'd been blessed with that gift, but most of the time, he wanted no part of it. He preferred to rely on his wits, his training, and, when necessary, his Baby Glock.

His memory was good enough when it needed to be. Like now. There had been an assignment a few years back when he'd been set up in a Glendale penthouse suite. It had been the perfect vantage point from which to monitor the comings and goings of a suspicious character the FIN wanted to flush out from a terrorist group plotting to blow up the L.A. library building. The operation had been a bust: The guy in question had turned out to be a member of the Sikh faith attending a comparative religion series at the local mosque, and someone at headquarters had confused the imam there with a radical activist because they had the same name.

Sometimes, the FIN was clueless. Sometimes, it was built on nothing more than hunches and longshots—like the hunch Carson was following now. But hunches could be better than nothing when lives were at stake. If a hunch was all you had, you owed it to yourself and the people who were depending on you to at least investigate it. Chances are, the penthouse he remembered *wasn't* the place Jules had chosen to take Raven, but the sooner he got there, the sooner he'd find out, and he didn't know how much time he had. He'd taken the car, and what if Amber got finished with Minerva before he got back? With any luck, dealing with Jules would help that situation, too.

Carson just tried to ignore the nagging feeling that dealing with Jules wouldn't be easy. Even with all his expertise, she had something he didn't.

The gift.

Traffic crawled a few feet forward, then stopped again.

Glendale was just a few miles up the road, but Carson had a feeling it was going to be a long trip.

Neurogenesis

"I've never seen anything like this before." Henry showed Amber the results of the EEG he had ordered on Minerva. There'd been no change in her status—she was still unconscious, and she still seemed to be in a state of REM sleep. It was as though she were stuck there, unable to follow the normal pattern into deep sleep or to emerge from her slumber into waking.

"Neurogenesis," Amber said. "It looks as though her brain is growing new neurons in the hippocampus."

Henry nodded. "That's not what's unusual," he said. "It's the *rate* at which they're being generated. That shot of adrenaline you gave her shouldn't be causing anything like this."

"No, it shouldn't," Amber agreed. "If anything, I was worried it might cause long-term brain damage. But who knows? She's a unique individual. Maybe her physiology reacted differently. Adrenaline's meant to accelerate blood flow; maybe it accelerated something else in her, too. Who knows? Or maybe it has nothing to do with that."

"And what makes her any different than anyone else? I need to know, if I'm going to be able to treat her."

Oops. Amber hadn't meant to let that slip. The last thing she needed was questions about Minerva—which might lead to questions about her. Henry had covered for them so far, but she didn't know him well enough to trust him on this.

"I don't need you to treat her," she snapped. "I just needed help with the tests. I can take it from here, thanks."

"Oh, really?" He took a step back, stared at her and threw up his arms dramatically . . . in the process knocking away the stethoscope around his neck so it went flying. He ignored it. "You come in here, dragging along an unconscious patient exhibiting unheard-of symptoms and you think you can solve it all yourself?"

"Well . . ."

He pulled her aside and shut the door to the room. In a low voice, he said, "I understand people are out looking for this woman. They say you died and she brought you back to life, but that now you're dead again. I don't know any more than that, but your secret—whatever it is beyond that—is safe with me. We need to figure out what's wrong with her, and the way I see it, two heads are better than one. Agreed?"

Amber looked him up and down. From his demeanor, he seemed sincere, and he did have a point. "You dropped your stethoscope," she said, then paused. "And as much as I hate to admit it, you're right. I'll take whatever help I can get on this one."

Henry bent over and retrieved the stethoscope, then shook it playfully at her as he stood up again. "That's not exactly a ringing endorsement, but I'll take it." He smiled.

That's good, she told herself, *because it's all you're going to get.*

Visitor

A flash of light slashed through the darkness like a starburst, and Raven staggered back a step.

"You think you can keep me out of here with a piece of flimsy cloth?" Jules demanded, pointing up at the curtain that still hung across the vent.

"I didn't . . ."

"Don't give me that!" she shouted. "This is your world, your creation. You can change the rules here. Don't play coy with me. I know you've figured that much out at least."

In truth, he hadn't even considered that possibility. He'd been too busy worrying about Minerva. But he was grateful for the information.

"But don't think it means you can go back on our agreement, darling," she said, her tone harsher than he had heard it in some time. "I know things about the Between you couldn't even begin to imagine, so if you even consider for a moment backing out on our deal, I'll make you regret it for the rest of what will be a very, very short existence."

Raven should have been scared. He had no idea at all what she was capable of, but instead, all he could think about was Minerva. She couldn't just continue to sleep like this forever. She would need to eat. . . . Did people even eat here? And if they did, was the food real? Or was it just some empty form of nourishment that did nothing to sustain you in the waking world? He didn't know how or why Minerva had been transported here, but he knew he had to get her back. Somehow. He couldn't let Jules get in the way of that. Perhaps it was best to play nice with her for the time being, get her what she wanted as quickly as possible so he could figure out how to save Minerva.

"What do you want me to do?" he asked.

Before she could answer, however, there was more pounding on the cellar door.

His parents.

Well, there was no sense in trying to keep them out any longer. He went over to the vent, climbed up on a chair and pulled aside the dusty curtain to let in some light again—flashing a challenging look back at Jules to put a point on the fact that he'd done so without using his gift. He still wasn't sure he'd done so the first time or, even if he had, how he'd accomplished it.

"Impressive," Jules said sarcastically.

Raven climbed down and unbolted the door at the bottom of the cellar, then opened it to let in just enough light for his adjusted eyesight to make out the steps. Then he climbed to the top and opened the main, outer door.

A look of relief washed over his mother's face when she saw him, but she didn't step forward to greet him, waiting instead until he was out of the cellar to throw her arms around him in a big, mama-bear hug.

"Did she hurt you?" she asked, pulling back to examine him closely, her eyes taking in every contour of his face, then running up and down his body to make sure everything seemed well.

"I'm fine, Mom," Raven said. "She's just down there sleeping."

She gave him a half-sidelong glance, the kind that said, *Are you sure? I don't quite know whether to believe you.*

"Mom, I know you think she's a witch, and I know what you think she did to you, but—look, I can't explain it all now, but I love her, okay? I mean, I really love her." It was strange how natural it felt to say it, although he realized he hadn't even told her yet.

Sharon Corbet stared straight at him, hands on her hips. "She's a witch," she said emphatically. "She's bewitched you, she has."

"Mom, there are no such things as witches." He wasn't sure whether he was telling the truth about that or not. Jules sure came as close to being one as anybody he'd seen. "Did you look at her closely?"

Jimmy Corbet broke in, making no attempt to hide the resentment in his voice. "No, son, we didn't have a chance to get a good look at her when we were tied up on that table!"

Raven was losing patience. Of course, they'd had a better chance to look at her since she'd turned up on their doorstep—or in their living room, or wherever it was she'd made her entrance. He didn't want to be hard on his parents, but he didn't have time to argue about how they should be treating Minerva.

"Well, if you two ever get enough courage to go down there and look at the woman sleeping on that bed down there, you might just recognize her. When she was a little girl, you used to take us everywhere together. Minerva Rus. I tried to tell you that before, back at that gingerbread house or whatever it was. Don't tell me you can't even remember her name."

His father looked chagrined, but his expression softened a bit, and his mother's certainty gave way to doubt. "I remember Minerva," she said. "Come to think of it, this girl *does* bear a certain resemblance. . ."

"That's because she *is* Minerva, Mom."

"How did she get all grown up?" his mother asked. "She's changed so much, and it seems like we just saw her yesterday . . ."

"Mom, that's because you and Dad have been dead for fifteen years. A lot has changed. A whole lot."

"Dead? Fifteen years? What are you talking about?" his father said. "I feel as healthy as a horse!"

Jules grabbed his sleeve and pulled his ear down to her mouth, cupping her hand to her lips. "You fool! They don't *know* they're dead. Everything here seems perfectly normal to them. That's how it works in the Between."

Raven's brow furrowed as he pulled back and looked at her. When Minerva had unwittingly revived him with her memories, he'd known immediately that he had been dead. But she'd called him into the waking world; the rules here must be different.

"I mean it feels like that long since I've seen you, that's all," Raven said hurriedly. It was a poor recovery, but he was counting on the fact that most rational people wouldn't even consider believing someone who told them they'd been dead for fifteen years. Even their own son.

His mother stepped forward and hugged him again. "Yes it does," she said, beaming. "It feels like every bit that long and longer. Look at how you've grown up! Maybe you're right. Maybe Minerva grew up, too. But why would she attack us like that."

"Mom . . ."

"Mrs. Corbet, I'm sorry to interrupt, but we have something important we need to ask you," Jules interrupted.

Sharon Corbet's eyes moved from Raven to the red-haired woman.

"If Minerva . . .," she said haltingly, looking back at Raven and then again to Jules. "If she's with Raven, then who are you?"

"Actually, Mrs. Corbet, I'm a private detective."

She's good, Raven thought. *She doesn't miss a beat.*

"Your son hired me to find you, but for something more as well. He wanted me to help reunite your entire family."

"Our entire family?" Jimmy Corbet said. "I don't understand."

"We want to find your grandmother, Mary Lou, and we think she can help us find your grandfather, too."

"I'm sorry, but Mama's been dead a while now."

So have you, Jules thought. This was going to be tricky, but if her hunch was right, she could bring Mary Lou Corbet to them just by getting Jimmy and Sharon to think about her. That's how it seemed to have worked with the dog—he'd just appeared out of nowhere because Raven had been thinking of his parents and, presumably, his parents had been thinking of the dog, wondering where he had run off to. If she were correct, she could forge the next link in the chain here and now. Then she'd be one step closer to her ultimate objective.

Jimmy was still speaking: "I never knew my father, and Mama never talked about him. Every time I asked her, she clammed up tight as a drum. The only thing she ever said about him was, 'It's best you didn't know.'"

Of course, that's what she'd say, Jules thought.

Just then, there was a knock at the door.

Right on time.

"Who could that be?" Sharon asked. "We never get visitors here."

"It's probably your mother, Jimmy," Jules said. "Why don't you go answer it?"

Jimmy went to the door and pulled it open. And sure enough, there in the doorway stood his mother, Mary Lou Corbet.

Tea

She was a slight woman, like Sharon, scarcely more than five feet tall—and she seemed shorter, because she walked slightly hunched over. Her hair, mostly gray, was nonetheless still streaked with traces of orange. The wrinkles etched across her face seemed to have skipped the sides of her eyes, where laugh lines usually formed. Mary Lou Corbet hadn't had much to smile or laugh about in her life, but she had tried to make the best of things. And she had survived, despite all she had been through.

"Mama!" Jimmy couldn't believe what he was seeing.

"Jimmy!" She did smile at that. Seeing him had always made her happy, even if few other things in life had.

Jimmy gave her a hug, then stepped back from the doorway and gestured for her to come inside.

"I'll put on some tea," Sharon said.

While Sharon went to the kitchen, the rest of them moved to the front room; Jules took hold of Raven's arm and directed him to a loveseat next to her, while Jimmy sat in an old recliner and Mary Lou took a padded, gold, straight-back chair that looked like something straight out of Victorian England.

"It's so good to meet you, Mrs. Corbet," Jules said to Mary Lou, who was eyeing her suspiciously.

"And you are . . . ?"

"Just a friend who's helping your grandson," Jules put in.

Sitting next to her like this was making Raven queasy, and he couldn't stop thinking about Minerva. "If you'll excuse me, I need to go check on someone."

Jules grabbed his wrist discreetly and locked onto it so hard he thought she was trying to break it. Maybe she was. She cupped a hand to his ear and whispered emphatically: "The sooner you fulfill your end of the agreement, the sooner you can go check on that precious waif of yours. In the meantime, you're going to stay right here until I say otherwise, got it?"

Raven acted like he didn't hear what she'd said, wrenched his wrist free of her grip and stood; then, without another word, he moved quickly toward the hallway and disappeared.

A low whistle reached their ears from the kitchen, growing gradually louder until it was cut off abruptly. A moment later, Sharon came in with a tray bearing five teacups with teabags and a pot of near-boiling water.

She looked around her. "Where did Raven go? And that woman?"

The loveseat was empty. Not only had Raven left, but suddenly, Jules just wasn't there.

Mary Lou shrugged. "She was there a moment ago. I don't care for her. There's something odd about her."

"Oh, Mama, she's just trying to help," Sharon said, patting her arm.

Down the hall, Raven was about ready to open the cellar door when Jules appeared out of nowhere in front of him.

He was only startled for a moment; he was getting used to her turning up when she wasn't wanted.

"Nice trick," he said. "Now if you'll get out of my way . . ."

"That's the least of my 'tricks,' as you call them. You have no idea how close you are to getting flung right back into the waking world. And that's if I'm feeling charitable. I could just as easily send you the other way."

"Not if Minerva's still thinking about me."

"And you think I couldn't just pop in there and choke the life out of her?"

Raven said nothing.

"Hadn't thought about that, had you, pretty boy?" She raised a hand and softly patted the side of his face. "There, there. We don't need to quarrel now. I just can't have your attention on her right now. I need you to focus on your parents and help me direct the discussion to your grandfather. We'll both get what we want that way. What's wrong with that?"

He pulled away from her. If only he knew how he had made that curtain fall across the vent in the cellar, he might be able to fight her—maybe lock *her* in that cellar and free Minerva. He tried focusing on the idea, but nothing happened.

"Are you listening to me, pretty boy?"

Raven nodded. He was getting tired of giving in to her like this, but he didn't know of any other choice at this point. Perhaps the best thing to do was just to go along with her and make sure she got what she wanted sooner rather than later. Not that he had any illusions of her keeping up her end of the bargain. But maybe if she got what she wanted, she'd be distracted enough for him to actually do something.

"There they are," Jimmy said as they returned to the living room.

"Who were you checking in on?" Mary Lou asked, taking a sip of her tea.

"Just a friend," Jules said. "She hasn't been feeling well, so she's resting now. Raven's been concerned about her."

"I see."

I don't care whether you believe me or not, you old bag. All I care about is finding that youthful indiscretion of yours.

"Raven, isn't there a question you've been wanting to ask your grandmother?"

Raven shot an angry glance her way. He'd go along with her, but was it really necessary to lead him along like some leashed puppy?

"Yes," he said. "It's so good to see you, Grandmother. Mom and Dad told me so much about you. I never thought I'd actually get the chance to meet you."

Mary Lou's expression softened, and he could see a wistful sadness in her eyes. "Your parents were bringing you home to meet me when something happened. I'm not sure what. But I don't remember anything after that until now."

Just then, there was a shuffling sound at the open window behind the loveseat, and a moment later, Raven saw a blur of orange flash past him out of the corner of his eye. The cat landed deftly on the floor, looked up and saw Mary Lou, then scampered across the floor and bounded into her lap.

"Petrushka!" she exclaimed. "Where did you come from?"

Jules knew exactly where the annoying feline had come from. Her chain theory was working perfectly, but she wanted it to produce a man, not a cat.

Mary Lou started stroking the rotund cat, tickling him behind his ears as he purred loudly enough for everyone else to hear.

"Grandmother, I was wondering," Raven began. "My parents told me so much about you, but they never mentioned anything about my grandfather. I was wondering whether you might be able to tell me about him."

Raven's father sent him a look that was one part confused, three parts annoyed. "Son, I told you," he began, but his mother held up a hand before he could say anything more.

"It's all right, Jimmy," she said. "I've held this in for far too long. It's more than past time that you know the truth. You, Jimmy, and all of you."

Connection

Minerva could hear the sound of muffled voices that seemed to be coming from somewhere in a room above her, and the sound of others that seemed to be right beside her. It was as though she were in two places at once.

She couldn't see anything—everything was dark. But the voices had been with her, coming and going, for a couple of days now, ever since she had lost all other contact with the outside world. She'd heard Raven earlier, but he'd gone away. Still, of course, she hadn't stopped thinking about him. She knew she couldn't. And she couldn't stop thinking about Amber, either. Hers was another of the voices she was hearing, but it seemed to be coming from a second place, nearer in one sense, but farther away in another.

At one point, she had heard her talking to another doctor about her condition. "Neurogenesis" was the word they'd used. Something to do with her brain creating new neurons, they'd said. But what did that mean? Did that account for the faint buzzing sound she seemed to be hearing and the lightheadedness she'd been feeling?

The voices from up above her were too faint to make out now, as though they were coming through several walls.

She'd heard Jules at one point, too. What was Jules doing here—wherever "here" was?

Someone had called her a witch. That wasn't anything new. Kids had teased her about her wheelchair and anything else they could think of for years during her childhood. They'd said she was a witch because she had dark hair and kept to herself. *Then why can't I cast a spell and stand up out of this wheelchair?* she'd always thought when they had said that. How ironic that she'd ended up doing exactly that. Maybe she was a witch, after all.

She wondered how she had gotten to where Raven was. She had tried for so long to reach him, but without success. Why now? Perhaps he had drawn her to him the way she'd pulled him into her reality in the first place. He was so close . . . what if she were to try to reach him now? Maybe he could free her from this dark place that seemed like a prison.

Raven. Can you feel me?

Nothing.

She felt like crying, he was so close—but she wasn't going to give up that easily.

Raven, please answer me. She visualized him in her mind, every memory of him at every point of their time together, as children first and now, since she'd revived him.

Minerva? Is that you?

Yes! He'd heard her. Or felt her. Or become aware of her in some way. She felt her heart starting to beat faster, but the darkness around her was still as dark as ever.

Where are we?

In the Between. My parents locked you in their cellar—don't ask, it's a long story. Jules is here. She's making me help her find my grandfather.

Your grandfather? I don't understand.

Neither do I.

Raven, I can barely hear voices, but they're very faint and I can't understand what's being said.

Raven thought for a moment. If he could create a chain to find his grandmother, perhaps he could forge a different kind of chain to help Minerva hear. Maybe he hadn't figured out how to use his control over this place to stop Jules—yet—but maybe he could make this much happen. He concentrated.

There! He could feel something happening, as though a part of Minerva's consciousness was being pulled into him. It felt like everything he had felt before with her, only amplified, almost like the time when they had made love.

Raven! Thank you! It's becoming clearer.

"I met your grandfather when we were both in our twenties. I was visiting Germany at the time, on an extended holiday with my parents. I was very young—I'd just turned 18—and it was still three years before the

United States had entered the war. The Nazis were making rumblings about going to war, but my parents were pacifists: They were convinced that the Germans would 'listen to reason' and there was nothing to worry about.

"As most children of that age do, I shared my parents' beliefs. I wasn't too aware of what was going on in the world, and to the extent that I was, their naivete rubbed off on me. I was more concerned with the romantic notion of falling in love and the dream I'd had since a little girl of becoming a nurse. Call me an unliberated woman, but girls from South Carolina just didn't grow up to be doctors back then.

"Anyway, you can imagine how excited I was when I met your grandfather. He was young and dashing, with a thick crop of dark hair and a smile that would have been perfect if not for that gap in his teeth. To me, it only made him seem cuter. We met at a dance in Frankfurt, and I suppose you could say he swept me off my feet. He had just joined the SS, but he was most excited about having just become a doctor. We talked for hours about life, medicine, and the German dream of building a new utopia. He even told me how much he loved children. He really opened up to me, even though he was nine or ten years older than I was. . . "

Jules looked briefly toward the door, trying to conceal her nervousness. With this the focus so clearly on Raven's grandfather, he should have shown up by now. Even the old lady's damned cat had made an appearance. Something was wrong.

She cast a sidelong glance at Raven. He appeared deep in concentration, which should have been a good sign . . . unless he was focusing on something other than his grandmother's words. What else could he be thinking about?

Raven felt an elbow in his ribs, jarring his connection with Minerva.

Trying to ignore Jules, he fought against losing the link.

How did you get here, Min? Do you have any idea?

I'm not sure. I haven't felt right ever since Amber brought me back . . .

Amber?

She kind of brought me back from the dead.

Wait. This Amber revived you?

Not exactly. Actually, I revived her. Before that. I'll tell you all about it someday. But I'm not sure that's what brought me here. I think maybe you pulled me here, the way I brought you to me in the beginning. I don't know, but . . .

Raven wondered. Maybe, if she'd been brought back from the dead somehow—even if she hadn't technically been revived—he had the same effect on her now that she had on him: an ability to somehow summon her just by thinking about her. But if he had brought her here, somehow pulled her into this place he had created in the Between, that meant he might be able to send her back.

Min, you don't belong here. It's too dangerous. I'm going to try something.

What?

I'm going to try to stop thinking about you. Just long enough to get you out of here.

Minerva felt a frustration welling up inside her. I'm fine, Raven. I can take care of myself.

Why did she always have to say that? He had to admit that most of the time, it was true. But . . . *Do you realize Jules threatened to choke you to death? You can't very well defend yourself if you can't wake up!*

Raven . . .

Sorry, Min. I've got to do this. You'll thank me for it later.

Raven!

Awake

"She's awake!"

Amber had fallen asleep in a cold, hard molded plastic chair beside Minerva's bed in the private room where they'd taken her after the tests. She felt Henry shaking her as she opened her eyes, struggling to focus through the bleariness as her vision settled on Minerva, who was sitting up in bed, eating a bowl of vanilla ice cream. She looked perfectly healthy, as if nothing had ever happened.

"It's about time you woke up, Doctor Snoozyhead," Minerva said, frowning. "Will you tell your friend here to please discharge me so we can get to Glendale and stop Jules before she revives some Nazi nutjob from World War II?"

"What?" Amber shook her head vigorously, trying to shake the cobwebs loose as she sat fully upright.

"Well, I'm not exactly *sure* that's what's going on. Raven kicked me out of there before I could find out for sure what was going on, but before he did, I heard his dead grandmother talking about a childhood crush on an SS officer, and Jules was there listening to the whole thing, so that can't be a good combination."

"Did you say Raven 'kicked you out?'" Amber said at the same time Henry spewed, "Did you say, 'His dead grandmother?'"

Minerva shook her ice cream spoon at Henry. "Welcome to my world, Doctor Nunya." Then she turned back to Amber. "As near as I can figure, when you brought me back with that shot of adrenaline, it opened a door or something for Raven to pull me into the Between. Not that he meant to do it. When he realized it, he said it was too dangerous for me there and kicked me back here. I tried to tell him I could take care of myself, but . . ."

She noticed Dr. Nunya—or Dr. Marshall (that's what his name tag said)—was staring at her through squinty eyes, shaking his head slowly back and forth. "I'm not sure what the bloody blue blazes you're talking about," he said, "but it sounds like whatever trauma you've been through has done a number on that noggin of yours. Until I'm sure you're all right, I'm afraid I can't, in good conscience, discharge you."

Amber cleared her throat to get his attention. "I'm sorry, Dr. Nunya" (she couldn't resist repeating Minerva's name for him—it was just too perfect), "but I'm afraid you couldn't discharge her even if you wanted to, considering she was never formally admitted in the first place. Remember?"

Henry scowled back at her. "Fine," he said. "If you want to thank me for helping you by putting your patient's health in jeopardy because we don't even know what's wrong with her yet, that's your prerogative."

Amber nodded a self-satisfied nod and was about to say, "Thank you," when her colleague produced a syringe he'd been keeping in the pocket of his smock.

"I'm afraid," he said to Minerva, "we're going to have to keep you here for a little while." And as she watched, he squeezed a few drops of fluid from the top of the syringe, took hold of her left arm, sanitized it with a cold, wet ball of cotton, and plunged the needle into her flesh.

"Hey! What's that?" Minerva demanded.

"Just a little something to put you out for a while so we can make sure you stay put until we have an actual diagnosis," Henry said.

"What the hell do you think you're doing to my patient?" Amber seethed.

"Don't you mean, 'our patient'?"

"Whatever, Doctor Stupidass. Did it ever occur to you that sedating a patient who's just come out of a coma isn't the world's most brilliant idea?"

"I thought we agreed she wasn't in a coma."

"Again. Whatever. The point is, *what happens if we can't bring her out of it?*"

Minerva felt her eyelids getting heavy and focused her energy on trying to keep them open. But the more she tried, the harder it got. Before long, her whole body felt heavy, and a feeling somewhere between relaxation and drowsiness seemed to permeate her. The ice cream bowl tipped onto her lap, and she was vaguely aware of a cold sensation trickling down the side of her upper thigh.

Someday, she thought, she was going to prove to all these idiots that she really *could* take care of herself.

In the meantime, though . . . sleep.

Crosshairs

Carson took his position and peered out from behind the low concrete barrier that kept people from falling off the roof of the Reeves-Cathcart Office Building. He opened a briefcase that he'd carried up twenty flights of stairs and began rapidly assembling a Vanquish .308 sniper rifle that he'd picked up from a hiding place in the basement of an abandoned service station off San Fernando Road. He had hiding places—stocked with a variety of things he had hidden—throughout the region, so he could properly equip himself at short notice as various needs arose.

The need for a sniper rifle didn't arise often. He hadn't taken many assignments like this since he had terminated Mary Lou Corbet. But each time he did, he thought back to the Corbet mission, and each time it got a little harder for him to pull the trigger—even when he knew the world would be a lot better off without the scum on the other end of his sights.

This wasn't a mission; he was doing this on his own, and if anything, that made it harder. There was no one to hold accountable except himself, but then, that was the way he wanted it. Orders or not, he'd lost a lot of sleep over Operation Death Trap, and while it might be ironic to find redemption through another successful hit, that didn't stop him from pursuing it. Besides, there was more than redemption at stake here. There were lives: If his instincts were right, a whole lot of lives. Steeling himself, he played back his favorite movie quote in his head: "The needs of the many outweigh the needs of the few. Or the one."

It helped that, this case, the "one" in question was a sociopath who needed to be stopped.

Methodically, he assembled the pieces. He'd locked the door to the stairwell behind him, so he was in no hurry. Better to do this right than to rush things and screw it all up. One good, clean shot was all he would need. He wasn't in the habit of missing, and he could see his target, even without the aid of the viewfinder, inside the window on the penthouse across and down a little from where he'd stationed himself.

Her captive was there, too, but neither one of them was moving, and with the exception of a few fronds from a potted plant, it appeared he could easily get off a clean shot from here with an unimpeded line of fire. Just to make sure, he scooted a couple of feet to his left, eliminating the plant from the equation altogether.

It was late afternoon, and the sun's reflection in the window didn't help matters, but the angle wasn't yet so severe that the glare would force him to squint. He had another ten or fifteen minutes before it would get to that point, and he wouldn't need nearly that long.

The weapon was almost fully assembled now. He clicked the last piece into place, tested it to be sure everything was secure and shouldered it.

It felt good there. Natural. He was sure of himself as he looked through the scope, finding his target. Then he felt that usual pang of doubt creeping up from the center of his chest and, with an effort, squelched it. This was the right thing to do. The only thing to do.

He heard a flock of seagulls squawking nearby as he waited there, seemingly for an eternity, balancing the weapon until he was certain the target had been acquired, that the aim was right, that the human head was fixed at the center of the crosshairs.

Then, with a slow, steady motion, he squeezed the trigger.

The rifle fired, and the seagulls, startled, flew away.

Geschenk

It had taken considerable effort, but Raven had forced himself to pivot his attention entirely away from Minerva and focus intently on the conversation in front of him.

". . . Because my parents didn't approve, I would sneak off to see him. He told me about some research he was doing—he said Hitler wanted to create a 'master race' and he had dreams of helping to make that happen. I wasn't too thrilled with the sound of that, let me tell you, but he seemed so excited about the idea of improving mankind. He quoted the Hippocratic oath to me. 'I want to harness our true potential for our highest good,' he would say."

Jules looked back at the door again, then at Raven, who now seemed to be entirely focused on the old woman's story. That was a relief. But the more the woman rambled on, the more obvious it would become to all those present that the man she wanted to show up on the other side of that door wasn't the kind of person anyone would want as a relative. When she got through with the telling, they wouldn't even want him within a hundred miles of this place.

Where is he?

Mary Lou took another sip of her tea and dabbed her mouth with a napkin. Her voice cracked a little as she continued. "He said he believed he knew how to enhance a person's memory through a simple procedure that would accelerate neural growth in part of the brain."

Jimmy Corbet put down his teacup and cleared his throat. "Mama, I think we've heard enough. I'm sorry I ever asked you about this. You don't have to say any more."

But Mary Lou only smiled. "It's all right, son," she said. "I've been holding this in for too long, now, and I thought I'd never have a chance to tell you. It needs to be said."

Her son sat back down, settling uncomfortably into the recliner as he looked at his mother, his expression one part concern and two parts apprehension. He remembered his history classes, and he didn't like where this was going.

Mary Lou continued: "He asked me if I wanted to be part of his experiments, and like a starry-eyed simpleton, I said yes. He took me to a lab and hooked me up to some huge, shiny metal contraption that looked like something out of *Frankenstein*. It was a giant, oval thing with wires sticking out of it that he said would amplify my brainwaves."

"My God. How could you . . .?" Sharon's tone was shocked and frightened, but not judgmental.

Mary Lou lowered her eyes, her voice trembling now. "I started to have second thoughts right then, but I was in love, and I trusted him. He said he would have to put me under, and I let him. When I woke up again, it was two days later, and I felt . . . different."

"Different how?" Raven asked.

"I could remember everything as though it had just happened yesterday. When memories came to me, every color was as vivid as it was if I were seeing it with my eyes. I could hear sounds, too. And I could even feel things as though they were happening to me again. It was maddening. Sometimes, it I could barely tell whether I was living something or reliving it. He said I would get used to it, and I did, but by that time . . ." Her voice trailed off.

"Really, Mama, you don't have to go on."

She raised a hand then picked up the napkin again, but this time, she dabbed at her eyes. "He left me," she said finally. "I was eighteen and already pregnant by this time, but a week or so after the experiment, he stopped taking my calls. I went to his apartment, but there was a guard outside. There'd never been a guard there before, but the man said Josef wouldn't see me."

Jimmy leaned forward, his eyes dark. "Josef? The man you fell in love with—his name was Josef."

Mary Lou averted her eyes again and nodded slightly. "Your father, Jimmy," she said in a voice that was barely above a whisper. "You must think me a monster."

Jimmy got out of his chair and rushed over to where Mary Lou was sitting. Kneeling there in front of her, he took her hand and said gently, "Look at me, Mama."

Mary Lou hesitated, but finally looked at him through glistening eyes.

"He's the monster, Mama. Not you," Jimmy said.

She nodded. "I know." She patted his shoulder and forced a smile. "You're such a good boy, Jimmy. You turned out nothing like him."

Raven saw his father smile back at her, then get up and go back to his seat. He wasn't sure what was happening, but he could see the recognition on his father's face. It was apparent that he knew who his grandfather was, and this knowledge had nothing to do with the fact that he was related to the man. He knew about him some other way, from a well-known reputation, it seemed. But if this man had been a monster, what did Jules want with him?

"What happened then?" he found himself saying.

"I went back home with my parents," she said softly. "What else could I do? It was only after I came back that I realized I was pregnant. In those days, it just wasn't something that happened to good girls. My parents helped me hide it as long as I could and, thankfully, once the war started, most people had better things to do than to worry about who'd had a child out of wedlock." She turned to face Jimmy again. "The important thing was, though, that I loved you. You were always my reason for living after that, Jimmy. You were always the pride of my life."

Raven had never seen his father blush before, but he thought he saw it now, and he also thought he saw that glistening in his grandmother's eyes reflected in her son's.

"Whatever happened to him—my grandfather?" Raven asked.

"After we went back home, I learned that he'd married some woman—I think her name was Eileen. It was only a year after we'd been together, and even though he had rejected me, I was still crushed."

"Irene," Jules said under her breath, without thinking and without realizing anyone could hear her.

"What?" Jimmy said.

Jules smiled her usual disarming smile, but it wasn't as effective as it usually was. "Nothing. Nothing at all," she said. *The name you're thinking of is Irene, bitch.*

Mary Lou, though, hadn't heard her. "I only heard from him once more after that. He sent me a telegram around the holidays in 1950 that said he had survived the war and had left his wife. He told me that his research into memory had gone so well he had been able to 'treat' hundreds of other people the same way he had me. He said people with *Das Geschenk*, as he called it, could use their memories to cure illness and even bring people back from the dead. A few people could do this naturally and had been doing it for centuries, he said. But through his experiments, he said, he could confer *Das Geschenk* on anyone he chose.

"He told me he planned to live forever, and he wanted to reconnect with me. He had always been arrogant, even when I'd known him before, but I thought he'd gone completely round the bend. I threw the telegram away and thought nothing more about it . . . until I discovered I had *Das Geschenk*, as well.

"What does that mean?" Raven asked. "I'm afraid I don't know German."

"The Gift."

That made sense. His parents had told him that his grandmother had urged them to adopt someone with the gift—and that someone had been him—to keep them revived after their death in the crash, just in case something should happen to her. And something *had* happened to her: She'd been killed by an assassin's bullet just after his parents had picked him up in South Africa. The shooter had never been found, and no one had ever figured out a motive. Could it have something to do with the gift?

His grandmother went on to tell them that she'd discovered her ability after her beloved cat, Petrushka, had died. She kept thinking about him, and then one day, shortly after she'd buried him, she woke up from dreaming about him to find him lying by her feet on her bed. At first, she'd thought some stray that looked just like him had wandered in off the street when she wasn't looking, but then she'd spoken his name, and he'd come right up to her, purring and head-butting her. Petrushka had always been one of those strange cats who acted a little like a dog: He almost always came when he was called, his silver name tag going jingle-jangle to announce his arrival.

When she'd looked closer, she'd noticed that the same name tag was still there around his neck, and that it said "Petrushka."

At first, she hadn't understood how it had happened—she had buried him herself. But then she remembered what Josef had written about bringing people back to life. The more she wondered about it, the more she thought there must be something to it.

"And, Jimmy, when you and Sharon died in that awful crash, I knew I had to see whether I could do it again."

Jimmy smiled. "And you did. I love you so much, Mama." He got up again and went over to embrace her.

Just then, a knock came at the door.

Contained

"Is somebody going to answer that?" Jules realized she sounded a little too eager, but with so much at stake, she forgave herself.

"Another visitor?" Sharon said. "My, my! This old house feels like Grand Central Station today."

She got up and headed toward the door, but stopped when her husband grabbed her arm as she passed.

"Let it be," he said, gazing up at her from the recliner, the softness in his eyes belying the firmness in his voice. "How long has it been since we've all been here together, the whole of our family? Truth be told, we never have been. Should we really risk letting someone spoil this moment, Sharon?"

She smiled down at him. "Remember, Papa," she said affectionately, "the last knock at that door was your mother, and the one before that was your son. Who knows what wonderful surprises the universe might have in store for us today?"

Jimmy let go of her arm and nodded, though the look in his eyes was more one of worry than agreement.

"Wait, I'm closer," Jules said, standing quickly. "I'm happy to get it."

Before anyone could object, she strode across the room, lay her hand on the doorknob and turned it, opening the door to reveal . . .

"You!"

She took a step back at the sight of Minerva there on the doorstep, grinning like a Cheshire cat that had caught some canary, then stashed it in some invisible hiding place.

"Surprise," Minerva said in an even tone, maintaining a straight face and doing her best to hide the nerves that were threatening to eat away like termites at her composure. Every time she had encountered Jules before this, she had come out on the short end of things. The last time, she'd been lucky to even survive. But she had known she'd have to face her again sooner or later, and since Amber's doctor friend had decided to put her back to sleep again, she had decided to forget about Glendale. There was no time like the present.

Jules, recovering from her surprise, stepped forward again, so she was no more than two feet away from Minerva. "How dare you!" she spat in a whisper. "Where's Josef?"

"Oh, that fellow with the space between his front teeth I saw coming this way?" Minerva asked. "I pointed him in the right direction: straight back to hell!"

"Liar!"

"What's going on here?" Jimmy stepped up behind her, Raven right beside him.

"Min!" he said.

Jules wheeled around and, before he could react, locked her eyes on his. "I told you what would happen if you went back on our deal," she growled. "I'm afraid this is the last time you'll ever see your beloved parents."

Raven reached out to grab her, but he was too late. The woman had done something that seemed to have frozen him in place. Desperately, he tried to figure out what he had done to make that curtain fall in the cellar, but no matter how he tried to focus, nothing seemed to matter.

"You might have created this little place in the Between, but you've forgotten: I have a lot more experience here than you do, and I can create spaces of my own. Spaces within spaces, if you will. That's where you are now: one of my spaces. And Minerva, before you try doing anything to stop me, you should realize that I can collapse that space—with your baby-faced boyfriend there inside it—with a single thought."

Minerva clenched her jaw. No matter what she tried, Jules always seemed to be one step ahead of her.

Then, suddenly, a thought occurred to her.

"Two can play at that game," she announced, and suddenly, a solid steel cylinder appeared around Jules.

"What are you doing to my house?" Sharon shouted throwing up her hands—including one that still held a teacup, which went flying across the room and shattered against the far wall.

"Sorry," Minerva said, feeling embarrassed and slightly relieved at once. Most of the relief stemmed from the fact that Jules' invisible space hadn't collapsed on Raven, who was once again able to move without being stuck to the floor.

He stepped forward and threw his arms around Minerva, grateful that they were finally back in the same place at the same time—even if the "place" wasn't exactly real—and, for once, both aware of each other.

"Where did you come from?" he asked, between kissing her cheek, her lips, and her forehead. "I thought I sent you back."

"You did. Then someone else sent me back here. Seems no one wants me around these days," she laughed.

Raven noticed his parents were standing about as far away from them as possible, so far away that their backs were nearly pressed up against the farthest possible wall. They doubtless still thought Minerva was a witch, and given the display she'd just put on, he couldn't really blame them. His grandmother didn't seem bothered by any of it. She was still sitting in that gold Victorian chair, fixing the two of them with a look of keen interest that seemed to indicate she was eager to see what would happen next.

"Who's going to clean this up?" Sharon lamented, pointing to the steel cylinder in the center of the room.

It almost sounded comical, and Raven had to keep himself from laughing. "No one's going to have to," he said. "I'm taking you back with me."

"Back?" said Jimmy. "Back where?"

"Back to . . . where I live," he said. But then he stopped himself. That was where Jules had come in. She was the one who knew how to get them back, and she'd promised to do so. But now that she was walled up inside Minerva's prison.

"We've got to get her out of there," he said.

"What? Are you serious?" Minerva said, looking at him like he'd just suggested impounding Santa's sleigh.

"I'm afraid so," he said. "Without her help, I don't have any idea of how to get my parents out of here."

Minerva looked at him askance. "Raven, I have no idea what will happen if I let her out. Every time I've tried to stand up to her before, she's gotten the better of me. I think I just got lucky this time."

"But maybe the two of us together . . ."

Minerva's expression was sober, but doubtful. "Maybe."

"You get on one side, and I'll take the other."

She nodded grimly and positioned herself opposite him, on the other side of the cylinder. "I'll count down from three, then be ready on my signal. Three. Two. One . . . Now!"

The cylinder disappeared, and the two of them waited, legs slightly spread and arms stretched out like a couple of linebackers ready to tackle a running back bursting across the line of scrimmage. But when the cylinder vanished, nothing happened.

Jules was gone.

Rope

Jules awoke to the sound of shattered glass and a burning feeling in her right shoulder. The bullet bored into her flesh for a couple of inches, then exited, leaving a moderately deep but not fatal wound.

Whoever had shot her had actually done her a favor. She'd had no clue about how she was going to escape Minerva's improvised prison, and she was almost as angry at having clued her in about how to create it as she was relieved to be alive.

Almost.

She turned around to look back through the broken glass window and felt a cool breeze waft in from outside. Twilight was approaching, and even if she'd looked in time to see the gunman scurrying away over the rooftop across the way, she wouldn't have been able to tell who it was. She couldn't see the seagulls that had fled at the sound of the gunshot, though if she had, she might have thanked them for throwing the shooter off just enough to keep the bullet from piercing her skull instead of her shoulder. Not that she knew any of that. And not that it mattered who had wielded the weapon. The gunman, at this point, was the least of her worries. It was Minerva she was most concerned about.

Minerva was the one who'd thwarted her plans to revive Josef—and just when she had been so tantalizingly close to bringing it off. Not only would she have been able to call upon his expertise and create a veritable army of the gifted, she would have been able to do it at the expense of the woman who had bedded her husband before she'd married him. The same woman he'd tried to go back to after their divorce. He always thought he was so clever. She'd managed to intercept all his attempts to correspond with Mary Lou Corbet—all except one. And one had been enough to do more damage that she could have imagined.

No, Minerva was her biggest threat. And Raven.

Or maybe not.

Glancing across, she saw Raven was still out like a light—which meant he was probably still in the Between. That meant she had time . . . and leverage: if she could somehow confine him before he popped back to the waking world. Jumping up and doing her best to ignore the searing pain in her shoulder (not to mention the blood dripping from the wound), she ran to the cedar chest and started rummaging through it, tossing one thing after another aside. An old Kolinsky coat. A black velvet cloak. A photo album. A hairbrush. . .

At last she found the rope she was looking for and yanked it out, sending several other items that had been tangled up in it spilling out onto the floor. Picking it up, she scrambled across the room and hurriedly tied him up. One of the many talents she'd picked up in nearly a century of existence on this planet, prolonged as it had been by her former husband's research, was tying a mean constrictor knot. Working quickly but carefully, she bound his hands and feet together behind him with a single length of rope. She stood back and surveyed her handiwork. There was still no sign that he was stirring to consciousness, so she went to the bathroom, opened the medicine cabinet and removed some gauze to bandage her wound.

It hurt like hell, but not as much as losing Josef had hurt that first time. In time, she had come to realize that the gift he had given her was worth far more than his pathetic excuse for romantic love. But she never forgot it when someone wronged her. And she had so been looking forward to reviving him now—so she could use him to accomplish her purpose. She had spent years savoring the prospect of seeing his face when he saw her now as a young, vivacious redhead, instead of that crushed and vulnerable blond daughter of a university professor she had been.

She'd tried to bring him back herself, but she had never been able to succeed. When he had altered her to receive the gift, somehow he had blocked her memory from fixing itself on him. How, she didn't know. It was another reason she craved to get to him. And it was the reason she'd needed someone to help her. When Hiram had refused to cooperate, she'd found Raven, and now that door appeared to be shutting, too.

Not if she could help it.

Chauffeur

When Minerva finally pushed her eyes open, it felt like she was shoving 200-pound boulders away from them. She'd been trying to wake up for the past two hours, but the sedative Henry had given her hadn't worn off sufficiently until exactly this moment. And it couldn't have happened soon enough.

The room was dark, and, this time, Amber was the only person there.

Thank goodness.

"Hey," Amber said when she noticed Minerva stirring.

"Hey,yourself. Listen, we've got to get out of here."

Amber laughed. "Hold your horses. Let's make sure you're okay first."

"The only horses I want at this point are like horsepower, as in the engine of a car that's gonna get us to Glendale."

"I don't think Henry's going to like that," Amber mused.

"And who's gonna tell him?"

Amber raised both hands and waved them slowly back and forth, palms outward, in front of her. "Not me, Sis." She walked over to the bed and put a hand on Minerva's left wrist, checking her pulse. She nodded approvingly. "Strong as an ox."

"Of course I am. Now can you get us out of here?"

"Yep." She tossed Minerva a plastic bag containing her clothes. "Get dressed quick. There's no telling when Henry might be back."

Minerva caught the bag and began rummaging through it as she pushed away the blankets and stood in her hospital gown. "On a first-name basis, are you?"

"Pffft," Amber said, exhaling through pursed lips. "I worked here a few times when he was on duty. He's kinda cute, but too much of a know-it-all. Besides, you *know* I'm not interested in getting involved again."

Minerva raised an eyebrow. "Did I say you were?"

Amber shook her head, flashing an irritated look. "I thought you were in a hurry. Now get changed before he comes back."

She left the room and went out to check the hallway. Visiting hours weren't over just yet, but it was just past dinnertime and pretty quiet. All the food trays had been collected from the patients' rooms, and there was only one orderly in the hallway. In one direction was the nurses' station; in the other were the elevator and the stairwell.

Amber got the orderly's attention and told him to go get some extra towels and a pillow. (It wasn't particularly inventive, but it was the only thing she could think of off the top of her head.) The man disappeared down the hallway toward the nurses' station, and Amber motioned for Minerva to follow her in the opposite direction. Once they were in the elevator, no one had any reason to suspect Minerva was anything other than a visitor leaving the hospital.

No one except Dr. Henry Marshall, who happened to be standing right in front of them when the elevator doors opened on the ground floor.

"Going somewhere?"

"As a matter of fact, we are," Amber shot back. She was in no mood for any delays, and she knew Minerva wasn't, either.

"And how are you going to get there?"

Minerva and Amber looked at each other.

Carson.

Amber hadn't seen him since they'd first entered the building, but in all the excitement, she'd forgotten all about him.

"The gentleman you came in with? I saw him walk out to the parking lot right after he escorted you in. I also saw him get into a vehicle and drive off in rather a hurry. Haven't seen him since. I mean, he *might* be here somewhere. It's not as if I'm spying on him or anything."

Yeah. Right, Amber said to herself.

"But," Henry continued, "I would have thought he'd come looking for you when—or if—he came back, and I haven't seen hide nor hair of him."

"Great," Amber said. "Then I suppose we'll have to hail a taxi."

Henry just shook his head and stared down at his feet, smiling. "You really don't get it, do you, 'Ber. I'm trying to help you here. It just so happens my shift ended a few minutes ago. I'm free as a bird, and I just happen to have a vehicle that I'll place at your disposal—as long as you let me do the driving of course. It's a '65 BMW, and I don't really fancy letting just anyone behind the wheel. You understand, of course."

"Of course," Amber said. She looked at Minerva, who nodded. "I suppose it beats hailing a cab. Okay, Henry, you have yourself a deal. On one condition: You don't get to call me 'Ber." *Yet. Or maybe ever. It sounds like you're just saying it's cold outside.*

"Deal," Henry said, smiling wider. "The jalopy's over here. Just follow me."

Minerva tapped him on the shoulder as they headed to the parking lot. "Thank you," she mouthed when he turned to look at her. And then, speaking up, she said, "Ever hear an old song about not being able to drive 55?"

Henry chuckled. "I think maybe," he said.

She nodded once firmly and just said, "That."

Roadblock

The first sensation Raven felt was the feeling of something coarse restricting any movement in his wrists and ankles.

"Welcome back, darling," Jules said. He looked up at her from the floor, where she'd left him lying on his side, and noticed that one of her shoulders was heavily taped in gauze. Even through it, he could see a crimson spot had stained it badly. If she wasn't still bleeding, it hadn't been stopped for long.

"What happened to you?" he said.

She laughed. "How touching that you're concerned for little old me. Honestly, I really didn't know you cared." Her voice turned suddenly from syrupy sweet to sharper than a freshly forged steel rail spike about to be pounded home. "Too bad you didn't show the same level of concern about *keeping our agreement!*"

He pressed against the ropes but only succeeded in causing rope burn as they gnawed at his flesh.

"I wouldn't bother trying to get out of there," Jules said. "I'm good with knots. Almost as good as I am at some other things. A pity you won't get to learn about that first hand. I had such high hopes for you."

Raven scrunched up his face as if he'd just smelled something putrid.

Hey! Somewhere back in the dim recesses of his mind, he heard the silent voice. *Where are you?*

I'm not sure. A penthouse suite somewhere. She's had me here ever since she moved me out of that dingy warehouse—except for when we went to the Between. I'm all tied up and can't move a muscle. Well, maybe a muscle or two here or there, but no more than that.

Minerva looked at Amber and shook her head. "He doesn't know where he is exactly. Just a penthouse. Somewhere. But we know he's in Glendale."

Before they'd left the Between, Minerva and Raven had made a pact to stay in touch with each other—if they could—once they got back to the mundane world. Somehow it was easier now than it had been before. Whether that was because they'd grown closer or whether it had something to do with what Amber called the neurogenesis in Minerva's brain, they weren't sure. Whatever the reason, the ease with which they connected was a relief . . . and would have been more than that if they hadn't been fighting for their lives. Minerva was worried. If Jules had Raven tied up, that meant he was her hostage. Still. Or again. Whichever way you looked at it, it presented a problem.

Wait, Min, Raven told her. *There's something else: The window to this place has been shattered. It wasn't that way before we went in, but now it's halfway blown out. If you drive around looking for it, maybe you'll be able to see it from the street.*

Henry steered the BMW into the fast lane. The needle on the speedometer edged past 80.

"We'll be looking for a shattered penthouse window. Somewhere," Minerva said.

"That shouldn't be hard to find," Henry said. "Glendale isn't exactly San Francisco. There are a few midlevel high-rises, but they're all mostly in the same area. It shouldn't take me too long."

Henry's eyes flashed to the rearview mirror in time to see red and blue flashing lights twirling a few car lengths back. He eased his foot off the gas, hoping he wasn't the object of the highway patrol's misplaced "affection."

Minerva, who was sitting in the back with Amber, slapped him on the shoulder. "Hey, why are you slowing down?"

"CHP behind us," he said.

"Sooooo, that means you should be speeding up!" Minerva countered. Her tone was part condescension, part rising panic. "We don't have time for this."

"I'm afraid we're going to make time for it, girls."

"Girls?!" Amber growled. Most of the time, Henry's Britishisms were endearing. But the rest of the time, they could be annoying. Or worse.

More lights had appeared behind them. Three cars now, all gaining fast.

Henry moved over to the center lane, then to the right.

"What are you *doing*?!" Minerva shouted. "We've got to get out of here!"

Henry sighed. "I'm sorry, but I'm a law-abiding citizen, and I don't fancy this buggy has enough horses in her to outrun these boys. I'd rather lose a few minutes to a ticket than spend a night or more in jail. Then we'd never get to Glendale." He took the car over onto the shoulder of the freeway and cut the engine.

"Sorry, ladies," (that was a little better, Amber thought) "but I'm here on a visa and I like my job. I don't relish the prospect of being expelled."

The three highway patrol cars that had been tailing them dropped out of traffic and onto the side of the road, two in front of them and one behind. A fourth arrived a few seconds later.

Henry rolled down his window, but the officer approached not with clipboard in hand but with gun drawn—and pointed straight at him.

"You. Get out of the car. Now," he demanded.

"Officer, I . . ."

"Didn't you hear me, Ringo? Nice and slow. Keep your hands where I can see them, *and step out of the vehicle.*

Henry did as he'd been ordered, as another officer moved to the passenger side of the car. "You, too. Both of you. Out of the car and put your hands where I can see them."

Minerva didn't move. If this had happened a couple of weeks ago, it would have been because she was too petrified—and still paralyzed. But now the paralysis was gone, and so was the fear. All that remained was pure, seething anger. She was vaguely aware of the other officer reading Dr. Nunya his rights and saying something about transporting a fugitive from justice. *Would that be me or Amber? Probably both of us,* she thought ruefully.

The officer shined a light into her eyes, but she didn't blink. He couldn't have done her a bigger favor.

As he stared at her, she conjured up a memory of being in the complete darkness that had surrounded her in Raven's parents' cellar. Then she directed it at him.

"Hey! I can't see anything!" he said, dropping the flashlight. "Hey!" he shouted again, and started groping around like some sleepwalking Frankenstein's monster.

"What's wrong, Sergio?" came a concerned voice from the other side of the car. Other officers were exiting their vehicles now. One. Two. Three.

Four. Five of them. This could be a problem. Minerva knew she couldn't force them all to look into her eyes at once. There had to be some other option.

She looked around frantically as she saw two officers escorting Henry—his hands now cuffed behind his back—toward one of the squad cars and usher him unceremoniously into its backseat.

It was a split-second decision. Minerva opened the car door, got out . . . and found herself face to face with the officer who'd run up behind his blinded comrade to offer backup. He drew his gun, held it in both hands out in front of him, and shouted, "Freeze!"

At the same moment, from somewhere behind them, she heard another voice shout, "My baby!"

It was Jessica.

What the hell is she doing here?

Then it clicked: Someone at the hospital must have tipped police that she and Amber had been there, and the police must have notified Jessica. Minerva couldn't fathom the police letting a civilian go out with them to find a "dangerous" fugitive, but then Jessica wasn't just any civilian. She was the most obnoxious, demanding, won't-take-no-for-an-answer individual Minerva had ever known. It looked like she'd followed the cops in her own car.

Minerva wondered whether Jessica had finally decided to start caring about her. What was she getting out of this? That was the question you always had to ask with her, but now was one of those rare occasions when she couldn't find an answer. Maybe she just hated the cops more than she hated her daughter.

You sure picked one helluva time to start caring, Mom. A little late, but I'll take it. I guess.

"Hands up!"

Minerva raised her hands slowly.

"Now, behind your head. No sudden movements!"

"What are you gonna do? Shoot me?" *C'mon Mr. Boy in Blue. Look me in the eyes.*

But he wouldn't. He was looking everywhere except her eyes. *Dammit!*

It was then that Jessica came running up from out of the darkness behind him. "Don't you hurt my daughter, you sonofabitch!" she shouted.

"Mom, I really wouldn't . . ."

"Shut up!" the officer shouted. Minerva couldn't tell whether that was meant for her or for her mother.

She looked around her frantically for some way—any way—out of this. Another officer was opening the other rear door to the BMW and escorting Amber away from the car. She had her hands on her head as well. If only there weren't so many of them and just the one of her. Minerva felt more helpless than she'd been at any time since she'd regained the use of her legs. She *needed* to get to Raven, or who knew what might happen to him? Jules had him tied up, and there was no doubt she'd do far worse to him than that as payback for double-crossing her.

What's happening there? It was Raven.

Umm. We're in a little trouble.

Trouble? What kind?

The kind that wears badges and rides around in black-and-white cars with flashing lights.

Uh oh.

Yeah.

Raven might have been talking to Minerva, but he hadn't taken his eyes off Jules. She'd gone into the kitchen and pulled a very long, very sharp looking knife out of the drawer.

"You do realize you aren't the first person I asked to help me with my mission," she said, holding the knife in front of her and inspecting the blade. "Your friend Minerva met my previous helper, a man named Hiram. He was very stubborn about refusing to help me. I kept giving him second chances, until I finally grew tired of waiting for him. Then I just forgot him, and he faded entirely out of existence. I don't even remember what he looked like now. Did you know I can do that? Forget things on purpose? Oh, yes. Your little princess hasn't a clue about some of the things she might accomplish if she just had the proper . . . expertise. But it takes years of practice to master these things, and I've had those years—and more."

Her tone was turning bitter. The change was gradual, but unmistakable.

"But I'm getting away from the point of this little soliloquy, Raven. And the point is, I kept Hiram around, even though he was stubborn, for a very long time, because at least he was honest with me. At least he never pretended he might be willing to help me, only to stab me in the back." She turned the knife nimbly over in her hand and made a sudden, downward slashing motion at the air. "Like you did."

Raven struggled against the ropes, but without even the faintest hint of success.

Jules knelt down beside him and smiled. Raven imagined that, if a vulture could smile when it saw a lioness take down an antelope, it would look very much like this. He didn't know whether Jules was the lioness or the vulture, or a little bit of both. Right now, it didn't seem to matter much.

"If I were the forgiving type, I might just use this knife to cut you loose, darling," she cooed pressing the side of the cold blade against his cheek. "But I'm afraid I'm not the forgiving type. I don't give anyone a second chance to *BETRAY ME!*" The last two words were shouted in a tone that seemed to cross over into madness, and Raven couldn't help but flinch as she turned the sharp edge of the blade against his cheek, pressing just hard enough to draw a sliver of blood.

"You can't kill me with that," he said, trying to summon up enough nerve to mask the fear he felt just beneath the surface.

Jules laughed almost hysterically. "Do you really think I don't *know* that, idiot? Or that I don't know that you're expendable? If I found you to replace poor, pitiful Hiram, I can find someone to replace you. And while I may not be able to kill a walking corpse, I'm perfectly capable of torturing you. Until I grow tired of it, that is, and send you back to the Between. Or did you forget I was the one who took you there the last time? The next time won't be nearly so pleasant. You see, you won't be going to a land of your creation, but to a place I'll be designing especially for you. A place from which you'll never be able to escape."

Raven closed his eyes. *Uh, Min, is there any way at all you might be able to get here? Like now?*

"Move!" the officer shouted at her, and she could see out of the corner of her eye that three other officers had taken up position off to her left, all with guns drawn and pointed directly at her. "I need you to start walking toward me, slowly," the officer in front of her was saying, "and I need you to do it right now!"

If only he would just look her in the eye, but he was focused instead on her hands. Did he think she was going to throw them into the air with a flourish like some medieval witch and cast a spell on the entire bunch of them? She wished she could.

Raven, what's going on there?

I'm not sure, but have you ever heard of a person being hanged, drawn, and quartered? Well, I think Jules is about to skip the first part altogether and go directly to the bloody part.

Holy . . .

Minerva took two steps toward the officer.

"That's it, lady. Nice and slow, and nobody here gets hurt."

She took two more steps, then stopped, frozen in place. She realized what she had to do. If they wanted a witch's incantation, they'd get the best damned attempt at one she could give them. With a single, rapid motion, she pulled her hands out from behind her head and thrust them in front of her as though she were sending two balls of pure, searing molten energy straight in the officer's direction. She saw his eyes widen, and finally, he looked her directly in the eye.

And in virtually that same instant, he pulled the trigger. So did the three other officers, each of them less than a dozen feet away.

There were no balls of flame. Not even a puff of smoke. Minerva was no witch; she felt in that moment just like the frightened little girl who'd run away to hide whenever the kids at school would tease her. Spit on her. Knock the books out of her hands. She had never been able to fight back before, and even with all her newfound power, she couldn't fight back now. But despite her fear, she could do something she hadn't been able to do back then: Even if she felt powerless to make a difference, at least she could make a stand.

The bullets ripped into her flesh in rapid succession, and she felt her body being jarred by their impact, followed at once by the excruciating pain of them tearing through flesh and bone and muscle.

She probably screamed, though she wasn't aware of it. With every ounce of her energy, she focused on the man who lay tied up less than five miles from where she was, a prisoner of the woman who had tried so hard to destroy them both.

Between ragged breaths and blinding pain, as she fell to the asphalt, Minerva managed to form one final, resounding thought in her mind:

Raven, I love you. Remember me.

Showdown

Jules was really enjoying this. So much had gone so badly recently, she was going to allow herself to relish this victory, however minor it might be.

"Where would you like me to send you, Raven dear?" she mused. "Perhaps I could cook up a molten hell for you. Get it? 'Cook up'?" She laughed. "Or maybe you'd prefer something a little cooler. Did I ever tell you I took a cruise to Alaska a few years back. Such beautiful country, but so very cold. A blizzard hit while we were there. I think I could re-create that for you, if you like. A perpetual winter whiteout for you. Maybe that's more to your taste."

She paused for a moment to look at him closely. To survey her handiwork. Was that a tear she saw running down his cheek?

It was!

She was better than she thought.

She reached down and stroked his hair, ignoring the fact that he was trying mightily to pull away from her. "What's the matter, Ray-Ray? Did someone steal your stuffed fluffy bunny?"

He spat at her, catching her on the left cheek just below the eye.

She pulled back and wiped her face with her sleeve. "Now, now. Is that the way you treat the women in your life? No wonder you're alone at the end of it. Except for me. My company isn't so bad now, is it?"

He closed his eyes and wished he could close his ears, focusing all his attention on Minerva. But try as he might, he still couldn't hear her voice. He didn't even have a sense that she was out there.

Anywhere.

It was that realization that had given rise to his tears. But he wasn't about to give up on her. Not without a fight. What had she meant by telling him,

"Remember me"? He didn't want to consider the obvious. He wouldn't let himself. It couldn't mean that.

Min, where are you! Answer me, Min. You're really worrying me here. I need to hear your voice. Min. What's going on there? Min, please!

Nothing.

His eyes flashed open and Jules jumped back at the sound of a gun blast at the front door. The doorknob, jarred loose, fell to the floor, and a second gunshot a second or two later shattered the wood around the deadbolt. A moment later, the door itself came unhinged, sent flying inward by a violent kick that was followed by the figure of a single man stepping across the threshold, wielding a Baby Glock and pointing it directly at Jules.

"I've had enough of this," Carson said, careful to keep her in his line of vision without looking her directly in the eye.

Jules frowned, then regained her composure and straightened her back, facing him. "Who have we here?" she said. "If it isn't Mighty Mouse come to save the day!"

Mighty Mouse? Who's . . . ? Raven stopped himself. He didn't care what happened here—whether Carson blew Jules' head off or whether she sealed him up like a turkey in some huge pressure cooker she created in the Between. All that mattered was that he somehow find some way to reach Minerva. But his mind couldn't find her. It was as if Jules had put up some block between them, but a sinking feeling in the pit of his stomach told him that wasn't it.

"Don't move an inch from where you are, Jules. Don't even think about giving me a reason to pull this trigger. Come to think about it, you've already given me a reason. A lot more than one. So maybe I should just. . ."

"Don't."

Jules' eyes widened, but it wasn't at the sight of Carson pointing that gun at her. She was looking past him, at the entryway, where a dark-haired woman was stepping over the shattered door and coming straight toward her.

"Stay back, Minerva," Carson said. "I can put an end to this right now."

Minerva shot him a withering look. "You don't want to do that. I'll explain it later, but hold your fire."

Carson wasn't used to being told what to do, but he eased off the trigger. For now.

"That's right," Jules laughed. "His conscience might not be able to handle the burden of killing me. I honestly don't think he's been the same since he killed that Corbet woman."

For the first time since Minerva had entered the room, Raven's feeling of relief that she was safe and sound was interrupted by a different emotion. For the first time, his eyes left her, shifting instead to Carson.

"What did she just say?"

"Go on," Jules said teasingly. "Tell him how you squeezed that trigger all those years ago and put his grandmother in the grave."

Carson said nothing.

"Is that true?" Raven asked. He had never known his grandmother in real life, thanks to whoever it was who had killed her, but he'd just come back from meeting her in the Beyond, and even in that short time, he had developed an affection for her. All the heartbreak she had been through, and then the hardship of having a child alone in a time when such things "just weren't done" . . . He felt for her.

"I'm sorry," Carson said in barely a whisper. "I was just following orders." The minute he had uttered those words, he wished he could take them back.

"Like the Nazis were 'just following orders,'" Raven said, disgusted.

"Yes," Jules said. "Just like the Nazis. Doesn't make you any better than they were, does it, Triage?"

Minerva strode directly up to Jules and stood directly between her and Carson, less than a foot away from her. In a way, she was amazed that she had the courage to get in her face like this, but a lot had changed since the last time the two of them had squared off. More than Jules could possibly have guessed.

"I'd back up a little if I were you," Jules whispered, the haughty laughter suddenly replaced by seething hatred.

"Oh? And why would that be?"

"Because of this." Jules gripped the handle of the knife she still held and plunged it outward and upward into Minerva's chest, twisting it and forcing it deeper with every bit of her strength.

Minerva took a step backward and looked down, seeing the knife sticking out of her chest, buried so deep that it nearly the entire blade had disappeared, up to the handle. Her eyes widened, as if in shock, and she looked at Jules as though she'd just been, well, stabbed with a very sharp, very lethal knife.

"How does it feel?" Jules gloated, meeting her gaze.

"Like. *THIS!*"

Jules staggered back as she felt the force of something she hadn't anticipated stabbing into her chest, cutting sinew, cracking her rib cage, arcing up into her.

She gasped.

"How . . . ?"

The intensity of Minerva's stare alone could have probably melted ice, but that was nothing compared to the power that lay behind it.

"You see, Jules, you can't kill me if I'm . . . already . . . *DEAD!* Only one person could do that: The gifted person who revived me, and I happen to have a pretty strong suspicion that he's quite fond of me." She wanted to glance back at Raven to see the look on his face when she said those words . . . but first things would have to come first.

Jules crumpled into a ball on the ground, unable to tear her eyes away from Minerva as she emptied every bit of agony she would have experienced from the knife still buried in her chest.

Would have.

If she had been alive.

Jules was gasping for air now.

"Oh, don't worry. You won't die," Minerva said. "I won't let you . . . because I don't want someone to bring you back the way I am. I don't want to take that chance. That's why I didn't want Carson to kill you. Don't think I was taking pity on you. I'm not that nice—especially to someone who tried to steal my boyfriend and *then* threatened to exile him to some artificial hell she created. Yeah, I overheard that. I have good ears . . . and good eyes, if I do say so myself."

Jules could barely breath. "Stop. Please," she managed to gasp.

Minerva ignored her. She was too busy trying to figure out what to do with her. She couldn't kill her, but she was far too dangerous to leave running around loose. Even putting her in a maximum security prison wouldn't do much good. The minute she got a fix on one of those guards with those beady eyes of hers, it would be over.

Then it hit her. Abruptly, she stopped sending the pain from the knife-wound to her and slid it out of her chest, watching with satisfaction as the flesh closed cleanly again over the wound. No wonder Amber had gotten such a kick out of that. It *was* a neat trick. Jules was shivering and whimpering on the floor like a dog that had been kicked to the point that it was no longer conscious of anything but the pain.

Minerva looked down at her and would have felt sorry for her—except for everything she had done to Raven.

Carson, seeing it was finally safe to lower his weapon, had bent down beside Raven and was undoing the knots that Jules had tied. Soon, he was up on his feet again.

Meanwhile, Minerva started flooding Jules with a different memory, something she had experienced all too recently: the utter darkness and hopelessness of a perpetual sleep from which she couldn't awake, no matter how much she struggled, no matter how hard she tried. Jules' eyelids slowly closed, and before long, her eyes began moving rapidly behind them.

"Stay there," Minerva whispered, and closed her own eyes.

It was done.

She'd have Amber arrange to put her on life support and keep her there when this was all over. . . . She caught herself in the middle of that thought. It *was* all over. Finally. She had somehow managed to win this fight *and* die trying. Not too many people could say that.

Raven, on his feet now, rushed across the room and picked her up in an epic embrace.

She looked down at him as he held her aloft, like heroes do in the movies. He was her superhero, and she was his. Now, after all this time, they were finally on equal footing. Each of them needed the other to stay revived, each equally dependent on the other.

"So you're . . . dead?" Raven said, finally setting her down.

She nodded. "Un-huh."

"Would it be weird of me to say I'm glad?"

"Nope," said Minerva, "because I am, too." She laughed. "Thanks for remembering me, Raven."

"How could I not?" he replied. "You're unforgettable."

Epilogue

"Not many people get to attend their own funerals, unless they've faked their own deaths for the insurance money."

Raven laughed at Minerva's snide remark.

Sure, he can laugh. He's been dead fifteen years. I'm still getting used to the idea.

She watched as they lowered the casket into the ground. Why were they burying her, anyway? She'd always wanted to be cremated, but her mother insisted on clinging to this particular Catholic tradition, even though she only went to Mass on Christmas Eve and had so many things to feel guilty about that any priest who heard her confession would be too worn out by the end of it to even bother giving her penance.

It was weird seeing her mother dressed in black—even if it was a leather jacket and black jeans—and crying over her, although Minerva had a hard time believing those tears were genuine. The woman had never shown her the least bit of affection during her lifetime; why should she start now that she thought she was dead?

She's probably just trying to get some rich guy at the funeral to feel sorry for her.

Not that her memorial service had attracted hordes of people. Minerva hadn't had too many friends, and most of the people there were extended family members who were attending out of a sense of obligation.

She tugged at Raven's sleeve. "Come on, let's go," she said.

There was no point in staying there, hiding in the shadows, to watch something that amounted to an unwitting charade and, for the two of them at least, a private joke.

Minerva wanted to get home while her mother was still out of the house. She wanted to see her room one last time, collect a few of her things—

the ones Jules hadn't stolen—and leave. She couldn't stay there anymore, although she had no idea where she would go. She only knew it would be with Raven. And Amber.

The Three Dead Musketeers.

They still had to get Amber out of jail, but first Minerva wanted to say a final goodbye to her old life.

"I have one stop I want to make on the way back," she said, figuring they still had a little time. If Jessica held true to form, she would want to hold an impromptu "wake" at Muskie's Tavern, drowning her imaginary sorrows in some very real whiskey and schnapps (and, she no doubt hoped, some drunken male's libido-driven attentions). "Come with me."

They walked down the street to a strip mall, and she led Raven into a store called E.T.'s Phone Home. E.T. stood for Edward Thurston, the owner, whose main product was, naturally cellphones.

"What are we doing here?" Raven asked.

"Since you're going to be around a while, I think it's time you put down some roots into the 21st century. So I'm buying you a cellphone."

Raven laughed. "Do we really need that?" They were getting quite good at reading each other's thoughts. "It's not like I could phone you from Between if I somehow get hung up there again. Get it? *Hung up* there?"

She punched him playfully in the shoulder. "Humor me. Most girls want their boyfriends to have their numbers programmed into their cellphones. It's kind of like a symbol, y'know? And a word of advice, Mr. Tech Not-So-Savvy: Mine goes at the top of the list." She paused for a moment. "Oh, and one other rule: You don't get to throw it at me."

"Okay, okay," he chuckled, remembering when she had thrown her imaginary phone at him in that dream of hers not so long ago. "I like the sound of you calling me your boyfriend. You've never said that before."

She couldn't stop herself from blushing. She had been hoping he would just accept that gracefully without pointing it out. Yes, she felt good about where they stood with each other, but she didn't know if her insecure self would ever feel comfortable being the center of attention. She thought about that for a moment. Well, she could probably get used to being the center of *his* attention, as long as he didn't make a big deal about her in public.

She signed him up for the phone, adding him to her account and handing over some of the money Carson had given her to cover living expenses when they were back at Amber's bungalow. Part of that had been spending money for food, but since she didn't need to eat now, strictly speaking, she could afford to splurge on a phone for Raven.

The salesman activated Raven's new phone and handed it to him.

"Okay, Min, what's your number."

She read it off to him, and he started typing it in. With each digit, however, his response became slower, and before she could say the last one, he said it for her.

"Seven."

"How did you know?"

Raven reached into his pocket and pulled out the crumpled scrap of paper he'd taken out of his father's desk in the Between. Unfolding it, he handed it to her. "Recognize this?"

Minerva frowned. "It's my number. But how . . .?"

"I don't know," Raven said. "The Between is a weird place. Jules told me I had created that reality, but maybe since you were there, it looks like you created part of it, too—even though you were asleep. Somehow, it seems like you put your number in that desk because you wanted me to have it."

She pursed her lips together. "Maybe." She had been annoyed that he hadn't left her a phone number before, after he hadn't shown up at the park to meet her.

"Wait," he said, a flash of inspiration appearing on his face. "I found something else there, too."

He reached back into his pocket and took out the poem he had found, the one in what he had thought was his father's wedding day card to his mother. "Do you recognize this?"

She took it and began reading the lines.

I love you as a friend
I cherish you, my lover
I love the treasures found
In every secret I discover

Of your heart and of your essence
Of your spirit and your dreams
Crashing in on me like thunder
From a desert storm that seems

A raging, swirling, mesmerizing
Echo of your soul
That, whene'er I find the source of it,
I know will make me whole

I loved you from a distance
I love you as a child
Loves all things when first he sees them
Wholly innocent and wild

A miracle believed in
Is a miracle come true
A moment out of timelessness
A moment spent with you

Minerva's face grew white. It was a poem she'd written for him after their first night together, but she wasn't about to tell him that. Not yet, anyway.

"What is it? You look like you've seen a ghost."

She smiled awkwardly. "I did. You."

"Not funny. You're one too, remember? But seriously, who do you think wrote this?"

"Well, you found it in your father's desk," she said. "I can tell you one thing: Whoever wrote this was very much in love."

Before he could ask any more questions, she turned to the sales clerk and handed over the payment in cash. Then she said, "Let's go," and, taking his hand, whisked him out the door.

~

Nobody noticed them as they walked up to the front door, their posture unassuming and their faces hidden by hoodies. The door was locked, but Minerva knew Jessica kept a spare key under the woodchips near the rose buses to the right of the door.

"Ouch!"

Her thumb caught a thorn as she retrieved the key, and she watched as the pierced skin drew closed before her eyes without spilling a drop of blood. She'd probably start taking that for granted after a while, she knew, but for now it was still pretty cool.

They stepped inside and went to her room, and they were surprised to find Minerva's candle still burning beside her bed.

"That's amazing," said Raven. "How could it have lasted that long?"

"It didn't."

They both turned at the sound of the voice behind them. There in the doorway stood Archer.

"Mom's kept that burning for you ever since you left. She said she wouldn't put it out till you came back. That's like the sixth or seventh one she's put there, always with the same flame. She lit each one with the one before it."

"Archer! What are you doing here?" Minerva said. Forgetting she thought that he thought she was dead, she ran over to him and hugged him.

Archer shrugged. "I stayed home," he said. "Mom stopped believing you were still alive after she saw the body. But I knew it wasn't you. I knew you'd come back, and I wanted to be here when you did. Besides, Mom wanted to go out drinking, so she dropped me here. I can take care of myself," he added, and Minerva realized he'd probably learned to say that from her.

As she looked at him, she couldn't hide the confusion in her eyes. "You knew? But how?"

Archer shrugged again. "I dunno. I just did. You shouldn't be too hard on Mom. I think she finally gets it now. She's even stopped smoking . . . well, I saw her sneak a cigarette once last night, but that was it. She flushed all the others down the toilet."

"Okay," Minerva said. "But she can't know I was here. It's better for her that way."

"I know," Archer said, smiling agreeably. "It's like 'Ghost in the Machine'"—that was one of his favorite video games. "It's better to be the ghost than the person who gets spooked." He laughed, and Minerva laughed right along with him.

"That's true," she said.

She hugged him again and kissed him on the forehead. "Gotta go. Take care of Mom for me, will you?" *She'll need it.*

Archer nodded. They collected a few things quickly and headed back toward the front door.

"Going somewhere?"

They stopped in their tracks.

It was Carson. "I thought you might need a ride."

Raven scowled at him. "Not from you we don't," he said.

Minerva untucked his shirt in the back and ran the palm of her hand up his back. She could never forgive him for killing Raven's grandmother, but she couldn't ignore the fact that he had done his best to look out for her.

Minerva tossed her head back slightly as a way of saying, "He's right," and Raven directed his scowl toward her . . . before it evaporated into a smile. He couldn't be upset with her.

Carson drove them from there to the county jail, where he politely asked the guard on duty to release Amber and Henry into his custody. He produced one of his many fake IDs—this one a badge with the L.A. County Sheriff's Department—but the guard shook his head and said, "No can do." That's when Minerva stepped forward, looked into his eyes and sent him a childhood memory of burning her mouth when she'd tried to gulp down a piping hot cup of apple cider. It was almost funny watching him hop around like a chicken in the midst of convulsions. Nothing on the level of what she'd done to Jules, but enough to persuade him to hand over the keys just as another guard showed up to ask what all those commotion was about.

Raven caught his eye this time and imparted an equally painful memory—of the time he'd disturbed a hornet's nest when he was four— that rendered the second guard irrelevant and largely immobile.

Nice job, Babe. You're learning.

Raven winced. *It's not the kind of talent I really want to get the hang of.*

Yeah. Neither do I.

A couple of other guards tried to stop them on their way to the holding area but met with similarly painful responses; fortunately, Amber and Henry were in cells that weren't too far away from each other, and the four of them were able to make a quick getaway before any of the guards recovered sufficiently to sound an alarm.

$\sim$

Carson took them all back to the old motel he used as his retreat from the world, no longer worried about Jules finding him there. On the way over, they filled Henry in on everything that had happened, including the fact that three of them were, technically speaking, dead. When they reached their destination, Carson poured the rest of them a glass of wine and grabbed a beer for himself—bypassing the ginger ale; he was no longer on the job. Then they spent the rest of the evening playing draw poker.

Amber seemed better than the rest of them at bluffing, and before long, she'd amassed a stack of chips larger than the rest of them put together.

"So, what do we do with *her*?" Amber pointed to the sleeping figure of Jules, who was lying on the couch. Carson had taken her with him after the Glendale incident.

Henry dealt the next hand.

"She's not going anywhere," said Minerva. "I was hoping you could hook her up to life support somewhere. The hospital has to take care of her if they can't find any relatives, right?"

"Yeah, except after that jailbreak of yours, I don't think either of us can get anywhere near a hospital without being arrested," Henry quipped.

"Oh. Right."

"I'll take care of it," said Carson. "Remember that lab where I took you to see Dr. Fitzgerald?"

Minerva glowered at him. Of course she remembered it. She remembered everything. But that was *not* a pleasant memory.

He ignored her withering look and continued: "It's a full-scale medical facility, off-limits to everyone except those of us with security clearance. I can leave her there with the proper instructions, and they'll take care of it. No questions asked."

Amber threw two blue chips into the pile, and everyone around the table matched her.

"So, what do the rest of us do now?" Amber asked, calling for three cards from the pile.

"The three of us have to stick together," Minerva said. "Otherwise . . ." She left the rest of the thought unsaid and asked for two cards, which Henry dealt to her.

"You're not bloody leaving me behind," he said. "I might not be dead, or revived, or whatever you call it, but I am a fugitive now, too. I can't very well go waltzing back into work tomorrow as if nothing's happened."

Raven took four new cards, and Minerva stood pat.

"Why do you think Jules was trying to bring back your grandfather?" Minerva asked.

"I'm not sure," said Raven.

Carson stroked his chin, and it wasn't clear for a moment whether he was pondering Minerva's question or the strength of his poker hand.

"I'm not sure, but from your description of him, I think I know who your grandfather was. Let's just say he was very high up in the Nazi hierarchy, and that he was a very, very, very bad man. They used to call him the Angel of Death, because his medical 'experiments' got so many people killed. Jews were no better than lab rats to him. If he's the one who figured out how to impart the gift, Jules might have been trying to revive him in the hopes of perfecting it. Or implementing it on a larger scale."

"For her own reasons? Or do you think your agency was behind it?" Raven asked.

Carson shook his head slowly, staring intently at his cards. "That's what I haven't figured out," he said. "It might just be a personal grudge, but there's no way of knowing if it went beyond that. Either way, bringing your grandfather back would have been a nightmare."

Amber increased her bid to five chips this time, and everyone else folded except for Minerva, who matched her bid and raised her five more.

Amber picked up five chips and started to drop them into the pile, then thought better of it.

"Fold."

Minerva reached forward for the pile and pulled it toward her.

"Thought you were bluffing," Amber said. "But I couldn't be sure."

"I never bluff," Minerva said. "Except when I do." She smiled broadly and winked.

Raven laughed. "I guess Jules sure found that out with that whole knife trick of yours. Pretty sneaky bluff there, pretending to be alive."

They all laughed at that.

Minerva looked over at Jules, lying motionless on the couch—motionless except for the rapid movements barely visible behind her closed eyelids.

She stopped laughing. She might have won this hand on a bluff, but at what cost? They were still all in, and this wasn't a game.

Raven saw the shadow pass across her face.

"Hey, beautiful," he said, leaning over for a kiss on the cheek. "I love you. Everything's okay."

She forced a smile. "I love you, too, Raven. Let's deal another hand."

ABOUT THE AUTHOR

Stephen H. Provost is a journalist and author. He has worked as an editor, reporter, and columnist at newspapers throughout California. He is the author of *Fresno Growing Up: A City Comes of Age 1945–1985*, a history of his hometown. Provost lives with his wife on California's Central Coast, where he is the editor of *The Cambrian* newspaper. Provost frequently blogs on writing and current events at his website, stephenhprovost.com.

CPSIA information can be obtained
at www.ICGtesting.com
Printed in the USA
LVOW08s1535110417
530416LV00003B/614/P